R
DL	DW	88	BT
DM	DX	BM 5/09	BV

WHISPERING GRASS

WHISPERING GRASS

Graham Ison

Severn House Large Print
London & New York

This first large print edition published 2008
in Great Britain and the USA by
SEVERN HOUSE PUBLISHERS of
9-15 High Street, Sutton, Surrey, SM1 1DF.
First world regular print edition published 2006 by
Severn House Publishers, London and New York.

British Library Cataloguing in Publication Data

Ison, Graham
   Whispering grass. - Large print ed.
   1. Brock, Detective Chief Inspector (Fictitious character)
   - Fiction 2. Poole, Detective Sergeant (Fictitious
   character) - Fiction 3. Police - England - London - Fiction
   4. Detective and mystery stories 5. Large type books
   I. Title
   823.9'14[F]

   ISBN-13: 978-0-7278-7715-4

Printed and bound in Great Britain by
MPG Books Ltd, Bodmin, Cornwall

One

The forecourt of Stone Mill prison is a desolate place at the best of times, but on a cold February morning with the rain lashing down it's particularly dire.

Within feet of the prison's massive wooden doors, a small tent had been erected which, I presumed, contained the body that was to be the subject of my latest murder investigation. If it didn't, I'd have wasted my time coming all the way out here from Curtis Green.

It is not generally known, but Curtis Green lies just off Whitehall between the fortress that is the Ministry of Defence and the grandiose apartments where our parliamentary representatives flog their guts out on our behalf, or so it is rumoured. It is where Serious Crime Group West has its offices, and from my discussions with various members of the Metropolitan Police its location appears to be a well-kept secret. From the police, that is.

The Serious Crime Groups are the outfits that handle murders likely to be too protracted for the local nick to investigate –

poor overworked darlings – and those 'specialized' deaths that the multifarious other squads at the Yard disdain to look into because they're 'specialist' squads. But I ask you, what's more specialist than common-or-garden murder?

But enough of that.

The usual blue-and-white tapes had been strung out around the area in such a way as seriously to obstruct entry to and exit from the prison. Deliberately, I suspect, but there's not a lot of love lost between the Old Bill and the screws.

Two or three police officers in oversized, unflattering yellow jackets marked POLICE – in case you didn't know – were standing around, arms folded, and overseen by a youthful Uniform Branch inspector from the local nick. The PCs looked bored, the inspector looked important, despite the rain dripping from the peak of his cap. Aware of his enhanced status as 'incident officer' he marched up to me waving a clipboard.

'And you are?' he demanded pompously.

'Detective Chief Inspector Brock, Serious Crime Group West.'

The inspector nodded, mumbled, 'Sir,' and wrote down my name on the piece of rain-sodden paper that adorned his clipboard. He pointed his government-issue ballpoint pen at Dave. 'And you?' he asked, looking down his nose. I suspected he had not long been an inspector and was intent on flexing the two stars on his epaulettes.

Dave Poole, my black detective sergeant, loved jousting with petty authority. 'Colour-Sergeant Poole, ditto ... *sir*.'

The inspector had obviously been on one of the ethnic-awareness-and-anti-discrimination courses that now lie at the heart of Metropolitan Police be-nice-to-everyone strategy. Unfortunately such 'diversity' courses did not cater for sergeants of West Indian origin who made racist remarks about themselves.

We moved on, leaving the important inspector wondering why his pen didn't work in the pouring rain.

The armed-response vehicle had been the first unit on the scene. Its crew, dressed in black combat suits and girt about with firearms, stood around and looked disappointed.

'I'm afraid we got here too late, guv,' said their sergeant.

'Bad luck,' I said, and sent them back on patrol. I was never happy working in close proximity to policemen with guns. People tend to get shot. And not always the right people.

I approached a man in civilian clothes sheltering beneath a colourful golf umbrella. I hazarded a guess that he was a CID officer, although it's not always that easy to tell these days.

'DI Newman?' I asked.

'Yeah, that's me.'

'DCI Harry Brock, SCG West,' I told him, 'and this is DS Poole.'

Newman laughed. 'You caught this one, then, guv?' he said. 'Bit tasty by the look of it.'

This is the sort of encouraging remark one gets from local detectives once they've discovered that a particularly tricky murder has been offloaded to the Serious Crime Group.

'I reckon so,' I said, making no pretence of being enthusiastic about my latest murder enquiry. 'So what have we got?'

'Guy gets released from the nick at eight this morning,' said Newman, waving at the prison's huge doors, 'and far from being greeted by the usual welcoming shapely blonde in nothing but a skin-tight dress and a Mercedes who's going to carry him straight off to bed, like it is on television, some finger takes a potshot at him from a passing vehicle. On closer examination, guv, you'll see a hole in the centre of the victim's forehead, thus killing him and rendering him unable to tell us who did it. Or to give us the index number of the said vehicle,' he added as an apparent afterthought.

'Who said it was a passing vehicle?' I asked. I always enjoyed having a dig at locals who've jumped to conclusions.

DI Newman thought about that. 'Well, now you come to mention it, guv, no one.'

'Thanks,' I said. 'Very useful. So you've no

idea where the shot came from.'

'Not really, no.' But Newman was clearly set upon not having his theory entirely discounted. 'Except I don't think it came from inside the prison.'

This is the sort of enquiry that my colleagues and I on SCG West always seem to get lumbered with, given that we're responsible for investigating all the serious crimes in that broad swathe of London that stretches from Westminster to Hillingdon in the west, Barnet in the north and Richmond in the south. Those enquiries, that is, that aren't the preserve of the aforementioned 'specialists'.

'We've got a name for him,' volunteered Newman helpfully.

'I suppose you would have as he's just emerged from doing porridge in there.' I indicated the prison with a slight jerk of my umbrella. 'So who is he?'

'Jimmy Gould, known as "Spotter",' said Newman. I raised an enquiring eyebrow. 'He was a lookout man, you see,' the DI added. 'Got a handsome bit of form too, even though he's only thirty-two. Just finished an eight-stretch for a blagging down Stepney way. Only did five, though. Paroled for good behaviour.' He laughed cynically and offered Dave and me a cigarette. 'Probably wishes he'd stayed where he was.'

'Any known enemies?' I asked.

'Hundreds, I should think.'

'Smart-arse,' I said.

Thanks to the diabolical state of London's traffic, not helped by the closure of the road outside the prison while policemen poked about in the gutters, it had taken me forever to get here. But somehow the crime-scene examiners had arrived before me, and so had Henry Mortlock, the Home Office pathologist. I opened the flap of the tent and found Henry on his knees, humming some vaguely sacred tune, and already at work with the tools of his trade.

'If you're offering up prayers to New Scotland Yard, Henry,' I said, 'you're facing the wrong way.'

Completely ignoring what, in my case, passed for humour (Henry thinks he's got the monopoly on witticisms and sarcasm), he stood up. 'I suppose you're going to ask the cause of death, dear boy,' he said. 'Well, it's almost certain to be that.' And he pointed at the hole in Spotter Gould's forehead. 'Mind you, it's always possible that he succumbed to the catering in there,' he continued, pointing at the prison, 'and would have died anyway. On the other hand, he might have had a heart attack seconds before being shot.' Henry was never one to make assumptions.

'In other words, Henry, you're telling me to wait for the results of the post-mortem.'

'Indeed, dear boy.'

'All right to move the body?'

'Yes. Usual place.'

Henry's 'usual place' was the Horseferry Road mortuary in Westminster. He had an ingrained dislike of working anywhere else. Don't ask me why, but that's Henry for you. I left him to his ministrations.

Linda Mitchell, the chief crime-scene examiner, walked over, all bright, bubbly and sexy in her white coverall suit, rubber boots and latex gloves. 'We're done here, Mr Brock,' she said. 'I'll let you have everything we've got ASAP. Incidentally, the victim had a prison-issue plastic bag with him, but it only contained the usual bits and pieces, like clothing, a razor and comb and that sort of thing.'

'Are you sure it's a prison-issue plastic bag?' I asked teasingly.

'Fairly certain,' said Linda. 'It's got "HM Prisons" written on it.'

DI Newman joined me again. 'I've got a team doing a fingertip of the road, guv,' he said, 'but there's nothing so far. The cartridge case is almost certain to have fallen into the vehicle ... ' He paused. 'Er, if there was one,' he added cautiously. 'But there's always an outside chance we might find something, I suppose.'

'Not when I'm investigating a topping there's not,' I said gloomily. Beside me, Dave nodded, also gloomily. 'And if it was a revolver, the cases wouldn't have been ejected anyway.'

11

'I doubt a revolver would have been used, guv,' said Newman, determined not to let me have it all my own way. 'Would have to have been a bloody lucky shot at that distance. And in the rain.'

I was bound to agree with him, unless a witness came forward to say that he saw a man approach Gould and place the barrel of a pistol against his head. I was forced to conclude that we were probably looking for a sniper. But from where? A house opposite? Or was Newman right, that Gould was shot from a passing vehicle?

A prison officer ventured out into the rain and joined Newman, Dave and me.

'Are you likely to be much longer, Chief?' he enquired, shoulders hunched, and hands in the pockets of his raincoat. 'We're supposed to be doing some transfers this morning, but we've had to send the van to Brixton, to hold them there until it can get in here.'

'As long as it takes,' I said, 'but now you're here, you can show me to the governor's office.'

The governor of Stone Mill prison was a tall, emaciated individual who looked as though he suffered permanently from a duodenal ulcer. I think I would if I was responsible for running this place.

'I've just ordered some tea, Chief Inspector,' he said once Dave and I had introduced ourselves. 'Would you care for some?'

'Thank you,' I said. 'Now, about Jimmy Gould.'

'Ah, Gould, yes.' The governor put on his glasses, pulled a clipboard across his desk and spent a few moments studying it. 'Released this morning.' He took off his glasses and afforded me a worried smile.

'Didn't get far,' I said. 'He's camping out in the tent that's obstructing your entrance.'

'Yes, I heard about that.' The governor spoke airily, obviously thinking that once Spotter Gould was out of his prison he could wash his hands of him.

But I know a thing or two about the law. 'He's still within the curtilage of your premises, though,' I said.

'Mmm! Yes, I suppose so. Well how can I help you?'

'I'm going to have to interview all the prisoners who knew him.'

'Good God, there must be hundreds.' The governor thought about that for a second or so. 'But none of *them* could have killed him, could they?' he added archly.

'Probably not,' I said, 'but they might know a man who did.'

'You could start with the prisoners on his landing, I suppose.' The governor was clearly unhappy about my intention of disrupting the routine of his correctional facility.

'I don't propose to start until tomorrow anyway, Governor, but in the meantime per-

13

haps you'd give me the address Gould was going to. Presumably he's still on licence until the termination of his sentence?'

'Yes, yes, of course.' The governor pressed a switch on his intercom and asked the responding, disembodied voice of his secretary for that information.

Moments later a willowy blonde stepped into the office, smiled sweetly at Dave, and put a tray of tea and a file on the governor's desk. Dave is black, six feet tall, well built and handsome, and women always seem to fancy him. Probably because he's black, six feet tall, well built and handsome. It's an unfair world.

'Walloch Street, Poplar,' said the governor. 'Flat 37, New Labour House.'

'With any luck that might be the right address,' said Dave. Dave had tried finding ex-prisoners before.

'But it's the one he was required to furnish as part of his parole.' The governor spoke in shocked tones as if it would be unthinkable for an inmate to give a false address when he was released. 'And it was checked out.'

Oh boy, you do have a lot to learn, I thought. And that turned out to be more prophetic than I realized.

'Well, if it happens to be wrong, we'll let you know,' said Dave. 'Then you can do him for it.'

The governor did not seem comforted by this.

14

* * *

Having arranged to start interviewing prisoners the following morning, Dave and I
made our way to Poplar.

New Labour House did not have the appearance of being a salubrious neighbourhood in which to live. The usual assortment
of vandalized cars, upturned wheelie bins,
hypodermic needles, used condoms and
other detritus abandoned by what Dave
describes as the 'effluent society' added a
pop-art touch to the council's vain attempt
at landscaping. Several feckless youths were
hanging about and eyeing our car with felo-
nious interest.

Dave, however, was ahead of the field. He
strolled across to the largest hooligan of this
group of unemployed burdens on the
taxpayer.

'What's your name?'

'Whatcha wanna know that for?'

'Because I collect interesting bits of information like that,' said Dave, standing menacingly close to his victim, who was in the
unenviable position of having his back to the
wall. In more ways than one.

'Wayne Gibbs.' The youth did not have to
enquire who Dave was. He knew. It was in
his genes. And as I mentioned previously,
Dave is six feet tall and a heavily built fifteen
stones in weight.

'Prove it,' said Dave.

Remarkably, Wayne Gibbs produced a

P45, the official government form given to persons whose employment has been terminated. In Gibbs's case it was a very old piece of paper, but at least it showed that he had been employed during some distant period of his life. 'Whatcha wanna know that for?' he asked again.

'Because my chief inspector and I are visiting this pearl of council architecture and if, when we return, there is any damage to that vehicle' – Dave gestured at the police car – 'I shall come and find you and hold you personally responsible, Wayne Gibbs of 64 New Labour House, Walloch Road. Like nicking you for it.' Dave recorded the information in his pocketbook and looked Gibbs straight in the eye. 'Got that, have you ... Wayne?'

Gibbs nodded dumbly.

'Good,' said Dave. 'Now you be a good boy while I'm away.'

We mounted the stairs to the second-floor balcony, and stepping over piles of accumulated rubbish and a bicycle frame, eventually reached number 37.

After a considerable delay, a small boy of about six opened the door. He had a dirty face and a T-shirt bearing the word 'STUFFED'. But what appeared to be the remains of a hamburger and a liberal quantity of tomato sauce obscured whatever other words might have appeared above it.

The child was clearly not in a conversational mood because he just stared at us. But the impasse was broken by the arrival of a careworn woman wearing jeans and a baggy sweater that reached almost to her knees. Her dyed blonde hair – black at the roots – hung in rat's tails about her shoulders. Perhaps it was the prevailing fashion among the female residents of New Labour House. She held the edge of the door with one reddened, chapped hand with chipped nail varnish, while the other clutched hold of a small girl of about three.

'What is it?'

'Are you by any chance Mrs Gould?' asked Dave.

'What if I am?' The woman gave Dave a suspicious glance. Not that he looked like a Mormon or any of the other assorted religious people who make a nuisance of themselves by knocking on busy people's doors.

'We're police officers,' I said.

'Oh yeah?' The woman gave Dave an even more suspicious glance. The small girl began to cry. 'Shut yer racket,' said her mother. I hoped she was the child's mother; I could do without dealing with a case of an unregistered child-minder.

We produced our warrant cards and I repeated my question.

'Yeah, I'm Terry Gould, but if you want Jimmy, he's in the nick. And as you lot put him there you oughter know.'

'I think we'd better come in, Mrs Gould,'

I said.

Untidy would have been a complimentary term to apply to the sitting room: it was a tip. In fact, I'd go further: in a competition with a council rubbish dump, the Gould abode would have come first. The nylon carpet was stained and torn in places, and the cheap threadbare three-piece suite shared the room with a Formica-topped dining table chipped at the edges. Where it didn't bear the marks of cigarette burns, that is. Broken toys littered the floor and a large television was showing a Western film. The noise of a radio came from somewhere else in the flat.

'I thought I told you to clear this bleedin' lot up, Craig,' shrieked Mrs Gould. She detached herself from the small girl. 'Take yer sister in the other room, and don't make no noise. And turn that bleedin' radio off. Go and play wiv yer computer or sumfink.'

Dave crossed the room and switched off the television, and Terry Gould screamed once again to Craig to turn off the radio.

'I'm afraid I have some bad news, Mrs Gould.' All right, so she was a villain's wife, but I took the unusually charitable view that that didn't necessarily make *her* a villain. In fact, she'd probably been holding the family together on very little while Spotter was weight-training, playing volleyball and watching television in the nick. 'Jimmy was killed this morning.' There was no easy way to do it, and over the years I've found that to

18

come straight out with it is the best way. Okay, so it's brutal, but then so is sudden death.

Terry Gould sat down. 'But he was s'posed to be coming out today. Who done 'im? One of the screws, was it?'

'I very much doubt it. He was shot just as he left the prison.'

'Left the prison?' she echoed. 'Who'd've wanted to do that?'

'That, Mrs Gould, is what I'm trying to find out,' I said.

Having escaped from her brother's custody, the small girl came back into the room and climbed on to the sofa next to her mother. Dave gazed briefly at the child, and I anticipated that he was doing mental arithmetic. If Terry Gould's daughter was three years old, and Spotter Gould had just done five in the nick ... Oh well, who cares these days?

We heard a key in the door and seconds later a shaven-headed yob with the obligatory earring and tattoos appeared in the room.

'Wass all this then?' he demanded of no one in particular.

'It's the law, Darren,' said Terry.

I thought that to be an unnecessary observation; I had no doubt that Darren had been forewarned of our presence by the aforementioned Wayne Gibbs into whose safekeeping Dave had placed our police car.

'What d'you lot want then?' demanded the shaven-headed one truculently. 'Can't you leave her alone? You've already got her old man banged up.'

'Jimmy's been murdered.' Terry looked up listlessly. 'Got a fag, Darren?'

'Who done him then?' said Darren, tossing Terry a cigarette. He did not seem overly concerned at the demise of Spotter Gould, nor for that matter did Terry Gould. There was little doubt in my mind that Darren was shacked up with Spotter's wife, and was probably the father of the infant girl now asleep with her thumb in her mouth. In fact, the death of Spotter had probably removed an impediment to the domestic bliss enjoyed by this unsavoury pair. Which made Darren of great interest to me.

'What's your surname and date of birth, Darren?' asked Dave.

There was a brief moment while Darren appeared to weigh the possibility of refusing to impart this information, but common sense overcame his carefully nurtured macho-man image.

'Walters,' he said and told us when he was born.

'And what d'you do by way of a profession?' enquired Dave.

'In the motor trade,' said Darren tersely.

The three of us – Dave, Darren and me – all knew that being 'in the motor trade' covered a multitude of crimes from charging for work that hadn't been done, right through to ringing stolen vehicles.

'And where d'you carry on this business, Mr Walters?'

'Got a lock-up, ain't I?'

'Where?' persisted Dave.

'Down East India Dock Road.'

Dave waited, pen pointed menacingly at the motor trader's chest. After a moment's pause, Walters yielded and gave the exact address.

'How well did you know Jimmy Gould?' I asked.

'Well, I knew him, like.'

'Yes, but how well?'

'We done a few jobs together,' said Walters.

'What, blaggings?'

'Nah, course not.' Darren Walters managed to conjure up a scandalized expression at my suggestion. 'We was in the trade together before he got sent down. Mind you, it was a stitch-up. He weren't nowhere near when that heist went down, but the Heavy Mob come round here and nicked him. Reckoned he was the lookout.'

The Heavy Mob, as the Flying Squad is affectionately known to its enemies, takes a great interest in armed robberies, and rarely makes mistakes in identifying those responsible for them. And that is because they have a stable of good informants. If 'Spotter' Gould was the lookout, and the gang was caught, perhaps 'Spotter' was a grass.

21

But that apart, it is in the nature of villains always to claim that they were somewhere else at the crucial time of such criminal activity, and that the police have got it in for them.

'Can you think of any reason why someone should want him dead, Mr Walters?' I asked.

'Yeah, sure. He grassed up a few fingers after that last heist went down. Otherwise he'd've got twelve years instead of eight.'

Oh deep joy! I'd guessed right. This was clearly going to be a fun investigation.

Two

Still mulling over the implications of Darren Walters's involvement in the Gould ménage, we went straight from New Labour House to Henry Mortlock's carvery in Horseferry Road, Westminster.

Henry made quick work of the post-mortem, wielding his electric saw with professional enthusiasm. The only piece of evidence, as far as I was concerned, was a 5.56-millimetre round he extracted from somewhere within Gould's cranium.

'That undoubtedly is what did for him, Harry,' said Henry. 'I'll let you have a full report in due course. I put the time at death at about eight o'clock this morning,' he added archly.

'I hope you're not guessing, Henry,' I said.

Dave took possession of the round that had killed Spotter Gould, filled up a few forms and we left.

We stopped off for a pint at one of the pubs near the mortuary because I did not intend returning to Curtis Green until after six o'clock. It's the commander's unfailing practice to leave at precisely that time, and I

23

didn't want to be subjected to one of his inane interrogations on the progress of the capital's latest murder. At least not until I had something more specific to tell him than I hoped he knew already: that one Spotter Gould had been topped approximately one minute after starting his homeward journey to 37 New Labour House in Poplar. And that right now I hadn't got a clue who it was down to.

'I somehow thought you'd be popping in here, Mr Brock.'

I recognized the voice instantly, groaned and turned to see the overweight figure of Fat Danny, pint in hand, approaching from the direction of the fruit machine. Fat Danny is the crime reporter of Fleet Street's worst tabloid newspaper, a difficult reputation to acquire among those who plumb the depths of depravity and sensationalism. And by association that made Danny the most odious of crime reporters.

'What d'you want, Danny?' asked Dave.

'Since you ask, another pint wouldn't go amiss, Mr Poole.'

'You've got that the wrong way round, Danny,' said Dave. 'You're supposed to buy us beer.'

With a sigh, Danny ordered three more pints. 'Bit of a juicy one you've got out at Stone Mill, eh, Mr Brock?' he said, wiping froth from his mouth with the back of his hand.

'Nothing I can't cope with.'

'Looks like Spotter Gould finally got what was coming to him.'

'Meaning?'

'Well, he was a grass.' Danny gave a half laugh. 'But you must've known that. If you finger your mates and get them put away, they're bound to get a bit arsey about it. Mind you, I shouldn't think anyone could've heard him. He could hardly talk, you know.'

'Really?'

'Oh yeah. Few years ago he got smashed across the throat with a baseball bat. Bit of a turf war, that was. Either that or he'd grassed up someone else.' Danny let out a grating laugh. 'Anyhow, he could only speak in a whisper. That's why they called him the whispering grass.' Danny took another mouthful of beer. 'But the idea is you give me information, Mr Brock, not the other way round.'

'Whatever made you think that, Danny?' I asked.

'Give me a break,' said Danny. 'You must have something for me. Our readers are crying out for a good story about a villain getting his just deserts.'

'Don't kid yourself,' said Dave. 'You know bloody well all your readers – if they can read at all – turn straight to the back page.'

'Yeah.' Danny nodded in agreement. 'I know they're all thickos, Mr Poole, but we do have to make money.' He faced me again.

'So, what d'you reckon, Mr Brock? Gang-land killing? Settling old scores? There's got to be a story there somewhere.'

'All I can tell you, Danny, is what you'll have read in a proper newspaper: Spotter Gould stepped out of Stone Mill and some-one shot him. Full stop.'

'But you must have some idea,' persisted Danny. 'I know you clever detectives. Always got a snout some place who'll finger the villain for the price of a double Scotch.'

'Unlike journalists, and to quote a well-known student of English literature: "I have heard it said that there is honour among thieves",' said Dave.

'Who said that?' asked Danny.

'I did,' said Dave.

'Yeah, but you must be following up leads, surely?'

'I'll tell you what, Danny,' I said. 'You give me some leads and I'll follow them up. Thanks for the drink.'

When we'd left New Labour House, Dave had telephoned Darren Walters's details to Colin Wilberforce, the detective sergeant responsible for the efficient running of the incident room.

'I've got a result, sir,' said Colin when we arrived back at Curtis Green. 'Darren Wal-ters has got two previous. Both for dipping. He started off nicking women's handbags out of their shopping trolleys in the supermarket, but then he graduated to Epsom races. Unfortunately, he tried to dip a Flying Squad officer's pocket at the Derby a year or two back.'

'Oh dear,' I said.

'It gets better, sir,' said Colin. 'This particular Squad officer always carries strong rat-traps in his pockets on race days, and guess whose fingers got nastily lacerated?'

'What did he go down for, Colin?' asked Dave, once the laughter had subsided.

'A month,' said Colin.

'A month?' Dave sounded disgusted. 'Must have been a bench of lay magistrates,' he muttered. 'And I'll bet he's up to more villainy that he's yet to answer for.'

'One other thing, sir,' said Colin. 'Mr Mead rang in to say that he's drawn a blank on house-to-house enquiries in the road outside the prison.'

Frank Mead was the ex-Flying Squad detective inspector in charge of the legwork team. And if he said there was nothing to be learned, then there was nothing. But it turned out, much later on, that on this occasion he was wrong.

We were at Stone Mill prison at eight thirty the following morning ready to embark upon what we knew from the outset would be a fruitless exercise.

Talking to villains who have been arrested for a crime can sometimes be quite profitable. If they think that there's the slightest chance of getting away with whatever they're being accused of, there is a tendency for them to sing like canaries. Sometimes.

But there is no reason why *convicted* villains should talk to the Old Bill about a crime, whether they are connected with it or not, because there is little profit for them in doing so. No one is going to wave a magic wand and let them out.

The governor had allocated us a room in which we could interview those inmates who had known Spotter Gould. We started with those who had been on the same landing.

However, the first prisoner set the pattern for all those who followed.

'Yeah, I knew Spotter. So what?'

'Was he a grass?'

'Not that I know of. He couldn't hardly talk.'

'Meaning what?'

'He got beat up a few years back and hit in the throat. Got his voice box damaged. He only ever whispered.'

That much we had learned from Fat Danny.

'An informant' – I wasn't going to mention Darren Walters's name – 'suggested that he got a lesser sentence for his last job because he grassed.'

'News to me, mate.'

And so it went on. Word had soon got round the prison that the Old Bill was in and was asking questions. We spent the whole day conducting similar interviews, all with similarly profitless results.

I glanced at my watch. It was five o'clock, and for the past eight hours or so, with a short break for lunch in the prison officers' canteen, we had interviewed countless prisoners. And got nowhere.

'I think we're wasting our time, Dave,' I said.

'Yes, sir,' said Dave drily. He always called me 'sir' when I made what he regarded as a stupid comment or asked a pointless question. It's Dave's form of a barometer that gauges the worth of my professional expertise.

'In that case,' I said, 'we'll get a list of recently discharged prisoners and have a go at them.'

'Good idea, sir,' said Dave.

'Ah, Chief Inspector, I was just about to go home.' The governor was standing in his office with his overcoat on. 'How did you get on?' he asked, making a point of glancing at his watch.

I wondered briefly if he was related to the commander, whose reputation for timekeeping is legendary.

'Despite information I've received that Jimmy Gould was a police informant, none of the prisoners I've interviewed is prepared

29

to confirm it, or that he received a lesser sentence because he fingered some of the others who took part in the robbery for which he was sentenced to eight years.'

'It's interesting that you should mention that, Chief Inspector, because I received some information from within the prison that Gould was an informant.' Clearly resigned to delaying his departure, the governor took off his overcoat and sat down behind his desk. 'I had a prisoner seek a confidential interview with me about a year ago, and he told me that Gould was an informant and had been threatened with violence.'

'What was this prisoner's name?' I asked.

Presumably as part of his thought processes, or even for want of regal inspiration, the governor levelled his gaze at the opposite wall and studied a government-issue picture of Her Majesty The Queen. 'Bernard Pointer,' he said eventually.

Beside me, Dave shuffled quickly through the list of prisoners we'd interviewed. 'Not on here, sir.' This was a different sort of 'sir'; Dave was always formal in the presence of outsiders.

'No, you wouldn't have done,' said the governor. 'He was released yesterday morning. At the same time as Gould.'

'Before or after?' asked Dave.

'Before or after what?' The governor looked a touch bemused, but then he wasn't as

30

accustomed to Dave's rapid-fire form of questioning as I was.

'Before or after Gould.'

'Oh, I see. As a matter of fact just after. He was being let out when the shooting occurred.' The governor smiled sadistically. 'He ran back in here at a very fast speed.'

'Don't blame him,' said Dave. 'But he was released eventually, I suppose.'

'Yes, he was.'

'And nobody thought to detain him on the grounds that he was a material witness to a murder?'

'We had no power to detain him, Chief Inspector,' said the governor loftily. 'He was a time-expired prisoner.'

'Very nearly time-expired permanently,' observed Dave drily. 'Presumably a prison officer also saw the shooting.'

'I imagine so. Do you want to interview him?'

'Yes, we do,' said Dave.

'How did this man Pointer know that Gould had been threatened with violence?' I asked.

'He claimed he had been told by another prisoner.'

'And *that* prisoner's name?'

The governor pinched the bridge of his nose, ferreted about in his pockets until he found his glasses and put them on. Carefully. He unlocked one of his desk drawers and eventually produced a small book.

'Record of confidential interviews,' he explained and began to thumb through the pages. 'Ah, here we are. Pointer claimed that the prisoner who told him that Gould was in danger was called Edward Jarvis.'

'We saw him this morning, sir,' said Dave. 'He never mentioned anything about that.'

'In that case we'll see him again.' I did not like being jerked about by villains.

'There was something else,' said the governor. 'Shortly after Pointer came to see me, I interviewed Gould and told him that it had been suggested that he was a police informant and could be at risk. I asked him if he wished to be segregated under Rule 43, but he declined, and he strongly denied being an informant. Oddly though, Pointer was assaulted shortly after he came to see me and applied for segregation, which was duly granted. He remained segregated until his release.'

'What was Pointer in for?' I asked.

'Embezzlement. He was a solicitor's clerk, apparently, and stole from his principal's client account to the tune of eight thousand pounds. He got five years at the Old Bailey, but was released on parole after thirty months.'

'And what address did he give when he was released, Governor?'

'I think my secretary's gone home,' said the governor, rising from his chair with a sigh, 'but I'll see if I can find the file.' Our enquiries seemed to be placing an unwarranted burden on him.

Minutes later, he returned from the outer office with a slip of paper in his hand. 'There you are, Chief Inspector. He's gone to 27 Capstick Road, Merton Park.'

'We hope,' murmured Dave.

'Oh, he will have done,' said the governor confidently. 'Before paroled prisoners can be released, the addresses to which they are going are checked by the Probation Service. It's his sister's place, apparently. Pointer wasn't married.'

'How old was he?'

'Forty last birthday,' said the governor. 'His date of birth is on there,' he added, pointing to the slip of paper.

Edward Jarvis was a surly individual with a broken nose and biceps that stretched the sleeves of his T-shirt.

'When I spoke to you this morning, Mr Jarvis, you denied knowing that Jimmy Gould was a grass.'

'Well, he wasn't, was he?'

'But another prisoner reported to the governor that you'd told him that Gould had grassed up some of his associates and that there were prisoners out to get him.'

Jarvis gave a mirthless laugh. 'You're talking about that weasel Pointer.'

'So what's the story?'

'Pointer was a poofy sort of geezer, full of

piss and importance, and we thought it was *him* what was the grass. So we fed him this bollocks about Jimmy just to see if he'd go running to the governor.'

'And he did,' said Dave.

'Too right, mate,' said Jarvis.

'And so you beat him up.'

'Did I?' Jarvis affected an air of injured innocence. 'Well, someone duffed him up, that's for sure. So the sneaky little git goes back up the governor's office like a rat up a drainpipe, begging for Rule 43.'

'So what did that achieve?' I asked.

'Bloody obvious, innit? We'd proved he was grassing to the governor, and we'd got him off the landing. In fact we got him out of the wing altogether. He couldn't do no more grassing to the honcho after that. Never had no one to talk to, see.' Jarvis laughed callously. ''Cept the screws, o' course.'

'How did you know he'd reported what you'd said to the governor?'

''Cos the governor sent for Jimmy and told him. Offered him Rule 43 an' all. So we knew Pointer had been shooting his mouth off. That's the bleedin' death wish in here, I can tell you.'

By some mysterious complexity of the duty roster, John Purvis, the prison officer who had been early-shift on the gate yesterday, was on the late shift today.

'Gould and Pointer were the only two inmates released yesterday morning,' said

Purvis.

'So tell me what happened.'

'The reception officer had gone through all the usual malarkey: restoration of property, getting signatures for it, and issuing all the usual forms and statutory notices that—'

'Yes, I'm sure that was all done correctly, but what happened next?'

'Well, it was done in alphabetical order, see. Gould first, Pointer second. So when the reception PO gives me the nod, I opened the wicket gate and bid Gould a fond farewell.' Purvis gave a throaty chuckle. 'And then I said what I usually say: see you again soon. Anyhow, Gould hadn't gone more than ten yards across the forecourt when he went down.'

'Did you hear anything, Mr Purvis?' asked Dave.

'Well, now I come to think about it there was a noise that could've been a shot, but there was a lot of traffic noise at that time of the morning.'

'What about Pointer?'

'Yeah, funny that. He reckoned straight off it was a shot. He'd just stepped out of the wicket and bloody near broke his leg getting back in again. I tell you, I've never seen a prisoner in such a hurry to get back into the nick. It was almost as if he'd sussed out that there was a bit of shooting going on and that he might be next.'

'You'll know now that Gould was in fact

shot,' I said, 'but have you any idea where that shot might have come from?'

'No. I just saw Gould go down and the next thing I was sent flying by Pointer rushing back in. If he hadn't been released already, I'd've done him for assaulting an officer.'

Capstick Road, Merton Park, was a street of well-kept semi-detached houses not far from Morden Underground station.

The door of number 27 was answered by a man of about forty who gave us the sort of suspicious glance that we've come to expect of men with a bit of form behind them, and who immediately recognized callers like us as police. But, as it turned out, he hadn't got any previous convictions.

'Mr Pointer?'

'No. Who wants to know anyway?'

'We're police officers,' I said.

'What d'you want with that loser now? He only came out of prison yesterday. Are you going to arrest him again?' the man asked hopefully.

'We think he may be able to assist us in our enquiries into a murder, Mr...?'

'Morrison. Geoffrey Morrison. You'd better come in, I suppose.'

Morrison led us into the front room of his house and we were joined shortly afterwards by a woman he introduced as his wife Karen. She was small and mouse-like with permed hair, and from her demeanour clearly in awe of her husband.

'What is it, Geoff?' Karen glanced nervously at Dave and me, then at her husband.

'It's the police, love. They've come to see your damned brother about a murder.' Morrison turned to us. 'Is this the shooting that happened outside Stone Mill prison yesterday? The one that was on the news last night?'

'Yes,' I said.

'Well, he couldn't have done it because—'

'I know he didn't do it, Mr Morrison, but he may have witnessed it. That's our interest and that's why we want to talk to him.'

'Well, I'm sorry to disappoint you, but he's not here.'

'Have you any idea when he'll be back?'

'Never, I hope. I threw him out. Some probation officer came round here a few weeks ago and said he was checking on where Bernie was going to live when he came out. Well, Karen here, who's Bernie's sister, said yes, it'd be OK. I wasn't here, you see. But I put the kibosh on it when I got home, and I told her I wasn't having any ex-con in my house, brother-in-law or no brother-in-law. So when he turned up yesterday morning, I gave him his marching orders. Full stop. I don't know where he's gone and I couldn't care less.'

Beside her husband, Karen nodded meekly. 'I suppose Geoff was right,' she said. 'I just felt sorry for Bernie, and he is my brother after all. But we've got children of an impressionable age to worry about. Geoff said that if we were having a criminal living here, all sorts of undesirables might turn up. I suppose Geoff was right,' she said again.

'Have you any idea where he went when he left here?' asked Dave.

'No, and I don't want to know,' said Morrison. 'The further away he stays from my family the better. And I'll tell you this much: if he shows his face here again, he's likely to get some of this.' And Morrison raised a balled fist.

'But he did say he'd let us know where he'd gone,' volunteered Karen Morrison.

I gave Karen one of my cards. 'If he does get in touch, perhaps you'd ask him to ring this number, Mrs Morrison. You can tell him he's not in any trouble. We just want to find out what, if anything, he saw yesterday morning.'

But I held out little hope that Bernie Pointer would tell his sister where he'd gone, and had a gut feeling that he was quite happy to disappear into the hinterland of Greater London. And that getting in touch with the police, for whatever reason, would be the furthest thought from his mind.

There was little else we could do that evening. Back at Curtis Green, I told Gavin Creasey, the night-duty incident-room sergeant, to put Bernard Pointer's name on the Police National Computer and mark it up for breach of parole. Unfortunately embezzlement is not what we call a repeat crime, and the chances were that Pointer would go straight now that he'd served his time. I made the mistake of putting that theory to Dave.

'Quite possibly, sir,' he said.

The next morning I decided to make enquiries of the solicitor whose client account Pointer had plundered.

It turned out to be a large firm with prestigious offices in central London, and the senior partner saw us immediately.

'Oh yes, I remember Pointer,' he said, somewhat ruefully, once we'd explained the reason for our visit. 'The trouble is that we tend to trust our staff, but it turned out to have been a mistake in Pointer's case. He'd obviously been stealing from the client account for some time before we rumbled what was going on.'

'How long had he been with you?' I asked.

'About six months, I suppose. I must say he was very good at accountancy. A touch too good,' the solicitor added.

'Where did he come from, sir?' Dave asked.

By way of a reply, the solicitor thumbed down a switch on his intercom and relayed the question to his secretary. Five minutes later a woman appeared and handed the senior partner a sheet of paper.

The solicitor glanced at it and then handed it to me. 'There we are,' he said. 'He was with that firm for about a year, so I understand.'

'Did he provide a reference?' I asked.

'Yes, he did.'

'And did you check it with the signatory?'

There was a distinct pause, and then, 'Er, no, I'm afraid we didn't. Very remiss of us, as it happened. But we've learned our lesson.'

I decided not to mention that it would ease the workload of the police if that sort of verification were to be made. But as usual, we were left to pick up the pieces once it had all gone pear-shaped and the losers came running to us in tears.

'Do you have a copy of the reference he provided?' I asked.

The secretary was summoned again, and eventually produced a letter typed on the headed notepaper of the firm for which Pointer had worked previously. As an accounts clerk with a firm of West London undertakers.

Having obtained a photocopy of Pointer's reference we made for the offices of the funeral directors whose address was on the reference.

A bald-headed man rose from his chair behind an ornate desk, an expression of suitable gravitas on his face, and in well-modulated, funereal tones introduced himself as *Mister* Crow. His shirt collar was about two sizes too big and he moved his head backward and forward so that he resembled the sort of nodding dog frequently seen on the back shelf of cars driven by idiots. 'May I begin by offering my condolences on your loss, sir,' he began.

'We're police officers,' I said.

'Oh!' said Crow, and began nodding again.

'I understand that some four years ago you employed a man named Bernard Pointer, Mr Crow.'

'Never heard of him,' said Crow, his expression and his accent changing quite dramatically. He was lying. I just knew he was lying.

I produced the copy of Pointer's reference. 'This was the glowing testimonial he produced when he went on to the firm whose client account he screwed for eight grand,' I said.

The undertaker laughed at that. 'Serve 'em right.' But the smile vanished when he took the document. 'I never wrote that,' he protested. 'I don't know anyone called Pointer. I'll bet it was that bastard Salter. He must have pinched some of our notepaper and forged it,' he said, with a show of outrage. 'And he was only here for six weeks, not a year.' He looked up. 'You going to nick him for that?' he asked.

'You knew him as Salter, then?' I asked.

'Yeah, Bob Salter. Why's he calling himself Pointer, I wonder?'

'Why did he leave?' asked Dave.

'Dunno. Like I said, he was here for about six weeks, but he never turned up after that. Never gave notice or nothing. No loss, mind you. Half the time he didn't come in anyway, and I had a shrewd suspicion he'd had his hand in the till, although I couldn't prove anything.' Crow waved the photocopy of the bogus reference. 'You going to do him for this?'

'Might consider it,' I said. 'If we can find him.' But I knew that there was no chance of the Crown Prosecution Service having a stab at that.

'Well, you can put me down as a witness. I'll happily swear that little bugger's life away.'

'You said he frequently didn't turn up for work. What was he, sick?' Dave asked.

'That's what he claimed,' said Mr Crow, 'but he was as fit as a flea. No, I reckon he was up to something. There were two or three occasions when I did a check by ringing him at home, but there was never an answer.'

'Did you confront him with it?' asked Dave.

'Too bloody true. But he said he was in bed and too ill to answer the phone. Well, if you believe that, you'll believe anything.'

'Where did he live?'

Crow paused. 'D'you know, I've no idea. It was his mobile number I rang. He reckoned he hadn't got a landline at home, but the little bugger could've been having me on.'

'Where did he work before he came to you?'

'The army. He produced a discharge book of some sort which said he'd finished his time and was given a character reference of "Very Good".'

'And did you take up references with the army?' I asked.

The undertaker scoffed. 'Have you ever tried to get a reference out of the army? They just said that his discharge book *was* his reference. They didn't even ask for details. I'll tell you this much, Chief Inspector, I'll think twice before I take on any other ex-servicemen.'

Three

Leaving the undertaker alternately vowing vengeance and feeling sorry for himself, Dave and I returned to Curtis Green, there to ponder what to do next.

The commander was lying in wait.

'Ah, Mr Brock, at last. A moment of your time, if you would be so kind,' he said, crooking a finger.

Such courtesy was disturbing and I followed him into the office that housed his paper empire.

'Now, about this suspicious death outside Stone Mill prison, Mr Brock. It's generated a great deal of publicity. I've even had the media trying to speak to me about it. I refused to discuss it, of course. Sub judice, you see.'

Thank God for that.

The commander took a small piece of chamois leather out of his desk drawer and carefully polished his glasses before delivering what he believed was his masterstroke. 'And the Assistant Commissioner is very interested in the outcome.'

Here we go again. He's trying to frighten

me. But a suspicious death? It was murder, plain and simple.

'I imagine he is, sir.'

The commander gave me a hard stare, suspecting that I was being sarcastic. Which, of course, I was. 'So, what progress have you made?'

I explained what I had learned so far, which was very little, but I'm not sure the commander understood even that much. Although purporting to be a detective, he had been transformed into one by the stroke of a pen whose wielder was, doubtless, secreted somewhere deep inside the walls of New Scotland Yard, detached from the horrors of the outside world.

All the commander's previous service had been in the Uniform Branch, where he dealt, not very well I'd heard, with such important matters as abuse of overtime claims, traffic flow in Willesden and the design of protective clothing and other accoutrements for female officers. He was also reputed to be a positive wizard at dealing with complaints against the police. But to his credit, he had a reputation for being able to pen a withering memorandum. And that was apart from an extended tour on the directing staff of the Police College at Bramshill, a post for which, at least in my view, he was ideally suited. In fact, so suited was he that I was sorry they ever let him go.

'I see,' said the commander. 'And d'you

think that this man Pointer had anything to do with it?'

I repeated what I'd already said, that Pointer had emerged from the prison *after* the shooting and that his involvement was, therefore, unlikely.

'Mmm! Yes, I see. Well, keep me posted, Mr Brock.' And with that, the commander waved an airy hand of dismissal.

Somewhere in the great metropolis there is a giant kaleidoscope that someone takes delight in shaking from time to time. Just to annoy me.

This time they chose to shake it the very next morning, a Saturday. Naturally.

Intending to have most of the day off, and perhaps take my girlfriend out to dinner, I had come to the office just to check whether anything of significance had occurred overnight. It had.

'Good morning, sir.' Colin Wilberforce was at his desk. There were times when I thought he actually lived in the incident room. 'I was just going to ring you.'

That was always an ominous statement. 'What's happening, then?' I asked.

'Bernie Pointer's been found, sir.'

'Excellent. Where?'

'On Hounslow Heath early this morning, sir. He'd been shot dead.'

'Oh, what a bloody shame.' This was not an expression of sympathy for the deceased

46

Bernie Pointer, but that he'd been found in an area for which SCG West had responsibility. And I was already anticipating what the commander would say about that. But I didn't have to anticipate for long. 'Has the commander been informed, Colin?'

'Yes, sir. I telephoned him first thing this morning. He's directed that you deal with it as it seems to him to be connected in some way with the Spotter Gould shooting.'

I wonder how he arrived at that conclusion.

'What's the SP?' I enquired, using a handy bit of racing terminology. Although it means 'starting price' to the aficionados of the turf, coppers use it when they want to know the story.

'Been shot once in the back of the head, sir. DCI Warner at Hounslow is dealing until you take over. He reckons it looks like a gangland killing.'

'Well, we can't do Pointer for breach of parole now, can we? Is Dave Poole in yet, Colin?'

'Yes, sir. He's getting the coffees.'

Brian Warner was in his office at the nick in Montague Road when Dave and I got there.

'What's the score, Brian?' I asked, once I'd introduced Dave. Asking the score is another bit of copper's jargon, lifted this time from cricket, but meaning exactly the same as SP.

'A jogger was pounding round the public

47

golf course on Hounslow Heath at around six o'clock this morning, Harry. He found Pointer on the seventh green. Single bullet to the back of the head.'

'Hole in one,' said Dave, and was ignored by both of us.

'Looks like an execution,' Warner continued. 'I checked the PNC and found you had an interest. What's that all about?' He didn't need to know because he'd already been told that the investigation into Pointer's murder was down to me. But CID officers are, by nature, inquisitive. It's what we're paid for.

I explained, as succinctly as possible, why Bernie Pointer had come to our notice, and gave Brian a rundown on his form.

'Yeah, I picked that up from CRO,' said Warner. By which he meant Criminal Records Office, although the admin wizards at the Yard are probably calling it something else now. Just to confuse us. 'It's possible, I suppose, that someone might have rubbed out Pointer because he'd seen whoever shot Spotter Gould. Just in case.'

'Maybe. Maybe not. What did the divisional surgeon have to say?'

'Certified death,' said Brian with a smile, 'and buggered off.'

'Where's the body now?'

'Under guard in the mortuary at the local hospital. Who's going to do the PM?'

'Henry Mortlock, if I've got anything to do with it,' I said. 'In fact, if you'd arrange for it to be shifted to Horseferry Road, you'd be doing me a favour.'

'Glad to get rid of it, Harry,' said Warner. 'And the best of British luck.'

'Yeah, thanks.'

'By the way, the crime-scene examiners did the business. I told them to send the report to you.'

Colin Wilberforce had called in my team, even those whose scheduled day off it was, and by the time Dave and I returned to Curtis Green, they were assembled in the incident room.

'Sorry to bring you in,' I began, but by the smiles on the faces of those who were incurring overtime, they weren't all that sorry. I explained about the discovery of Bernie Pointer's body. 'It's possible that Pointer was topped because he saw who shot Spotter Gould on Wednesday,' I said, rehearsing Brian Warner's theory. 'On the other hand it may be that Pointer was the intended Stone Mill victim, and that Gould's murder was a mistake.'

'Oh, what a bleedin' tragedy,' said one of the DCs.

'Perhaps it was just Gould's bad luck to come out of the prison first,' I continued. 'We interviewed the screw who let Gould and Pointer out, but he claimed to have seen nothing of the shooting. However, he did tell us that the minute the bullets started flying

Pointer ran back into the nick as fast as his little legs would carry him.'

'Don't blame him,' said an anonymous voice.

'While Pointer was in the nick he was segregated under Rule 43 because he'd taken a beating for informing to the prison governor. But he might have known that someone was gunning for him and engineered the whole thing. Apparently he told the governor that Spotter Gould was a grass and was in danger of getting worked over. But another prisoner denied that, and told me that Pointer was the one they thought was talking out of turn and had set him up with the story of Gould grassing. Whatever the reason, Pointer got topped.'

'Looks like whoever was after him succeeded,' commented DI Frank Mead.

'DCI Warner at Hounslow is organizing house-to-house enquiries in the roads nearest the golf course, although I doubt they'll get much. The houses are a long way from the seventh green and I don't suppose Pointer was shot where he was found. More likely that he was murdered some place else and dumped there. I don't see him walking out to the seventh green in the middle of the night just to get some air.'

'So what's next?' Frank asked.

'The priority is to find out as much as possible about Bernie Pointer,' I said, and told the team about how Pointer had been given his marching orders by his brother-in-law Geoffrey Morrison. 'I suspect that there is more to Pointer than meets the eye. Get everyone out asking questions – and there's no time like the present – to see if anyone knows anything about him that might help. It's a long shot, I know, but someone must have something on him. Otherwise, why's he dead?'

'When's the PM, guv?' asked Tom Challis, one of Frank's detective sergeants.

'I've already spoken to Henry Mortlock and he'll begin carving on Monday morning. But I suspect that he'll not tell us anything we don't already know.'

'Anything on the bullet that killed Gould?' asked Frank.

'Yes, a 5.56-millimetre probably fired from a sniper rifle of some sort. We'll have to wait and see whether the round that killed Pointer is the same calibre. And, if we're extremely lucky, came from the same weapon. But somehow I think that Pointer's killer used a handgun close up.'

'What about the golf course?' asked Frank.

'It's still cordoned off, but Brian Warner hasn't searched it yet. Get out there and arrange for the local Territorial Support Group to do a fingertip. The CSEs have done an examination for footprints and tyre marks and I'm waiting for their report.' I stood up. 'Okay, that's it. Dave and I are going out to Merton Park to see the Morrisons again.'

51

It was three o'clock that afternoon by the time Dave and I arrived once more at the Morrisons' house in Capstick Road to break the news of Pointer's death.

Karen Morrison was in the house on her own. Her husband, she told us, had taken their sons to a football match.

Naturally enough, Mrs Morrison was distraught at the news of her brother's murder and her first reaction was to telephone her husband on his mobile and ask him to come home.

'What happened?' she asked. 'You say he was murdered? Who would have wanted to do that?'

Her response was a typical one. The innocent relatives of murder victims could never understand, and often could never accept, that their loved ones might not have been all they thought they were to the extent that someone would want to kill them. I had already come to the conclusion that Pointer was involved in more villainy than we had so far discovered, but there was no point in telling Mrs Morrison that.

'We don't know at this stage,' I said, 'but we're doing our best to find out.'

A few tears ran, unchecked, down Karen Morrison's cheeks. She took a tissue from her handbag and dabbed at her eyes. 'Whatever you might think, he was a good brother, you know,' she said. 'He never bullied me when we were children.'

Maybe so, but it is not beyond the experience of police that nice little boys sometimes grow up to be violent criminals.

'When he arrived here on Wednesday, Mrs Morrison,' I asked, 'how long did he stay before your husband threw him out?'

There was a long pause before the woman answered. 'He never actually came here, Mr Brock,' she said.

'But I thought your husband said—'

'I know what he said, but Bernie didn't come here.'

'I think we'd better start again,' I said. 'I was told that a probation officer came here to check on the suitability of your house as a place of residence for Bernard. I was told this by the prison governor, and by you and your husband. And your husband said he'd thrown him out.'

'I know. But the last time I visited Bernard in prison, he said that he'd given our address because he knew it would pass the test. Those were his very words. And he also asked us to confirm to the probation officer that this is where he'd be staying. But then he told me that he wasn't going to come here. He wasn't very forthcoming about where he intended to go, but I got the impression that he was frightened of something. He said that he intended to disappear and that I might not hear from him for some time.'

'Did he say what he was frightened of?'

asked Dave.

'No. We'd always been open with each other, even as kids, and I tried to get him to tell me. But he wouldn't say.'

'Well, did you have any idea?'

'No.' Karen Morrison gave a convulsive sob. 'It came as a complete shock when Bernard was sent to prison nearly three years ago.'

But, we later learned, he'd been to prison before that, and presumably had kept it from his sister.

'Did he ever talk about going to prison?' Dave went on.

'He said that there'd been a mix-up with the money at the place where he was working and that they thought he'd been stealing. Anyway, he couldn't prove that he hadn't and as he was the accountant the police reckoned it must have been him.' Karen gave us an apologetic smile. It was as though she was not blaming me personally for what her brother had probably persuaded her had been a miscarriage of justice.

'Did you know where he was working, Mrs Morrison? When he was arrested, I mean.' Dave was obviously pursuing his own line of questioning, and knowing how good he'd been at it in the past I let him continue. We knew where Pointer had been working, but it would be interesting to hear what he'd told his sister.

'I think it was a solicitor's office, but I

don't know where.'

At least that much was true.

'Did he ever work for an undertaker?'

'I don't think so.' Karen shook her head. 'Well, if he did he never mentioned it. To tell you the truth, Bernie was a bit squeamish, and I can't visualize him working with dead bodies.'

'When did Bernard leave the army, Mrs Morrison?' Dave asked suddenly.

There was a look of astonishment on Karen Morrison's face, followed by a brief laugh. 'Army? Bernard was never in the army.' She laughed again. 'He was the last person on earth to become a soldier. Much as I loved him, I can tell you that he wasn't very brave, and he could never have stood the discipline. He was quite a gentle person, you know.'

I tried one last question. 'Did your brother have any connections with Hounslow, Mrs Morrison? Did he know anyone there, for example?'

'Not that I know of.' Again an expression of bewilderment crossed Karen's face. 'Why d'you ask?'

'Because that's where his body was found.'

We stood up to leave, but as we reached the front door, Geoffrey Morrison arrived. His young sons promptly disappeared to their room announcing that they were going to 'surf the net', whatever that meant.

'What's this all about?' asked Morrison.

55

'Karen phoned me at the match. We had to miss the second half.' He seemed more concerned at that than hearing of his brother-in-law's demise.

I explained what had happened to Pointer and put the same questions to Morrison as we had put to his wife. And got similar answers. With one addition.

'There was one thing,' said Morrison thoughtfully. 'He seemed to spend a lot of his time abroad. Before he was arrested, I mean.'

'On holiday?' asked Dave.

'I doubt it. He was always off to France for a few days. Perhaps as often as once a month.'

'Did you ever ask him what he was doing?'

'No. There wouldn't have been any point, anyway. We didn't get on, Bernie and me. We hardly ever spoke to each other.'

I turned to Karen. 'Have you any idea what your brother was doing in France so often, Mrs Morrison?'

'He said it was business.'

'Connected with this job he had in a solicitor's office?' asked Dave.

'I don't know. He was always very secretive about it. Although he did say once that it was confidential because it was to do with clients.'

'I understand from your wife, Mr Morrison, that you knew Bernard was not going to stay here.'

Geoffrey Morrison gave Dave and me a guilty look. 'Yes, but I didn't think it mattered too much. I know I said we didn't get on, but as he'd told Karen he wasn't coming here anyway, I didn't see any harm in telling the probation officer that this is where he'd be staying. After all, he'd served his time.'

'As a matter of fact, he'd only served half of it,' said Dave drily.

It was obvious that we would have to speak again to the solicitor and to the undertaker Bernie Pointer had worked for. Even if the solicitor undertook the sale and purchase of properties abroad, I doubted that Pointer would have been visiting France on as regular a basis as his brother-in-law had revealed.

And we would have to dig more deeply into Pointer's claim to Wilfred Crow that he'd been in the army.

We returned to Curtis Green and I went quickly through the messages. Nothing had occurred that demanded my immediate attention, and there was little we could do before Monday morning when our first job would be attending the post-mortem.

'What's Madeleine doing this evening, Dave?' I asked. 'Dancing, is she?'

Dave's wife Madeleine was a principal dancer with the Royal Ballet and spent most of her evenings working at either Covent Garden or, less often, at the London Coliseum or the Festival Hall. Occasionally she would even be on tour. Which is why Dave never minded working late.

'No, guv, she's off tonight.'

'You'd better have an early, then, Dave,' I said. 'I don't want to get into Madeleine's bad books, even for a double murder.' A rumour still persisted in the canteens of the Metropolitan Police that Dave sometimes got beaten up by the petite Madeleine, all five feet two of her. But I think that's all it was: a persistent rumour.

Dave grinned and took off, and I telephoned my girlfriend, Gail Sutton, and suggested dinner in Town.

My former girlfriend Dr Sarah Dawson, at the time a rope and yarn expert at the forensic science laboratory, had dumped me in favour of an army major whom she had since married. But then I had the good fortune to meet Gail, a chorus girl who was appearing in a show at the Granville Theatre when I was investigating the murder of one of her colleagues.

Gail was a tall blonde with a fabulous figure and the sort of impish sense of humour that matched mine. And there was the added advantage that she lived in Kingston, very close to my flat in Surbiton. She had been married previously, to a director called Gerald Andrews whom she'd met when he was directing a musical in which she was appearing. However, she had returned home early one night to find him in bed with a nude dancer. And that was the end of that.

'Have you been working today?' she asked, when I met her at Waterloo. The fabulous figure I mentioned was wrapped in a full-length black leather coat and knee-high boots, the whole topped off with a fur hat.

'Nothing unusual about that,' I said. 'After all, you used to work on a Saturday.'

'Yes, and I'm disinclined to go back to it,' said Gail.

I'd selected a restaurant in Covent Garden and we sat over an aperitif watching the snow beginning to fall outside. Under an awning in the corner of the piazza, a five-piece jazz band, warmed by a patio heater, was doing its best to emulate the style of Dave Brubeck.

'So why *were* you working today, darling?' Gail took a sip of her gin and tonic.

'Because two people have inadvertently got themselves murdered,' I said. 'One last Wednesday, the other this morning. Or, more likely, during the night.'

'Oh!' Gail had known me long enough to know that such a case was likely to make serious inroads into my free time. But having been in show business, she understood un-social hours. 'Was that the murder outside the prison?'

'Yes, that's the one.' I broke off to place our orders.

'But why have you got *two* murders to deal

with? Isn't there anyone else who can do the second one?'

'It's because they're connected,' I said, but forbore from explaining the intricacies of this particular criminal investigation. Or at least, how the commander saw them. 'And what about you? Anything in the offing?'

I knew that Gail, having tired of what she called 'hoofing', had been seeking an acting role, but the theatre business was struggling at the moment and shows had been closing after very short runs. The producers blamed it on the terrorist situation and the concomitant demise of tourism, but the realists, Gail among them, knew that many of the productions would have failed anyway simply because they were not what the theatre-going public wanted to see.

The jazz band finally gave up and departed to a lukewarm round of applause from those brave souls, cowering beneath umbrellas, who had formed its diminishing audience.

'So what are you going to do?'

'Nothing,' said Gail and gave me a ravishing smile. 'At least not for the time being. Daddy's quite happy for me to give up the theatre altogether, but I can't live on the allowance he gives me.'

'Isn't it enough, then?'

'On the contrary, it's very generous, but I can't just let him pay for me to be lazy. I'm not sure what I want to do.'

I wondered whether this was a veiled hint

at marriage but dismissed the thought immediately. Gail wasn't devious.

It was still snowing when we left the restaurant and, as is always the way in such circumstances, it was a good twenty minutes before we managed to find a taxi.

The snow had abated by the time we got to Surbiton, leaving the pavements slushy.

Gail paused for a moment in the entrance to the railway station, and linked arms with me. 'Your flat or mine, darling?'

'What for?' I asked, in an attempt to match her teasing.

'Well, I'm not talking about a cup of cocoa,' she responded, and dug me in the ribs with her elbow.

Four

Gail and I had eventually decided to spend the night at my flat rather than her house, and after a leisurely breakfast we spent most of Sunday lounging about playing CDs. We did venture out to a local pub at lunchtime, but wished we hadn't. The snow had started again, and there was a biting wind. And when we got there the pub was full of bikers in leathers that reeked of engine oil.

Having spent most of Saturday working, what remained of the weekend had gone much too quickly. But despite having two murders on my plate, I'd not had a single call from the office.

On Monday morning I met Dave at the mortuary for the grand opening of Bernie Pointer. Henry Mortlock was awaiting our arrival with an impatient expression on his face. I don't know what drives the medical profession, apart from money, but they always start work early.

'Good morning, Harry,' he said, glancing pointedly at his watch.

With a practised skill that he had developed over the years, Henry finished the post-mortem in about ninety minutes flat. Apart from the fact that Pointer had died at around eleven last Friday evening as a result of a gunshot wound to the head, the only evidence of real value to me was the bullet that had killed him. Even though I lacked the expertise of the forensic science laboratory's ballistics experts, I could see that it was of a different calibre from the one that had done for Spotter Gould. But that didn't preclude the possibility that the same finger had pulled both triggers.

From the mortuary we went straight to the offices of the solicitor whose funds Pointer had embezzled.

'Since we were here on Friday,' I began, 'I have learned from Pointer's previous employer that he had a poor sick record. Was that the case when he worked for you?'

'Yes, it was, Mr Brock. He was absent quite often.'

'Did he ever telephone to say he'd be taking the day off?'

'Yes, always. He said something about having recurring stomach pains. To be perfectly honest, I thought he was malingering, although I have to say he always put in a good day's work when he was here.' The solicitor paused. 'Most of it for himself, it transpired,' he said ruefully. 'And those frequent absences were one of the reasons why I arranged for our accountants to look closely at the monies for which Pointer was responsible.' He brushed a biscuit crumb from the top of his otherwise virgin desktop. 'I did a bit of amateur detective work' – he gave an embarrassed little laugh – 'and curiously enough the days when he wasn't here always seem to coincide with a race meeting somewhere or another in the Home Counties. Call it suspicious of me if you like, but I did wonder if he was spending our money on the horses.'

What a clever old lawyer you are, even though I think you were wildly mistaken in your theory.

'Did he ever have occasion to go abroad on your firm's business?' I asked.

'Good heavens, no.' The solicitor seemed quite appalled at that suggestion, and I wondered just how far he'd trusted Pointer even before he'd had the accounts checked. 'There'd've been no reason. He was the book-keeper. One does not send book-keepers abroad on business,' he added with a slight lift of his nose. There was another pause. 'As a matter of interest, why are you making enquiries about Pointer?'

'Because someone murdered him on Friday evening,' I said.

'Good God!' said the solicitor.

'Incidentally, what address did you have for him?'

Once again the enquiry was relayed to the secretary, who eventually came up with an address in Lambeth.

Needless to say, when one of Frank Mead's team went looking for it, it didn't exist.

Mr Crow, the undertaker for whom Pointer had been working prior to taking employment with the solicitor, looked hopeful when we entered his establishment.

'You've come for a statement, I presume,' he said.

'Why would I want a statement?' I asked.

'Well, aren't you going to do Salter for forging that reference?'

'Not unless Salter and Pointer are different people. Bernie Pointer was found on the golf course at Hounslow Heath on Saturday morning. Someone had shot him in the back of the head.'

'Really?' said Mr Crow. 'I never took him for that bad a golfer. In fact I never took him for a golfer at all.' He laughed at what he thought was a joke. But then I'd discovered before that undertakers have a macabre sense of humour similar to that of coppers. 'Well, much as I might have felt like doing him in, it wasn't me. We're not that desperate for business. Anyway, what was that all about?'

'At the moment, I haven't any idea,' I said, 'but we're working on it.'

'The last time we were here you told us that Salter was often absent,' said Dave.

'Yes, I did, and then I told you that one day

65

he was absent for good. What about it?'

'We've been told,' Dave continued, 'that he often visited France. Perhaps as much as once a month and for two or three days at a time. Would that have been on your firm's business?'

'Not bloody likely,' said Crow. 'I'd've trusted Salter about as far as I could throw a grand piano. I certainly wouldn't have relied on him to do any business for me, especially abroad.'

'What exactly did he do here, Mr Crow?' I asked.

Crow looked foxy. 'A bit of this and a bit of that. Sort of general help really. Oh, and he did the books.'

'This claim of Pointer's about having been in the army,' I said. 'D'you remember anything about the discharge book he showed you?'

'Not really, no. I seem to recall it was a red book with crossed swords on the front. But as I said, when I rang the army some snotty-nosed civil servant said that they didn't give references and that everything I needed to know was in the book. There was a reference of sorts, I must admit, but it was only about his service as a soldier. No damned good in the funeral business, I can tell you.'

Back at Curtis Green, Dave spent some considerable time on the phone to the Ministry of Defence before he was put through to

66

someone who could answer our query. And then it came to nothing.

'The short answer is that they don't know, guv. If we can tell them which regiment he was in, and provide them with an army number, or a personal number if he was an officer, they could check for us. But we couldn't give them that, or a date of joining or leaving. There are thousands of ex-servicemen and it would take them hours to trawl through their records, even though they're on computer. Apparently different regiments' records are held in different parts of the country. Anyway the guy I spoke to said that there's bound to be hundreds of ex-soldiers called Salter or Pointer and unless we could narrow down the search, we'd be wasting our time. And his, apparently. He said that there are probably so many that we wouldn't know if we'd got the right one even if they did turn up something. Actually, I think it was all bullshit; I got the distinct impression he didn't want to be bothered.'

'I reckon Pointer or Salter, or whatever his bloody name was, nicked that discharge book, Dave. If he'd Tipp-Exed out the original name and written his own over the top, I doubt that our Mr Crow would've noticed.'

'But why should he do that?'

'Because he didn't want Crow to know what he'd been up to before, Dave.'

Amazingly my optimistic speculation was

confirmed by the crime-scene examiner's report that arrived half an hour later.

'So they are the same according to this, Dave,' I said, skimming through the document. 'The fingerprints that Linda Mitchell took from Pointer's body don't only go out to Pointer with a single conviction for embezzlement, but also to a Robert Salter with a string of previous for petty theft.'

'He obviously didn't want Crow to know he'd been in the nick before,' said Dave. 'Hence the army discharge book,' he added, tossing me a cigarette.

I hesitated before lighting it. When I was at school one of the masters had caught me smoking and told me about his brother dying of nicotine-induced lung cancer. But I've still not summoned up the willpower to break the habit.

'But why the hell wasn't that picked up when he was nicked for embezzlement, then?' asked Dave. 'They must have taken his dabs when he was knocked off.'

'We don't know that it wasn't picked up,' I said.

'But he only got a five-stretch, *and* he got paroled after half of it. Looks like a bent copper who got a backhander for leaving out his previous,' Dave said darkly, even though there were checks in place that largely prevented that sort of thing these days. But if there was one thing guaranteed to infuriate Dave, and me for that matter, it was a corrupt police officer. 'What are you going to do about it, guv?' Once Dave gets wound up there's no stopping him.

I heard the unmistakable steps of the commander coming down the corridor.

'I shall mention it to the commander,' I said loudly, knowing that it was the sort of thing he loved getting his teeth into. But I was only doing it to aggravate him; there was no proof that Pointer's previous convictions hadn't been taken into consideration. But it would give our beloved commander something to do. And to worry about.

'Mention what to me?' asked the commander from the threshold of the incident room.

'I just thought that you ought to know about this, sir,' I said and suggested – only suggested, mind – the possibility of some malpractice. 'There's probably nothing in it, but I think it's always advisable to keep you informed,' I added once I'd explained my suspicions.

'Quite right, Mr Brock, quite right,' said the commander, all stiff and bristling. 'It's positively outrageous. How on earth are we expected to fight crime when this sort of thing goes on?'

Then he ruined it. Alan Cleaver, the detective chief superintendent who sometimes stood in for the commander, would have made a few notes on his pad and then made a phone call. Or he'd've told me to check it out before coming up with some half-baked theory.

But the commander wanted a full written report, as if I hadn't got enough to do, that he intended forwarding, with suitable comments I've no doubt, to the Department of Professional Standards, or in copper's jargon the rubber-heel squad. Serves me right for antagonizing a senior officer.

However, confirmation that Pointer was also Salter, and had previous convictions under that name, gave us some more addresses to check out. Not that I had much hope of finding anything useful after all this time. Even the latest address shown on his record was four years old and I suspected that Bernie Pointer, alias Robert Salter, was a guy who tended to move about frequently. And not to leave a trail. What interested me now was to discover why.

Of the four addresses shown on Pointer's record, in his guise as Robert Salter, three proved to be bum steers. Frank Mead's team banged on doors and interrogated occupants. Each address was a rooming house of bedsits in different parts of London, and there was nobody living there now who had ever heard of either Pointer or Salter.

But the fourth address, in Shepherd's Bush, proved to be a breakthrough that led ultimately to the arrest of the murderer of Gould and Pointer. But even so it was to take some time.

'The CSEs are still going over the room he occupied, Harry,' said Frank Mead, 'not that I think it'll yield much after almost three years, but the guy who owns the place hung on to some documents he found in Salter's room. He said that after Salter was arrested he didn't know what to do with them, but kept them in case Salter ever came back. Apparently he put them in a drawer and forgot about them.' Foremost among the documents that Frank put on my desk was an army discharge book and, believe it or not, the original name had been covered with whitener and the name Robert Salter written over it.

'That was careless of him, leaving that lying about,' I said.

'Seems he didn't have much choice,' said Frank. 'I spoke to the officer who dealt with the embezzlement and he arrested Pointer at his place of work. He searched Salter's room but by that time the helpful landlord had put the documents away and forgotten about them. Incidentally, Pointer's other cons, as Robert Salter, were known to police. So the magistrate refused bail and remanded him in custody until his trial.'

'Blimey!' said Dave. 'He won't last long on the bench. Doesn't he know he's supposed to worry about the villain rather than the victim?'

'There are also a number of used plane tickets for flights between Southampton and

Dinard in Brittany among that lot,' said Frank, gesturing at the little pile of documents. 'There are only about four there, all dated within the two months prior to Pointer's arrest, but it's possible, I suppose, that he may have crossed to France even more often.'

The discovery of airline tickets at Pointer's last address confirmed what Geoffrey Morrison had said about Pointer going abroad quite often, but it still didn't tell us *why* he had gone. To discover the reason now became a priority because I was becoming increasingly sure that these trips had some connection with his murder.

'I wonder why Pointer kept them,' I mused. 'Any bank statements or credit card accounts among them?'

'No,' said Frank, 'but the guy who arrested him seized a number of documents from his person. Might be worth having a look at them. If he can find them,' he added.

But before we did that, I had to destroy the commander's euphoria.

'It seems that Bernard Pointer's previous convictions, in the name of Robert Salter, *were* taken into consideration at his trial, sir,' I said, and went on to explain what Frank Mead had learned from the officer who had arrested Pointer for embezzlement.

'I see,' said the commander glumly. 'In that case I shall not be requiring a report, Mr Brock.'

He seemed quite disappointed.

A detective sergeant called Peter Ledger had arrested Pointer, and Frank Mead had asked him to come to Curtis Green with any property the police still held in the Pointer embezzlement case.

Ledger proved to have been a painstaking officer, thank God! Producing a plastic bag of papers, he explained that he'd searched Pointer's desk at the solicitor's office and had taken possession of a briefcase. The desk and the briefcase had yielded a number of bank statements in the names of both Pointer and Salter. There was also a credit card statement in Salter's name. 'And once Pointer's fingerprints had been taken,' continued Ledger, 'his previous convictions had been discovered. We also found that he had skipped bail on a previous occasion, so that was submitted to the court as a reason for objecting to bail on the case currently before the court.'

'I think Mr Mead's told you about the stuff he found at Pointer's home address,' I said, 'but did you find anything useful there when you searched?'

'No, sir, nothing at all.'

After filling in a few forms and exchanging signatures, the remaining documents passed into the custody of Serious Crime Group West as evidence in a murder case.

But despite my initial optimism, the documents themselves did little to assist us in discovering who might have killed Pointer and Spotter Gould, convinced though I was that there was a connection. They did, however, prove to be the first step in a lengthy journey of investigation.

The ballistics report arrived later that afternoon. It confirmed that the bullet that killed Gould was of 5.56-millimetre calibre, and the writer hazarded a guess that it might have been fired from an M16 carbine, a weapon that was widely available in the criminal community.

The calibre of the bullet that had killed Pointer was 9-millimetre and, said the expert, almost certainly came from a handgun.

Comparisons had been made with police records of weapons previously used, but with no success. So until we found the weapons, we were no further forward.

On Tuesday morning, Dave and I made for Southampton Airport, just outside the city to the north of the M27 motorway.

The surveyor of customs, who told us he was in charge of several ports along the south coast, was as helpful as he could be, but was unable to shed any light on Salter's frequent journeys, or on anyone called Pointer. Until a long serving two-ringer joined in the conversation.

'I remember this guy Salter,' he said.

'Worked for an undertaker. Used to bring in coffins. Haven't seen him for, what, must be about three years now.'

I explained *why* he hadn't seen him for about three years and told him why he wouldn't be seeing him again.

'But tell me more about these coffins,' I said.

'There's not much to tell. I chatted to him once or twice, and he said he worked for an undertaker who specialized in repatriating Brits who'd died on the Continent. Either expats or holidaymakers.'

'And this was definitely Salter, Robert Salter, was it?'

'Yes. I particularly remembered him because my mother's maiden name is Salter.'

'Were these coffins ever opened ... or even X-rayed?'

'No, we don't bother with that now. The families would probably go screaming to the European Court of Human Rights,' the customs officer added with a laugh.

'Did Salter say who he was working for?' Dave asked.

'No, and I never thought to ask him. Is it important?'

'Might be,' I said, underplaying the value of what the customs officer had just revealed.

We were back in London by midday and after a quick lunch, we made for Mr Crow's funeral parlour.

'We have recently learned from an official source, Mr Crow, that on several occasions about three years ago, Robert Salter brought coffins through Southampton Airport from Dinard. This would have been at the time he was working for you.' The last part of my allegation was guesswork, but I wanted to see if Crow would deny it. He did.

'Nothing to do with me,' he exclaimed vehemently. 'He must have been moonlighting, the cheeky bastard. That would certainly explain his frequent absences.'

'Have *you* ever brought coffins in from abroad?' I asked.

'No, never,' said Crow. 'Our business is very local. There are much bigger firms than ours who specialize in that sort of thing.'

'Who owns this business?' asked Dave.

There was a short pause before Crow answered. 'I do,' he said.

Back at the office, I mulled over what we'd learned so far.

'I think we're going to have to go to France, Dave,' I said, 'and visit the customs at Dinard Airport. See what they've got to say about the mysterious Mr Salter and his coffins.'

But the first hurdle that had to be overcome was to convince the commander of the necessity for such a trip. His initial reaction was always to worry about the

76

budget, and getting permission to make an enquiry abroad tended to bring him out in a sweat. He usually resolved the problem by duck-shoving the decision on to the deputy assistant commissioner. The next five minutes proved that nothing had changed.

'But is it really necessary, Mr Brock? Have you not thought of using the services of Europol?'

Time to blind the commander with science, I thought. 'There is a certain urgency about this enquiry, sir,' I said, 'and Europol is in The Hague. My enquiries are in Dinard ... in France. It would take forever.' I was trying to imply that someone would have to catch a bus from The Hague to Dinard to undertake our enquiries.

'But this is precisely the sort of enquiry it was set up to deal with.' The commander loved anything that involved an excessive amount of administration and paperwork. But he was beginning to get out of his depth and changed tack.

'What proof is there that this man was acting in any way unlawfully?'

'For a start, sir, he was operating under a name not his own: Robert Salter. Secondly, as I mentioned the other day, he has convictions under that name and under his own of Bernard Pointer. There's little doubt in my mind that his murder is in some way connected with what I see as nefarious activities.'

See if you can wriggle out of that, I thought. After all, the commander was convinced that there *was* a connection because it was he who'd landed me with the enquiry into Pointer's murder. Nevertheless he tried.

'Well, I, er, I'm not sure. For all we know, he might have been working for another funeral director at the time. Despite your saying that he was only working for this, um, Crow...?'

'Yes, sir, Crow.'

'Yes, for six weeks, I think you said.'

'Yes, that's correct, sir.'

The commander pondered the problem for a moment or two and then came up with the response I'd been expecting all along. 'I think I'll have to refer it to the DAC, Mr Brock. I'll let you know.'

Unusually for the now familiar chop-and-change career moves that have devastated the Metropolitan Police, the DAC had been a detective for most of his service. And didn't give a damn about budgets if the crime was going to be solved.

Ten minutes later, the commander rang through to my office to tell me that permission had been granted. I presume he'd rung me, rather than coming in, so that I wouldn't see the look of disappointment on his face.

Five

Thanks to the services of a detective sergeant in the Interpol office at Lambeth, I was eventually put in touch with Maréchal des Logis chef Jacques Bloyet, an English-speaking officer of the Gendarmerie National in Dinard. He promised to meet us when we arrived and oil the wheels for our discussion with customs at the airport.

On Tuesday morning, having decided that the easiest way to get to Dinard would be to follow the same route as Pointer had done, Dave and I drove to Southampton and caught an early flight.

Jacques Bloyet met us at the foot of the aircraft steps. 'Mister Brock, is it not?' he asked, a broad grin on his face. I was surprised to see that he was in uniform, but he later told me that a gendarme only has authority if he is clothed in the livery of the Republic. I hoped that the European Union wouldn't suddenly think that was a good idea for us too.

Dave and I introduced ourselves and within seconds we were Jacques, Harry and Dave. But that's the way the coppering game works: instant friendship. It has to be that way or nothing gets done in the short time we usually have for international enquiries.

'This is Odette Gouret, the 'ead *douanière*,' said Bloyet when we arrived at the customs post. 'I think she will be able to 'elp you. Afterwards we will 'ave lunch, *non*? *Moules marinière*, perhaps? You like *moules*?'

'Splendid,' I said, and shook hands with the attractive, Titian-haired woman who was in charge of Dinard customs. She too, I was pleased to learn, spoke passable English.

'Since the European Union abolished frontiers, M'sieur Brock ... ' said Odette, and then paused. 'Except for your country,' she added archly, but with a twinkle in her eye. 'Since then, we have not bothered so much with ordinary customs work. Nowadays it is all about terrorism and drugs and illegal immigrants. But' – she took a file from a large metal cabinet – 'we do occasionally ask, er ... ' She paused, seeking the right word. 'Embarrassing questions, *n'est-ce-pas*?'

'I'm pleased to hear it.'

'And we did ask some questions of this Robert Salter about three years ago.' Odette flicked open the file and flashed me an engaging smile. 'You see, m'sieur, at this airport we 'ave nothing else to do but write things down! All we seem to 'ave these days are what we call *seau-et-bêche* flights.'

'What on earth are they?' I asked, turning to Jacques Bloyet.

'It's what you call bucket and spade, 'Arry,' said Bloyet. ''Olidaymakers, *non*?'

'M'sieur Salter was carrying a coffin.' Odette laughed. 'No, that is not right. 'E 'ad a coffin with 'im. So for something to do, we asked to see 'is papers.'

'Anything interesting?' I asked.

'Well, the documents were in order, so we didn't open the coffin.'

'Do you remember anything about those documents, Madame?' I asked.

'Oh yes, we made a photocopy of it.' Odette handed me the file. 'We are very efficient in the French customs.'

The form, naming Robert Salter as courier, showed the deceased to be an Englishman named Charles Dobson.

But the form was signed by an undertaker called Wilfred Crow.

I passed it to Dave. 'Well,' he said, 'ain't that something?'

We really enjoyed the lunch to which the gendarmerie treated us, a lunch made more pleasant by the presence of Odette Gouret.

But the euphoria was short-lived. We arrived back in London at about four o'clock and made straight for Wilfred Crow's funeral parlour.

There was a sign on the door stating that the business had closed down.

'I think we're getting nearer to solving this job, Dave,' I said.

'Not right now, we're not,' muttered Dave. And as usual his forecast was accurate.

We made for the local nick and spoke to the duty officer.

'Don't know much about it, sir,' said the inspector. 'I knew it was there, of course. But as far as I was concerned it was just another undertaker's. We never had any problems with it.'

Which was the answer I expected. Police don't usually have trouble with undertakers. After all, one doesn't expect race riots or binge drinking in a funeral parlour. I explained our interest and asked the inspector if he would make enquiries of the street-duty officers to see if they'd ever noticed any coffins being taken in and out. And if there was any local gossip about why Mr Crow had suddenly shut up shop. The inspector promised to let me know.

'Any idea where we can find the local vicar, guv?' asked Dave of the inspector.

The inspector looked a little surprised, and so did I, but he pulled out a dog-eared folder and gave us an address.

'What was that all about, Dave?' I asked as we left the police station.

'If anyone's likely to know if an undertaker's kosher, it's going to be the local vicar, guv.'

'Unfortunate combination of words,' I murmured.

★ ★ ★

'Of course I know of the existence of Mr Crow, Chief Inspector,' said the vicar, 'but I've never officiated at a funeral conducted by him.' He sighed. 'Apart from the fact that the deceased may have been of a different religious persuasion, I regret to say that there are all too many people today who've forsaken the Christian way of life.' He shook his head dolefully. 'It's possible therefore that Mr Crow did conduct funerals other than those requiring the attendance of a clerk in holy orders.'

'A planting without benefit of clergy, you might say,' commented Dave drily.

The vicar cast a puzzled glance in Dave's direction and laughed nervously. 'Well, not quite,' he said. 'Benefit of clergy was an exemption from criminal proceedings back in the Middle Ages, but it was—'

Dave held up his hand. 'I know,' he said. 'I'm a policeman.'

Just to make as sure as we could, we visited the local Roman Catholic priest, who, after insisting we took a glass of Bushmill's whiskey with him, assured us that he had never had any dealings with Mr Crow.

Finally we spoke to one or two other undertakers in the area. Although they knew of Wilfred Crow's business, they had never known him conduct a funeral. But that was not wholly reliable. Commercial competition being what it is, they may just have been trying to do his legs for him.

'It's a front, guv'nor,' said Dave, summing up the situation in his usual succinct way.

I had to agree, but one other thought came to me. 'We could try the VAT office, Dave.'

'Funerals are not liable for value-added tax, sir,' Dave replied, somewhat smugly I thought.

The next morning, Dave and I visited our old friend John Fielding at the City of London headquarters of the Customs National Investigation Service. Some time ago I had investigated a double murder that finished up involving alcohol and tobacco smuggling, and John had been a great help in resolving it.

After exchanging a few niceties, an equal amount of professional badinage and consuming the obligatory coffee, we got down to business.

I told John about the deaths of Spotter Gould and Bernie Pointer alias Robert Salter, and what we had discovered since about the transit of coffins through Dinard and Southampton Airports.

'Drugs,' said Fielding. 'It's got to be drugs.'

'Seems the most likely explanation,' I said, 'although the French customs said the paperwork on one occasion named the deceased as a Charles Dobson.'

'But did they see the body?' asked Fielding, getting to the nub of the matter.

'No,' I said.

'Didn't think so,' said Fielding. 'On the other hand we have some pretty efficient sniffer dogs. They'd be bound to have detected drugs if they'd given it the once-over at Southampton.'

'Even in a lead-lined coffin?' asked Dave.

'Not sure about that,' admitted Fielding. 'However, we'll most certainly look into it.'

'And what'll you do if one of your dogs finds a positive trace, John? Nick the guy bringing in the coffin?'

Fielding laughed. 'Give us *some* credit, Harry,' he said. 'Of course not. He won't be working solo. No, I'll have a team down at Southampton and we'll do a following job. See where he goes.'

'What if it's not drugs?' asked Dave. 'It might be alcohol or tobacco. What then?'

'Could be, I suppose, but the routine would be the same.' For a moment, Fielding gazed pensively at the ceiling. 'I think the best idea is to keep a watch for say two weeks. If we draw a blank we'll have to think again. But you're sure that there's something dodgy about this business, Harry, are you?'

'My thinking so far, John, is that when Gould left prison he was murdered in mistake for Pointer. And then we have the situation where, according to your chaps at Southampton, Pointer, using the name of Salter, was importing coffins from Dinard. When we first suggested to Crow that Pointer was escorting them on his behalf, he

85

denied it. However, when we went to Dinard the customs there turned up a copy of an authority signed by Crow that Pointer had produced some three years ago. And when we went back to Crow to front him with it, he'd done a runner.'

'Yeah, but all this was three years ago, you said.'

'Maybe, but Crow was still in business, if you can call it that, up to a few days ago. That seems to imply that whatever criminal activity they were up to was still going on, even though Pointer was in the nick. What's more, we could find no one in the area – police, clergy and other undertakers – who'd ever known Crow conduct a funeral.'

Fielding sat back and linked his fingers. 'Seems pretty convincing that there's something going on,' he said reflectively. 'OK, Harry, leave it with me. I'll get something organized and let you know when we're up and running.'

It seemed to me that from our original investigation into the deaths of Gould and Pointer, we'd strayed into some sort of smuggling racket. Loath though I was to get involved in something that primarily was the preserve of Her Majesty's Revenue and Customs, I was convinced that the murders were in some way connected to the smuggling, if that's what it proved to be. And I was now in the unenviable position of being dependant upon another law-enforcement agency to dictate the running.

However, there were still things to be done. That afternoon, having persuaded a somewhat sceptical district judge that Crow's premises might yield evidence of a serious arrestable offence, I managed to extract a search warrant from him. I think the beak thought it might be politically incorrect to search a funeral parlour.

Accompanied by Linda Mitchell and her team of crime-scene examiners, and a few heavies from the Territorial Support Group, Dave and I arrived at the now-defunct funeral parlour. One of the TSG constables obligingly opened the door with the aid of an instrument specially designed for the purpose, and to which he referred as his fourteen-pound key.

The result was disappointing, although not unexpected. The telephone had been disconnected, there was no paperwork anywhere in the office and the workshop appeared not to have been used recently.

'There's no sawdust, guv,' observed Dave laconically. 'Dead giveaway.'

'Could have been swept up, Dave,' I said. Dave scoffed. 'Yeah, maybe.'

Admittedly there were a few planks of wood and the sort of power tools one would expect to be used in the manufacture of coffins, but little else. There was one partly constructed coffin on a couple of trestles, but I didn't anticipate that it would provide us with anything in the way of evidence. And it didn't.

Linda Mitchell's team searched the entire place for fingerprints and managed to lift one or two. I suspected that they would be Crow's and Pointer's and very few others. But you never know. I have been lucky in the past.

The next morning, I had three telephone calls.

The inspector we had spoken to on Wednesday about Crow's activities told me that he had questioned the members of his relief and someone he referred to as the BIO.

'What the hell's a BIO?' I asked.

'The borough intelligence officer,' said the inspector. 'He's what used to be called the collator, or in our case "she". But the Yard keeps changing the names of things. God knows why.'

'You have my sympathy,' I murmured. I could have given him a list of departments and functions that had been subjected to a recent name change. But it wouldn't have been complete; I hadn't read that morning's 'Notices'.

'Anyway,' continued the inspector, 'nobody has ever seen a coffin being brought out of Crow's place. What's more, sir, no one has ever seen any hearses, either outside the premises or in his yard. Looks like you were right. Anything else we can do?'

'Not really,' I said, 'but if any activity is seen there, and it's more likely to be at night, let me know. Whatever the time.' But now that the funeral parlour had been closed, I had little hope that anything would be seen. You never know, though.

The second call came from John Fielding to say that he had arranged for a team of his investigators to begin surveillance at Southampton Airport first thing on Monday morning. He didn't have to explain why he was waiting until then. I knew all about budgets and overtime and extra payments for call-out. And what I didn't know, the commander frequently told me. Anyway, we'd waited three years, so another couple of days wouldn't matter much.

The third call was from Linda Mitchell. Of the fingerprints lifted at Crow's establishment, only one had been identified so far: that of Bernie Pointer, otherwise Robert Salter. Surprise, surprise.

'Ah, Mr Brock, are your enquiries proving profitable?' The commander appeared silently in the doorway to my office.

I thought about mentioning that I'd won ten pounds on the National Lottery, but I didn't think that's what he had in mind.

Instead I explained what we had achieved so far, not that it amounted to much, but at least it put his mind at rest that the trip to Dinard had been worth spending the commissioner's money. Just.

'What have you done about tracing this man Crow, Mr Brock?'

'The standard procedures, sir,' I said. That had him. I knew that this pseudo-detective wouldn't have the balls to ask what those standard procedures were. As a 'detective' he should have known that it meant putting Crow's name on the Police National Computer as wanted for questioning.

'Good, good,' said the commander and retreated.

In the meantime, Dave had been doing some ferreting of his own.

'I checked with British Telecom, sir, to see where they were sending the final account for Crow's disconnected telephone.'

'Ah, good. And?'

'Not good, guv,' said Dave. 'The address doesn't exist. Well, the road exists, but it doesn't go up as far as the number Crow gave them.'

'What appalling bad luck. For BT, I mean.'

'But I did get a record of the numbers he'd called over the last six months.'

'Anything interesting?' I asked.

'Don't know yet, guv. Colin Wilberforce is checking them out. I'll let you know ASAP.'

And that, for the moment, was that.

As I was waiting for reports and the results of various other enquiries, it seemed that I had little to do until Monday.

* * *

I spent Saturday morning attempting to restore some order to my flat. The problem with being a busy detective living alone is that things like housework tend to get neglected.

I have a splendid lady called Mrs Gurney who comes in twice a week and 'does' for me, but even she is fighting a losing battle with the uncontrollable disorder that stems from my irregular lifestyle. Within a day of Gladys Gurney's latest blitz the place is in chaos again. I just hope she doesn't give up on me altogether.

I really don't know how working women manage. My ex-wife Helga, with her customary Teutonic efficiency, always kept our home immaculate, even though she was a busy physiotherapist at the local hospital.

My relationship with Helga had all started wonderfully. I was a young constable walking a Westminster beat when I dislocated my shoulder in a punch-up with a crowd of yobs. Helga Büchner, as she then was, was the physio who pummelled and prodded me until the shoulder was in working order again. There followed a whirlwind romance, frequent nights together and marriage. Great.

But it was her insistence on continuing to work even after our son was born that eventually caused the rift between us that led to divorce. Each day Helga would leave our four-year-old son Robert with a neighbour.

And then on one awful day he fell into her pond and drowned. I still have a vivid recollection of the day my detective superintendent called me into his office to break the news.

The marriage endured for a few years after Robert's death, more for economic reasons than anything else, but with the rift between us widening almost by the day. Eventually the relationship degenerated into daily rows about trivial things, and we decided to make it official. So finally we parted company the best of enemies, and Helga is now married to a doctor from her hospital with whom she had been conducting an affair for some time before our divorce.

But all of that is in the past.

I rang Gail and suggested dinner somewhere local that evening.

'I've got a better idea, darling,' she said. 'Come round at about half-seven and I'll cook for us.'

I know I said that Gail wasn't devious, but this time she'd conned me. I suppose I should have suspected something from the Rolls-Royce parked on her small drive.

She opened the door, greeted me with a hug and a kiss and led the way upstairs to the sitting room of her town house.

'Harry, I'd like you to meet my parents,' she said.

George Sutton was a jovial fellow, shorter

than his daughter and certainly stockier. His wife Sally was an older version of Gail. Given that Gail had admitted to being in her mid-thirties, her mother must have been at least fifty-five, but looked to be nearer forty. She had the same natural blonde hair as Gail and had kept her figure. I wondered if she too had been a dancer.

'So you're the copper Gail's been talking about,' said George Sutton, springing from his chair with an agility that belied his age, which must have been about sixty. 'She tells me you're on the Murder Squad.'

'Not exactly,' I said, resigned once again to talking shop to a civilian who affected interest in what I did. 'I'm a member of the Serious Crime Group. We don't only deal with murder, although it sometimes seems like it.'

'Gail says you're investigating a murder at the moment, the chap who was shot outside the prison. Must be absolutely fascinating, your job.' Sutton took out a pipe and waved it in Gail's direction. 'D'you mind, love?' he asked.

'Not at all,' said Gail. 'They're your lungs.'

'I thought about becoming a copper myself when I came down from university,' Sutton went on as he filled his pipe. 'Wouldn't have minded if I could have gone straight into the CID, but I didn't fancy being on the beat for two years. Mind you, I wouldn't have finished up with a Rolls-Royce,' he added with a

93

chuckle.

I'd lost count of the number of people who'd said that to me. People who thought that being a beat-duty copper was boring, and who had some wild notion that the CID was a romantic and adventurous job, and whose members raced around London in fast cars arresting gentlemen jewel-thieves who looked like a cross between James Bond and Leslie Charteris's 'The Saint'. But I decided against telling him what being a detective was really all about. The weary, seemingly endless hours spent on fruitless observations, the nights in freezing obo vans, or the winter days in the pouring rain following suspects who eventually turned out not to be suspects at all. And searching filthy 'flops' in the East End inhabited by drug addicts and aged, syphilitic prostitutes whose stench seemed to stay in your clothing for days afterwards. Or the sight of a pretty young woman who'd been raped and strangled and dumped in a ditch. And then having to tell the parents what had happened.

'Walking a beat's the best bit,' I said. 'It's where you have all the fun.' But even as I said it, I was aware that being a foot-duty constable today was nowhere near as enjoyable as it used to be.

Dinner passed pleasantly enough, although George dominated the conversation with stories of Formula One motor racing, about which he was a great enthusiast. And despite Gail's mother frequently telling him that he was talking too much, and to shut up, he insisted on relating the history of the land-speed record, and talked about drivers whose names meant nothing to me, like Malcolm Campbell, Henry Segrave and Bruce Lockhart.

I bore all this with fortitude, if only for Gail's sake.

In a quiet moment in the kitchen later, when I was helping with the coffee, Gail suggested that it would be embarrassing if I were to stay the night. 'You know what parents are like,' she'd said. 'Probably did it themselves before they were married, but take a poor view of their daughter doing it.'

So at half-past eleven, I left.

'I'm sorry to have put you through all that, darling,' she whispered at the front door as she saw me out.

So am I, I thought. Parents!

I spent the Sunday morning catching up on my housework. I didn't think I could stand another of Mrs Gurney's censorious looks. She had this habit of standing in the centre of my sitting room, hands on hips, and gazing round at the detritus while humming softly to herself. I can tell you, I've faced a few nasty villains in my time, but Mrs Gurney's silent criticism was something else. To be honest I'm terrified of her.

At six o'clock that evening Gail arrived at the front door.

'I've come to apologize, darling,' she said. 'And this needs to go in the fridge,' she added, handing me a bottle of champagne.

'Apologize for what?' I asked as I escorted her into my almost tidy sitting room.

'Inflicting my parents on you last night. It wasn't fair to do that without warning. And my father can be such a bore at times.'

'Think nothing of it,' I said, handing her a gin and tonic. 'I thought they were a very nice couple, and your mother's a really good-looking woman. Was she a dancer?'

'Yes, a long time ago. I think that's why she was against my going into the profession.' Gail took a sip of her gin. 'But you've got to admit that my father's a bit of a bore with all his talk about motor racing,' she said again.

'I thought it was very interesting,' I said.

'Liar,' said Gail and gave me a playful punch. 'Anyway, I've come to make it up to you.'

'Oh, really? How?'

'Guess,' said Gail.

Six

'Colin Wilberforce has checked the phone numbers on Crow's account,' said Dave as I arrived in the incident room on Monday morning. 'And they make interesting reading.'

'Enlighten me.'

Dave shuffled through a few pieces of paper until he found what he was looking for. 'There are some with 00 33 prefixes – that's France – and some with 00 387 prefixes.'

'Where the hell's that?'

'Bosnia-Hercegovina, guv.'

'Why should he be telephoning Bosnia, I wonder?'

'Could be where the trail begins,' said Dave, 'because there are also numbers that go out to Salzburg in Austria, Stuttgart in Germany and finally Lyon and Dinard. If you follow that on a map it's almost a straight line from Bosnia to Dinard. Here, I'll show you.' He produced an atlas and traced the route with the point of a letter opener.

'Do we know the addresses that these

numbers go out to?' I asked.

'Not yet, guv, but I've got a guy in the Interpol office working on it. He'll let me know as soon as he gets a result. He's got some mate at the headquarters of Interpol, which funnily enough is in Lyon, and who's got some shortcut to tracing subscribers.'

If what Dave had discovered proved to be a route, then Wilfred Crow was involved in a well-organized and sophisticated operation. But I doubted that whoever was controlling it would be too happy to know that the bogus undertaker had left this information for the police to find. More to the point, though, what were they bringing in? Sure as hell it wasn't dead bodies, despite what had been on the photocopy of the document that Odette Gouret at Dinard had shown us.

I telephoned John Fielding with this latest piece of intelligence and promised to let him have more details as we received them.

Fielding, being a cautious man, merely commented that it was 'interesting'.

'A thought occurred to me, John,' I said. 'Suppose that the coffins are going the other way.'

'What are you talking about, Harry?'

'Well, the coffins might be going out with something in them, but coming back empty.'

'It's a thought, I suppose,' said Fielding, 'but given the state this country's in, what have we got that's worth smuggling *out*?'

'I don't know, John,' I said. 'You're the

customs officer.'

But then Fielding scotched my idea. 'If they were coming back empty, Harry, they'd come in as freight. There'd be no point in pretending they're on their way to a funeral.'

'They will be if I get my way, John,' I muttered. 'Their own funeral.'

During the first week of the customs team's observation only one coffin arrived at Southampton Airport from Dinard. The documentation was in order and Crow's name did not appear in it; nevertheless Fielding's men followed the hearse containing the coffin. However, it was taken to an old-established funeral parlour in Winchester the reputation of which was way beyond suspicion.

I was beginning to fret. I had two murders on my hands, the commander breathing down my neck and no end in sight.

Just for the hell of it, I was tempted to search the garage used by Darren Walters, the guy who was undoubtedly shacked up with Spotter Gould's widow. But there was no evidence to suggest that he was connected with Gould's murder, even though he was fairly near the top of my list of suspects; it was not unknown for one third of an eternal triangle to take out one of the other thirds. But that said there was even less to indicate that he knew Bernie Pointer or Wilfred Crow, or was aware of their activities. But if he was, and I spun his garage, I might well foul up the operation now being conducted by customs.

We just had to wait patiently.

In the meantime, our colleagues in the Interpol office had finally come up with the addresses that went out to the numbers that had appeared on Crow's telephone account.

But even then, I was loath to alert the police forces of the appropriate countries for fear, once again, of treading on Fielding's toes.

And when I called him, he agreed.

'Let's wait and see, Harry,' he said. 'After all, from what you say, it's been going on for at least three years.'

But things started to come together ten days later with an early morning call on my mobile.

'What on earth's that, darling?' Gail awoke with a start and sat up in bed, clearly in a bad temper at having been disturbed.

'Sorry, it's my mobile,' I said, reaching out to grab the offending instrument.

'Another coffin arrived from Dinard at six thirty this morning, Harry,' said John Fielding. 'My guys are following it as we speak.'

'Anything suspicious about it, John?' I glanced at my watch: it was twenty minutes to seven.

'Not so far. But according to the paperwork it's some firm of undertakers in Birmingham. My lads did a check with the local police up there, but their enquiries indicated that the address is a florist shop.'

'Seems right,' I said. 'Perhaps they're calling in to collect some wreaths.'

'I'll keep you posted,' said Fielding, ignoring my little joke.

Attempting to placate Gail for having disturbed her, and refusing breakfast, I raced to Surbiton station and reached Curtis Green forty-five minutes later. I definitely had a gut feeling about this one.

My mobile rang again as I arrived at the office.

'John?'

'I think we've struck gold, Harry. The coffin arrived at a warehouse in a back street of Portsmouth about five minutes ago.'

'D'you think they sussed your guys, John?'

There was a short, cynical laugh from the other end. 'If they did I'll have my blokes' guts for garters,' said Fielding.

'So what's next?'

There was a pause. 'Hold on, Harry, I think that's probably the team leader on my other phone now.'

A minute later Fielding was back on the line. 'They've gone in, Harry, and I was right. There's a body in the coffin.'

'Well, there's a surprise.'

'Yeah, but this one's alive.'

'So that's it,' I said. 'People smuggling.'

'Looks like it, Harry.'

'How many in the warehouse?' I asked.

'Four. And I suppose you want to talk to them.'

'Too bloody true I do, but it'll take me a while to get to Portsmouth. Where are they now?'

'At the moment still in the warehouse, but they're about to be taken to the nick. Portsmouth Central.'

'Right. I'll get down there ASAP. And thanks, John, you might just have found some guys who've got the answer to my murders.'

Even so, I was not too hopeful about that. I've had many disappointments in the past and coppers are, by nature, pessimists.

Having decided that my journey to Portsmouth was of sufficient urgency to make use of a traffic car, Dave and I covered the seventy or so miles from London to Portsmouth Central police station in slightly under the hour. But not without a few terrifying moments that our highly qualified driver not only anticipated but laughed at. Nevertheless, I learned a few new expletives from him, and that, for a CID officer, is saying something.

But it turned out to be worth it.

The customs investigator in charge of the operation introduced himself as Ron Taylor.

'The guy who was in the box, Harry, is an

educated Bosnian. Speaks perfect English and claims to be a doctor of medicine. The others are British, including the guy who brought in the coffin and the two who were waiting in the warehouse. The Hampshire boys have put them in separate cells for the time being. A couple of my blokes are still searching the warehouse, but you might want to get some of your guys down here to give it the once-over.' Taylor passed me a slip of paper. 'Those are the names of the Brits.'

One name caught my eye immediately: Wilfred Crow.

'Well, well, well,' I said.

Crow did not look at all happy when Dave and I confronted him in the interview room.

'Oh, fancy seeing you, Mr Brock,' he said in a lame attempt to make light of his predicament, and glanced nervously at Ron Taylor. And even more nervously at Dave.

But I was in no mood to engage in small talk with this ersatz funeral director and told Dave to switch on the tape recorder and administer the caution. I had yet to learn the words of this complex and, in my view, totally unnecessary piece of stultifying legislation. Anyway, I'd lost the little card with it all on.

'You are entitled to the services of a solicitor if you wish,' I said, once Dave had finished. 'If you do not have the means, one will be provided for you.' At least I remembered that bit.

'They only get in the way,' said Crow, confirming my own view of the usefulness of the legal profession in such circumstances.

'So what's your part in this scam?' I began.

'I'm only a pawn in all this,' said Crow in an attempt to row himself out right from the start.

Dave looked up. 'Did you say pawn or prawn?' he enquired with a straight face. Despite the tape recorder whirring away, he was still making written notes.

Dave's comment only served to discomfit Crow even further. He had yet to learn, as I had learned some time ago, that it's not always easy to tell when Dave is joking.

'These are dangerous people, Mr Brock.' Crow's voice had developed a whining tone and his head was doing its nodding-dog imitation again.

'Very likely. So tell me about it.'

Crow gazed beseechingly at me. 'If I tell you all I know,' he said, 'will it help me?'

'Possibly, but that's a matter for the Crown Prosecution Service. And they're not very charitable when it comes to serious crime.' *Oh, if only.*

'And I'll want protection,' Crow went on, trying desperately to negotiate a deal. 'You know, this witness-protection thing. A new name, and a safe house somewhere.'

'You've been watching too much television,' commented Dave. 'Plea-bargaining is an American practice.'

'Ramo Aniç,' said Crow.

'Bless you,' said Dave quietly enough for the tape recorder not to pick it up.

'And who is Ramo Aniç?' I asked.

'He's the guy in Bosnia who runs things.' Crow licked his lips and glanced around as though the aforementioned Aniç might appear at any moment.

'Address?'

Dave flicked over a couple of pages in his pocketbook. 'Number 4 Dragan Bana, Banja Luka,' he said, repeating the information that Interpol had gleaned from Crow's telephone account.

An expression that was a combination of fear and wonderment settled on Crow's face. 'How the hell did you know that?' he asked.

'You'd be surprised just how much we do know about you, Wilfred,' I said. 'But there's more, isn't there? Much, much more.'

'Yes.' Crow spoke in a croaking whisper and beads of perspiration began rolling down his face to disappear inside his capacious shirt collar and drip on to his black tie.

'So this guy Aniç is the *grand fromage*, is he?' Dave was deliberately disconcerting Crow with his throwaway lines. It was a technique that often worked successfully with suspects of Crow's calibre because it made them think Dave was a lightweight. Bad mistake.

'The what?'

'The big cheese,' said Dave.

Clearly afraid to commit himself, Crow merely nodded.

'Tell me how this business works, Wilfred,' I said. 'There must be a lot of money in it if they're prepared to set you up as an undertaker and arrange these expensive trips.'

Crow licked his lips again. 'There are some very rich people in Bosnia, Mr Brock, but they want to get to England. The country's too unstable, you see.'

'England or Bosnia?' asked Dave.

'No, Bosnia,' said Crow, still taking Dave seriously. 'And they're willing to pay handsomely to get out of there.'

'So you bring them over in coffins, is that it?' I asked.

'Yeah.'

'And Robert Salter, alias Bernie Pointer, was a part of it, was he?'

'Yes, he was. Until he got greedy.'

'What does that mean?' I had the feeling that we were about to get close to the motive for Pointer's murder.

'Well, Bernie reckoned he was the one taking all the risks. Bringing in the coffins and that. He reckoned he should get paid more.'

'And how much *was* Pointer getting?'

'A grand a run.'

'What did he have to do for that?' Dave asked.

'Pick up the coffin at Dinard and escort it

over to Southampton. And he had to look the part in a tiddley suit, and sweet-talk customs if it started to get a bit iffy. Then he had to make sure the casket got to the right destination.'

'And where was that?'

'Different places. Sometimes my place.'

'And was Dinard to Southampton always the route that was used?'

'As far as I know. There might have been others. For all I know there might even be another set-up altogether. I did hear a whisper about a Nigerian run too, but I don't know if there was anything in it. We was only told what we had to know, like.'

'Where did your "passenger" get put in the coffin, Wilfred?' I asked.

'In Dinard.'

'Obviously, but where?'

'Look, I'm sticking my neck out here,' moaned Crow, and followed it up by sticking his neck out physically. 'If these guys catch up with me and find I've been grassing, they'll top me for sure.'

'Probably,' said Dave. 'But you might as well tell us, because even if you don't, I'll still tell the court you did. On the other hand, if you *do* tell us, I *won't* tell the court you did. Know what I mean?'

From the confused expression on Crow's face, I wasn't sure that he *did* know what Dave meant, and I knew from experience that Dave would never do such a thing. But it was a damned good ploy for getting the Crows of this world to spill their guts.

Fearful of allowing the information to be tape-recorded for posterity, Crow beckoned for Dave's pocketbook and scribbled down an address. Where it was recorded for posterity.

Dave glanced at it and nodded. 'Yes, we know about that one too.'

'Now for the big question, Wilfred,' I said. 'Who murdered Bernie Pointer?'

'Bloody hell, Mr Brock, you don't know what you're asking.'

'Yes I do. Who murdered Pointer?'

'I don't know.'

'Well, *why* was he murdered?'

'I told you that just now. He got too greedy.'

'Yes, go on.'

'Well, that's it, really.'

'Oh, but it's not, Wilfred. What you said was that he thought he should be getting more than a grand a trip. Presumably he made demands to someone, and that someone didn't like what he heard.'

'I suppose it was Ramo Aniç.'

'You suppose? Well, who else would he have made his case to?'

'It could have been one of the others along the route. Salzburg or Stuttgart or Lyon, but he probably meant for it to get back to Aniç.'

'And Aniç put out a contract on Pointer. Is that what you're saying, Wilfred?'

108

Crow licked his lips yet again. 'I s'pose it must've been what happened,' he said.

'Good. Now we're getting somewhere. So who are the other guys along the route?'

'I don't know,' Crow said, a little too hurriedly.

'If you don't know who they are, why did you telephone them?'

At last the truth dawned on Crow. 'Have you been going through my telephone account?' he demanded crossly, as though his civil rights had just been seriously impinged upon.

Dave laughed. 'I don't suppose your Mr Aniç will like that too much. But you can sue us for invasion of privacy if you like.'

'Right,' I said, 'we'll have a few names, Wilfred. Let's start with this country.'

There was a distinct pause while Crow appeared to be weighing up the dangers inherent in furnishing me with the names of his co-conspirators. But eventually he yielded.

'Well, there was Bernie Pointer...'

'We know that, Wilf,' said Dave, leaning forward menacingly. 'We're investigating his murder. So don't ponce about.'

Reaching once more for Dave's pocketbook, Crow wrote down a name.

I pulled the book towards me. 'And who's Darren Walters?' I asked. I had no intention of telling Crow that I'd already met Mr Walters or that he was, in my view, not only an extremely dodgy character, but also featured fairly high on my list of suspects.

'Christ, Mr Brock, *please*,' whined Crow. 'Not out loud. I could get in serious grief about all this.'

'You're in deep shtook already, Wilf,' Dave put in. 'So you might as well go for the five-card trick.'

'He's the geezer who takes care of things at this end. He's what you might call Mr Aniç's right-hand man.'

'And where does this mastermind live?' I knew of two addresses: New Labour House, Poplar, and the garage. But there might have been others.

'Dunno, but I can give you his phone number.' And once again Crow scribbled in Dave's book.

'That's his East India Dock Road garage,' said Dave.

Again Crow's face registered shock at how much we knew, but he said nothing.

'Let's get back to Bernie Pointer, Wilfred,' I said.

'What about him?' asked Crow in a whisper, his face now bearing the expression of one who hoped this nightmare would soon end. By now his chin had almost disappeared inside his collar as though he was attempting to vanish altogether.

'How long did he work for you?'

'A couple of years.'

'So all this story about him only being with

110

you for six weeks is crap, is it?'

'Yeah. See, I heard the word that someone was after him, so I told him to clear out and find somewhere else. Get out of the picture, like.'

'And who did you hear this word from, Wilfred?'

'Can't remember,' said Crow unconvincingly. Realizing that he'd said too much already he seemed unwilling to say anything else. 'Sort of round and about, like.'

'And you wrote the reference for him that you claimed he forged. Right?'

'Yes.'

'So you gave false information to the police in alleging a crime of forgery,' said Dave. 'Serious offence, that.'

'So what?' Compared with the other charges Crow must have realized he was facing, even he recognized that the offence of wasting police time must seem unimportant. I had to agree with him.

'And this business of the army discharge book was a lie too, was it?' persisted Dave.

'No. It existed, but the bit about me ringing up the army was all balls. I bought the book off a geezer.' But even now, Crow was lying.

'Name?' demanded Dave.

'Christ, I don't know, but I reckoned you'd never get any change out of the army. Seemed like a good way of stopping dodgy questions about Bernie's background.'

111

'So off goes Bernie and gets a job with a solicitor.'

'Yeah, but then the stupid sod buggered it all up by nicking cash. I ask you, what sort of idiot nicks cash from a solicitor?'

'You should know all about idiocy,' commented Dave. 'You haven't been too clever yourself.'

And with that, I decided to let Crow sweat for a while and he was returned to his cell.

'What d'you think, Ron?' I asked the customs investigator, who, throughout our chat with Crow, had remained silent. But his next comment made clear why he had said nothing.

'One thing's for sure, Harry,' said Taylor. 'None of this is anything to do with customs. It's between you and the Immigration Service.'

'Yes, I suppose I ought to tell them,' I said, 'but time enough when we've got what we want out of this merry band.'

Seven

I decided to interview the Bosnian next. Somewhat dishevelled from having spent an hour in a coffin, albeit a cunningly ventilated one, he regarded the three of us with a mixture of concern and fear. It was an expression that intensified once I told him who Dave, Ron Taylor and I were. That was natural enough, I suppose, given what I'd heard about the methods of the police in the country he had just left. I told him that he could have a solicitor at the public expense, but he declined. Probably thought it was a trap.

'What's your name?' I asked, once Dave had dealt with the tape recorder and administered the caution.

'Dr Gavrilo Lemez,' he said after a pause, during which, I imagine, he was wondering whether to refuse this information. Or wondering what would happen if he did refuse. Perhaps he was visualizing strong lights, wet towels and rubber hoses.

'And where have you come from, Dr Lemez?'

'Dinard.'

113

'Yes, I know that, but originally?'

'Bosnia.'

'Yes, I know that too, but where in Bosnia.'

There was another pause, and then, 'Zenica.'

'And you practised medicine there?'

'Yes.'

'How did you get here?'

Lemez closely examined all three of us in turn, his gaze lingering especially on Ron Taylor. Perhaps the Bosnian customs have a particularly nasty reputation. 'A man in Sarajevo arranged to get me here,' he said.

'Yes, I've no doubt, but how did you actually get here? Physically, I mean.'

'I had to meet a man in Sarajevo.'

'Do you remember the address there?'

'No, I didn't know. I do not know Sarajevo and it was dark anyway,' said Lemez.

'And from there?'

'One night two men took me in a van to somewhere in Austria. I had to lie down in the back under some sacks. That is because they told me that there are still frontier controls between Bosnia and Austria, but the border guards didn't bother to search the van. Then I went by car to Germany and finally to France. The next day I was taken to Dinard. Then a man put me in the coffin for the short flight here to the airport in Southampton.' Lemez gave a shrug. 'It was uncomfortable, and very cold because the coffin was put in the hold of the aircraft.'

'Do you know the names of any of these men, Dr Lemez?'

'No. I think they were very careful not to use names.'

'Do you know where in Dinard you were put in the coffin, Dr Lemez?'

'No. It was dark and I do not know that place at all. I was kept there until early the next morning.'

'And what did this journey cost you?' I asked.

There was a long pause.

I prompted him. 'Doctor?'

'Forty-five thousand US dollars,' Lemez said.

Dave did a brief calculation and let out a low whistle. 'Bloody hell,' he said, 'that's near enough twenty-five thousand pounds.'

'And where did you get that much money from?' I asked, not that I thought I'd get a straight answer. And I was right.

The Bosnian doctor shrugged. 'There are ways and means,' he said. 'I have friends,' he added enigmatically.

'Why didn't you come to this country by a more conventional route and apply for asylum once you'd got here?'

'Because Bosnia is now considered to be a safe place. Not one in which my life was in danger. I would not have been considered for political asylum.'

'But do you think your life would have been in danger if you'd stayed in Bosnia?'

'I don't know. Possibly. But I was told this was the only way to get here. Otherwise, they said, I would be turned back at the border of England.'

'And the money you paid was for the passage to England, was it?'

'Yes. That and the papers.'

'Oh? What papers?' I asked. This was starting to get interesting.

'A passport, work permit, driving licence. All that sort of thing, you know?'

'What sort of passport?'

Lemez gave a sigh of impatience, as though treating with a complete fool. 'A British one, of course.'

It seemed as though this man, professional and well educated though he might be, had been the victim of a confidence trick of outrageous proportions. Whoever had convinced him that to be smuggled across in a coffin was the only means of travel, had also persuaded him that a British-passport holder would need a work permit. But that apart, the National Health Service would probably have welcomed an English-speaking, qualified doctor to its ranks without giving a damn where he'd come from. Furthermore, I doubted that any of the promised documents would have been forthcoming. Somehow, I suspected that Lemez would have been dumped in a country lane in some outlandish place and left to the mercy of the authorities. There had been reports of such things happening in the past.

'What will happen now, sir?' asked Lemez. 'Will you let me stay? Or must I go back?'

'I'm a police officer,' I said. 'It's not a matter for me. My only duty is to inform the Immigration Service of your arrival, and you will be kept in custody until they decide whether you'll be allowed to stay in this country. But I must warn you that it doesn't look too hopeful.'

Lemez' shoulders slumped at that, and I couldn't help feeling sorry for him as he shambled back to his cell.

But, as usual, it was Dave who put the whole thing in perspective.

'He might not be a doctor at all, guv,' he said. 'We've only got his word for it. I can't see a guy who's medically qualified coming over here in a box and setting himself up with false papers. I reckon there's more to this than we've found out. He's probably a villain.' But Dave always worked on the basis that everyone was a villain until proved otherwise.

And in due course, Lemez did turn out to be a villain.

After a quick cup of tea, I interviewed the other two men who had been detained at the Portsmouth warehouse, but it seemed that they had been locally recruited; what in the trade we call front-line expendables. Certainly neither of them knew anything about the finer points of the immigrant-smuggling

117

scam that had got in the way of our murder enquiry. And they didn't know the names of any of the people involved. They didn't even know the names of Crow or Dr Lemez. And as for Ramo Aniç, they confessed never to have heard of him. Reluctantly, I believed that to be true. The whole conspiracy was probably run on a cellular system: names were only provided to those who needed to know them. And then they were probably false.

I did, however, glean one important piece of information from the man who had accompanied the coffin from Dinard. He said that the empty coffins were collected from the Portsmouth warehouse by a long-distance lorry driver who took them back to France to await the next consignment.

'Name?' Dave demanded.

'No idea,' said the courier.

'Where in France?' Dave asked.

The man shrugged. 'Search me,' he said.

But it was likely that this mysterious driver crossed either to St-Malo, the nearest port to Dinard, or to Le Havre, being a shorter voyage from Portsmouth. But there again he might have travelled from Dover to Calais and then driven along the coast as a means of deflecting police interest. On both sides of the Channel.

'What are we going to do about that lot, guv?' asked Dave when, later, we were mulling over what we had learned.

'Nothing,' I said. 'It's down to Her Majesty's Immigration Service, God bless 'em. We've got a couple of murders to solve. And something tells me that Mister Darren Walters might know more than we've extracted from him so far.'

'So what do we do? Turn over his garage?'

'That'll certainly be a start, Dave,' I said.

The next morning, we obtained a search warrant for Walters's garage in East India Dock Road. And, just for good measure, another one for Flat 37, New Labour House, Walloch Street, Poplar.

Having mustered half of the local Territorial Support Group and our own CSE team, we arrived at the garage. To no one's surprise, it was locked and apparently deserted.

One of the TSG guys made short work of the padlock and slid back the heavy double doors.

'Well, if we don't find anything else, I reckon the Stolen Vehicle Squad will have a field day in here,' said Dave as he stood, hands in pockets, surveying the interior of the huge garage.

There were several stripped-down cars, and a great number of vehicle parts scattered about the floor and littering the several benches.

We searched every inch of the place and found nothing that would incriminate

119

Walters, apart from the aforementioned vehicles and parts thereof. There was no paperwork of any consequence and no telephone either. Presumably Walters had a mobile and laboured under the misapprehension that the police, should they wish to know, would be unable to find out where he was calling from.

'There's a package up here on the rafters, sir,' said one of the TSG constables from the top of a ladder. 'It's wrapped in oilskin.'

'Bring it down,' I said.

The constable descended with his find, swept aside a few carburettors and laid the package on the bench.

Donning latex gloves, Dave carefully unwrapped the mysterious parcel to reveal an M16 carbine and a Walther P38 automatic pistol.

'Well, ain't that something?' he said, standing back and surveying the weapons. 'Looks as though all we have to do now is to find Darren Walters.'

'Yes,' I said, 'and that may turn out to be more difficult than just visiting the Widow Gould.'

Nevertheless, that's exactly what we did next.

Leaving Linda Mitchell and an escort from the TSG to take the firearms to the ballistics examiner at the forensic-science laboratory, we made for Walloch Street, Poplar.

We left the remainder of the TSG outside, an act that caused great alarm among the Walloch Street layabouts, all of whom vanished like mist in the early morning sun.

Mrs Gould surveyed us with an expression that was a unique combination of boredom and hostility. Without a word she left the front door open and walked back into the flat. I took this as an invitation to enter, and Dave and I followed her into the sitting room, where we were greeted by the same depressing sight of chaos that had existed on our previous visit. There was no sign of the children and I offered up a silent prayer that she hadn't murdered them; sure as hell the commander would saddle me with that too.

'Well? What d'you want this time?' Terry Gould sat down and waited.

'We'd like a word with Darren,' I said.

'I bloody well would too,' said Terry before I could continue.

'Have you any idea where he is?'

'No. And I ain't seen the bastard since yesterday morning. He got a phone call, packed a bag and fucked off.'

'Didn't he say where he was going?'

'Not a bleedin' word, but he seemed a bit uptight. All he said was that it was business.'

'To do with his garage business?' Dave asked. But we both knew it wasn't.

'Search me,' said Terry.

Thankfully, Terry Gould's invitation was merely a figure of speech, and one I'd've declined even if it hadn't been.

'Who was this phone call from, Mrs Gould? Any idea?' I asked.

'No, he wouldn't say. He never tells me anything, the bastard.'

But I guessed that someone connected with the immigrant racket had called him. The mystery was how they'd managed it. As far as I knew all the participants in the coffin scam at Portsmouth had been arrested by customs. I was pretty sure that none of them would have been allowed to make a telephone call. Whatever the law says. Someone else must have known about the arrests. But how? And who?

'D'you mind if we have a look round his room, Mrs Gould?' I asked, even though we had a warrant.

Terry Gould scoffed. 'It's my room an' all,' she said, 'as if you didn't know. But go ahead. If you find anything that'll tell you where the bastard's gone, p'raps you'd let me know. He owes me.'

'Owes you what?' asked Dave with an air of innocence.

'Money, what else? He's been shacked up here living off of my social security for bleedin' ages.'

'Doesn't he make any money from his garage, then?' Dave asked.

'Well if he does none of it comes my bleedin' way and that's a fact.' Terry Gould had clearly become disenchanted with her live-in

lover. But I suspected that the disenchant-
ment went further back than yesterday
morning.

I wondered whether to aggravate her even
further by telling her that Darren Walters
had been making a great deal of money from
smuggling witless aliens into the country.
But I was not absolutely certain of that, and
for all I knew Mrs Gould's protestations
might well be play-acting. Play-acting on the
instructions of Darren Walters. It was even
possible that she was involved in some way.

We had cursory look round the room
shared by Mrs Gould and, until recently, the
errant Darren. We opened all the drawers in
the solitary chest, and in a white-painted
bedside cabinet. But apart from discovering
that the bed was unmade and that the sheets
were well past the point at which they should
have been changed, and that there were piles
of dirty clothing on the floor and on most of
the tatty furniture, we found nothing that
immediately attracted our attention. If you
discount the overpowering stench of un-
washed flesh, that is.

'If he gets in touch, Mrs Gould, perhaps
you'd tell him that we'd like a word,' I said,
once we'd returned to the sitting room. I
gave her one of my cards. 'There's no rush.'
But as I said it, I knew that such a casual
attitude would not fool Walters for a
moment. Or that the last person he'd want to
talk to was me.

'Did Darren get on well with your late husband, Mrs Gould?' I asked.

'Dunno. As far as I know he only ever met him at the garage. Why?'

'I'm investigating your husband's murder, Mrs Gould.' I didn't think she'd need reminding, but her next utterance proved that she did.

'Oh, that. What's that got to do with Darren?'

'Nothing as far as I know,' I lied. 'It's just that he might know of someone who'd had a grudge against Jimmy,' I added, playing the dumb copper.

'Well I'll ask him for you,' said Terry sarcastically. 'If I ever see the bastard again.'

Despite having told Dave that I intended to do nothing about the quartet arrested by customs at Portsmouth, I had arranged for them to be brought to London. Having spoken to the Crown Prosecution Service, and the Immigration Service at their headquarters in Croydon, we had collectively agreed that, for a start, the four could be charged with conspiracy. That at least would secure their remand in custody, I hoped, while we delved into the possibility that one or more of them, particularly Crow, had been concerned in the murders of Jimmy Gould and Bernie Pointer.

The next thing I did was to enter Darren Walters's name on the Police National Computer as wanted for questioning. In view of the firearms we had found at his garage, I deemed it prudent to add the caveat 'may be armed and dangerous'. I somehow doubted that we'd found all the weapons that this little team possessed. And that was borne out by something that happened the following evening.

On Saturday night, a traffic unit of the Lancashire Constabulary had attempted to stop a stolen car in Whitegate Drive, Blackpool. However, people who steal cars have an ingrained dislike of stopping for the police. True to form, this driver declined to do so and was chased into Church Street. At one point the bandit car struck a stationary van, but still managed to carry on.

It then turned into the Golden Mile, which at that time of a Saturday night, even in winter, was thronged with people, and drove south towards Lytham St Annes at speeds approaching eighty miles an hour. By now other police vehicles had joined in the chase and an attempt was made to stop it by putting a police car across the road.

It was a strategy that proved to be unwise.

The escaping driver steered his car on to the pavement, narrowly avoiding a group of girls with 'Kiss-me-quick' hats, and coats of faux fur and denim, and succeeded in quite severely damaging the front of the police car.

Having taken a guess at which way the

vehicle was heading, another traffic unit placed a 'stinger' across the road clear of the town. This cunning device is designed to deflate the tyres slowly and bring the offending vehicle to a standstill.

It certainly achieved that, but at that point the driver leaped out and fired several rounds from a handgun at the approaching police officers.

Not unnaturally the officers retreated, thus allowing the gunman to disappear into the maze of side streets. A widespread search was carried out, but to no avail.

Unfortunately for the Lancashire police, and for us as it happened, the man escaped.

The abandoned vehicle was taken for scientific examination and the fingerprints of Darren Walters were discovered all over it.

But we knew nothing of this until the emailed report landed on my desk on Monday morning.

'Well, at least we know where he went,' I said.

'I'll bet he's not in Blackpool now, though,' said Dave. 'Come a long way from nicking purses and picking pockets, hasn't he, guv?' he added.

'I reckon the murders of Gould and Pointer must be down to him if he's prepared to shoot his way out, Dave.'

'So what do we next, guv?'

'There's not a lot we can do except sit and wait for another force to pick him up.'

'That could take for ever,' rejoined Dave gloomily. 'How about putting an obo on Terry Gould's flat at Poplar?'

'I doubt he'll return there now. Anyway, we don't have the manpower to do that. And even if we did it'd be an impossible task. They'd be sussed out in no time at all. Unless you want to give it a go, Dave.'

'I'm a bit busy at the moment, sir.'

That same afternoon, I received the ballistics report on the two weapons we'd found in Walters's garage in East India Dock Road. The test-firings indicated that Gould had been shot with the M16 carbine and that Pointer had been killed with the Walther P38 automatic.

So far so good. But as police officers we knew that Walters's possession of the weapons did not necessarily mean that he was responsible for the murders. And that would not be resolved until we had Walters in custody. And perhaps not even then.

'The next thing we have to do, Dave, is find this long-distance lorry driver who collects coffins from Portsmouth and takes them to Dinard.'

'Easier said than done, guv. I don't suppose he'll turn up at the Portsmouth warehouse now. If Walters was tipped off, it's a racing certainty that someone will have warned the driver as well.'

'In that case, we'll have another go at

Crow. I have a feeling that he's more into this scam than he's admitted.'

'Didn't strike me as being clever enough,' said Dave. He dipped into the nylon bag he used as a briefcase and took out an orange. 'Madeleine says they're good for me, guv,' he added, seeing my glance of disapproval.

'That's all right, then,' I said. Who was I to argue with the gorgeous Madeleine?

Eight

Wilfred Crow carved a pitiful figure as he was escorted into one of the interview rooms at Brixton prison. Still wearing the clothes in which he'd been arrested, the black suit, white shirt and black tie were now crumpled and strangely out of keeping with the surroundings.

'I don't know why I've been banged up here, Mr Brock,' he said plaintively.

But I did. Although I was by no means certain of it, I had managed to convince the district judge at Horseferry Road court that Crow was part of a conspiracy responsible for the murders of Spotter Gould and Bernie Pointer. I had also emphasized that other suspected co-conspirators were still at large – that was true of course – and that Crow's release might hinder my enquiry and result in interference with witnesses, et cetera, et cetera.

'Wilfred Crow, I've a mind to charge you with the murders of James Gould and Bernard Pointer.' I thought that would do for openers and sat back to await Crow's reaction.

'Bloody hell, guv'nor,' exclaimed the anguished Crow, leaping to his feet. 'I never had nothing to do with that.'

The bogus suavity with which Crow had first greeted us in his role as an undertaker had now given way to the familiar posturing of the common villain.

'Sit down, Wilf,' I said, 'while I explain the way the Crown Prosecution Service is likely to view the situation. You are an associate of Darren Walters and that makes you a suspect. I certainly don't believe that Mr Ramo Aniç of Bosnia came across here to top Gould and Pointer himself. Therefore I have to assume that the aforesaid Mr Aniç had an agent or agents in this country.' I had no intention of telling Crow that we'd found the murder weapons at Walters's garage.

'But all I did was to feed you Darren Walters's name,' whined Crow, his head nodding back and forth again.

'Precisely. That makes him what in criminal law is called an accomplice. An accomplice of yours, and that makes you an accomplice of his. A co-conspirator, even.'

'Just like a Rubik's cube,' said Dave. 'It all fits together.'

'I never met him. Honest, Mr Brock, I never met him,' Crow protested. 'He was just a name, see.'

'The law says that co-conspirators don't have to meet each other,' Dave said mildly. 'Like Mr Aniç is also a co-conspirator of

130

yours, just because you telephoned him from time to time.'

'And you telephoned Walters frequently,' I said.

'Yeah, well, I had to pass on messages.'

'What sort of messages?'

'About when the next consignment was coming in and that sort of thing.'

'Or telling Walters what Ramo Aniç told you to tell him? To go out and murder Bernie Pointer, for example. The man you said had got too greedy for Mr Aniç's liking.' I gave it a second. 'Or telling you to go out and murder Bernie Pointer yourself, even.'

'No, I swear it. I never had nothing to do with Bernie getting topped. It was me who tried to get him out of Aniç's way. Don't you remember me telling you?' pleaded Crow. 'I told him to go and get another job and change his name.'

'But Pointer *was* his name.'

'Yeah, but I mean change it back, like. You know, from Bob Salter back to Pointer.' Crow lapsed into confused silence, a perplexed frown on his face. 'Or was it the other way round?'

All of which might have been true, but there again it might not. It is a truism that Pointer was no longer here to confirm Crow's account of what took place.

'So how did you know there was a contract out on Pointer?'

'I never. Well, I heard a whisper,' said Crow

131

and then looked as though he wished he hadn't spoken.

'Really? And where did you hear this whisper?'

'Can't remember.'

Although such reticence was an impediment to my investigation, I didn't altogether blame Crow for suffering a quick onset of amnesia. Nevertheless, I was fairly sure that the mysterious Aniç had given Crow instructions for the murder of Pointer, and that he'd passed them on to Walters.

'What's the name of the long-distance lorry driver who collects the coffins from Portsmouth or wherever, and takes them to Dinard?'

'Eh? What lorry driver?' Crow was momentarily thrown by the sudden change in questioning. 'I don't know nothing about that.'

Dave decided to join in again. 'Well, how d'you think they get there, then? Magic carpet, perhaps? Bounced off a satellite, maybe?'

'Honest, I don't know. Mr Aniç was very secretive about everything. He wouldn't tell me nothing I shouldn't know.'

I was beginning to think that Mr Aniç was a very wise man.

'Well, Wilf,' I said, 'I'm now going to get that friendly screw outside to tuck you up in your nice warm little cell. And I suggest you do some deep thinking, because I shall come and talk to you again. And next time it'd be a good idea if you had some answers.'

'You haven't got a fag to spare, have you, Mr Brock?' asked Crow as I reached the door.

'No,' I said.

By Tuesday morning things were starting to come together.

Lemez, Crow and the other two had been fingerprinted when they'd been arrested at Portsmouth. And the three Brits all had criminal records. Which was no more than I'd expected.

We had already discovered from the fingerprints lifted at the funeral parlour that Crow had form spread over the last twenty-five years. But most of it was minor: at least a dozen for petty theft including an intriguing one for stealing from the Royal Mail while employed as a postman. And ten years ago he'd been fined and dismissed for 'being drunk while on duty as a railway porter at Waterloo mainline terminal to the detriment of passengers'.

'I knew he wasn't a professional,' said Dave scathingly.

The remaining two were also petty criminals and I wondered what had persuaded the apparently shrewd Ramo Aniç to recruit such lowlifes.

Dr Gavrilo Lemez was, however, a different matter. There was no record of him at New Scotland Yard, but then I didn't expect there to be. But the ever-resourceful Dave Poole had spoken to a mate of his in the Interpol office who had undertaken to send Lemez' fingerprints to Bosnia by dint of some computer wizardry.

There was even a suggestion that the Royal Military Police unit with the British army in Bosnia had been involved in our enquiry. But who cares so long as the job gets done?

'It says here, guv' – Dave flourished the note he'd got from Interpol – 'that Gavrilo Lemez is definitely not a medical doctor.' He looked up. 'He's not even a doctor of sociology,' he added scornfully. Dave, a graduate in English from London University, took the view that sociology was the pits when it came to higher education. His grandfather was a medical doctor who had come over from the Caribbean in the fifties to set up practice in Bethnal Green, and in Dave's view, the only people entitled to call themselves doctors were medical ones. 'In fact, he's wanted by the Bosnian police for a variety of offences including a massive fraud on a bank. And that probably explains how he came by forty-five thousand US dollars for his fare over here. What's more, the Bosnian police have expressed a desire to interview *Mister* Lemez. Preferably in a prison in darkest Sarajevo.'

'I think that's a distinct possibility, Dave,' I said.

Given the route and method by which

Lemez had arrived, and what the Immigration Service would shortly learn of his background, they were certain to return him to Bosnia. Perhaps. On the other hand the mere fact that he was wanted by the Bosnian police might well put him into the political-asylum-seeking category.

Funny place, Britain.

In the meantime, the Lancashire Constabulary, which takes grave exception to anyone shooting at its policemen, had circulated a description of Darren Walters as wanted for questioning in connection with attempted murder. What was more, the national press had got hold of the story and had given it widespread coverage. It also published a photograph of the wanted man. It certainly wasn't the one on his criminal record.

Dave rang the Blackpool incident room and was told that the photograph had come from Terry Gould. And when DS Challis went to Poplar to check on that, Terry Gould told him that she'd been paid a thousand pounds for it. And for sure, Darren Walters wouldn't see a penny-piece of it. And no, she hadn't seen him since he left, and never wanted to see him again.

The next day, I decided that Wilfred Crow had sweated long enough. Dave and I returned to Brixton prison determined to get more of the story from him. And I was sure he knew more than he had so far disclosed to us.

Escorted by a huge prison officer, Crow shuffled into the interview room, a hunted look on his face.

'Well, Wilf,' I began, as I settled down and lit a cigarette.

Crow looked hungrily at the packet, but I decided to let him wait.

'You know more than you're telling.'

'I can't think of anything I haven't told you, Mr Brock.'

'You'd better think again then, Wilf.'

'What can I say?'

'The truth. You see, Wilf, this little band of brothers with whom you are associated are going down big time.'

'What my guv'nor means is that it would be unwise of you to buy a five-year diary, Wilf,' said Dave.

'Oh Gawd!'

I pushed my cigarette packet across the scratched surface of the table and Crow almost snatched a cigarette from it.

'Speak, Wilfred,' I said.

'I've told you all I know.' Crow puffed smoke into the air.

'No you haven't. For example you haven't told me why Bernie Pointer got topped.'

There was a pause while, I imagine, Crow considered his position, as politicians are wont to say when they're in shtook. Which these days seems to be most of the time.

136

'Yeah, I did. I told you he got greedy, Mr Brock.'

'But I'm interested in the mechanics, Wilf.'

'What mechanics? I don't know no mechanics.'

'The mechanics of why Bernie was murdered.' I was beginning to get exasperated, and wondered whether Crow was being deliberately obtuse. Not that I'd blame him.

'Bernie sent a message up the line.'

'What line?'

'Well, like, Bernie let it be known that he wasn't happy with only getting a grand for bringing the coffins in.'

'Yes, you already told me that, but who did he tell?' I asked.

'Don't know, but word eventually got to Mr Aniç, and Mr Aniç didn't like what he heard.'

'Are you telling me, Wilf, that Bernie Pointer got topped merely for protesting that he was underpaid?'

'There was a bit more to it than that,' said Crow.

'Thought there might be. Go on.'

'Well, just to make his point, he rolled one of the passengers—'

'Hang on. Just explain that, will you?'

'One of the geezers what was being brought in. Just to let Mr Aniç know that he wasn't happy, Bernie robbed the next passenger of all he'd got on him and then took him down the beach at Dinard in a van.

Told him that that was part of the routine, see, and then told him to get out and hang about. Seems he told this geezer someone'd pick him up later.' Crow gave a brief laugh. 'They did an' all, 'cos then Bernie rang the local Old Bill, anonymous like, and told them there was an "illegal" roaming about looking to swim the Channel. Well, that was it. The "illegal" told the French law what was going on and they got all arsey about it.'

'Would've done, I suppose,' I said.

'Well, that put the kibosh on things for a while, until it'd all quietened down. See, the French law was crawling all over the place for the next few weeks. I reckon it must've cost Mr Aniç a packet. He wasn't happy. Not at all.'

'So he decided to have Bernie rubbed out. Was that it?'

'More or less,' said Crow dolefully.

Dave laughed. 'More rather than less, I should think, Wilf.'

'Obviously Aniç didn't come over and do the job himself, so who did?' I asked.

'I don't know, Mr Brock. Stand on me, it's the God's honest truth.'

'And what was your part in all this? You know this much, so you must have known how it went down.'

'Mr Aniç told me to tell Walters and that Walters'd fix it.'

I nodded at Dave. Although it would have been sufficient to warn Crow that he was

138

still under caution, Dave played safe and recited the magic words all over again.

'It's very likely, Wilf, that you will additionally be charged with conspiring with others not in custody to murder Bernard Pointer,' I said. 'And if there's any evidence of your association with the Gould murder, you'll cop a few years for that too.' Not that I thought the Crown Prosecution Service would wear any of it on the slim admission we had so far.

'Christ, Mr Brock, all I did was pass on the message. I never told Walters to top Bernie. All Aniç said was to tell Walters to deal with the Pointer problem.'

'And that,' I said, 'is called conspiracy.'

'But if I hadn't passed on the message, Bernie would have been topped just the same. And probably me an' all.'

'It's a hard old world, Wilf,' said Dave, busily recording the latest exchange in his pocketbook.

'D'you know Darren Walters's garage in the East India Dock Road, Wilf?' I asked.

'No. Like I said, I never met the guy.'

'And did Walters murder Bernie Pointer?'

'I haven't a clue, Mr Brock,' said Crow.

And that made two of us. Just because we'd found the weapons in Walters's garage didn't mean that he was the guy who'd pulled the trigger. Or in this case, the triggers. When eventually we found Walters, he'd probably claim that the guns had been planted and

139

that he'd never seen them before. And he did.

'What happens now?' Crow asked in a wheedling tone of voice.

'I told you that just now, Wilfred. The next time you appear in court, you'll probably be further charged with conspiracy to murder.'

'But I never had anything to do with it,' Crow pleaded, still trying to escape the inescapable.

'And to think that if only you'd stayed sober, Wilf,' said Dave, 'you could still have been a porter at Waterloo station.'

'How did you know about that?' Crow raised his eyebrows in astonishment.

But Dave just laughed.

'Now then,' I said, just when Crow thought I'd finished, 'when Pointer robbed this illegal immigrant in Dinard, and the heat was on from the French police, was there a change of route?'

Crow scoffed. 'You'd better believe it, Mr Brock. We had to switch from Dinard–Southampton to Calais–Dover. Just till it all died down, like.'

'So the coffins were brought in by ferry, yes?'

'Yeah, course.'

'And in view of your unfortunate arrest is the route from Calais to Dover operating once more, Wilf?'

'Christ, Mr Brock, you don't know what you're asking.'

140

'Yes, I do, Wilf. Are illegal immigrants being brought in by ferry from Calais?'

'Probably. But it wasn't me who told you.'

'When did you last meet Aniç, Wilf?' I asked.

'Oh, I've never met him,' said Crow. 'Only ever spoke to him on the phone. An' I don't want to meet him either. He's a right nasty bastard by all accounts.'

I was pretty sure that Crow had reached the point where he would tell me anything he thought I wanted to hear, probably seeing his 'information' as self-serving. There was certainly no proof that the people smugglers were still using the crossing from Calais to Dover – if, in fact, they had ever used it.

But we'd have to check.

I was loath to get entangled in this business of illegal immigration – primarily the responsibility of the Immigration Service – but there still existed the possibility that Pointer's murderer was to be found somewhere within the coffin-runners' set-up.

And I was sure that someone had warned Walters of the arrests at Portsmouth. But who?

It was time to indulge in a little of what the Job refers to as interdepartmental cooperation.

Dave and I went to Croydon, home of the Immigration Service. Thanks to fears of terrorism and the number of immigrants who frequently lay siege to its headquarters, it was no easy matter to gain admittance to what had become a veritable fortress. Unfortunately that high level of security in no way reflected the policy of Her Majesty's Government with regard to immigrants and asylum-seekers.

'Yes, well of course this is an immigration matter,' said the pompous official who eventually deigned to grant us an interview. 'I don't really see why the police are involved. We deal with problems of this sort day in and day out.'

'The police are involved,' I said, 'because one, if not two, of the participants in this little scam was murdered.' I had yet to be convinced that Spotter Gould was an innocent party. 'Undoubtedly by another of those involved,' I continued. 'And until I have that man in custody those concerned in this business are of great interest to me.'

'Mmm! Yes, I see. So how can I help?'

'I have received further information that a similar enterprise is being conducted by ferry between Calais and Dover.'

'Oh dear!'

'What sort of check is made on coffins coming into the port of Dover?' I asked.

'Well, the accompanying documents are checked, but you have to realize that Dover is a very busy port.'

'And if they come in aboard a container lorry?' The information about the long-distance lorry driver taking the 'empties' back to Dinard did not exclude the possibility that he was coming back via Dover. Fully loaded, so to speak.

'Good God!' The official looked aghast. 'But there are over five hundred lorries a day through that port.'

'Looks like you're going to be busy, then,' said Dave.

Back at the office, I telephoned Maréchal des Logis chef Jacques Bloyet, the gendarme who had introduced me to Odette Gouret, the head of customs at Dinard airport.

I told him Crow's story of the abandoned illegal immigrant and asked him if he could confirm it.

Half an hour later, he was back on the line.

'This was before my time 'ere, 'Arry,' he said, 'but I 'ave looked up the records and it is exactly as you say. The *adjudant-chef* who was 'ere at the time interrogated this man, but 'e was unable to tell us anything. 'E did not know where 'e 'ad been taken in Dinard or where 'e 'ad come from before that. 'E did not know what sort of van 'e was in, and 'e could not describe the man who 'ad left 'im on the beach. Some enquiries were made 'ere in Dinard but nothing was found. The *adjudant-chef* wrote on the file that 'e thought it was all nonsense. 'E thought that the immigrant was making it up, *non*?'

'So, no further action, eh, Henri?'

'The man was 'anded over to the Police de l'Air et des Frontières and I suppose was sent back to where 'e came from. Case closed, *non*?'

The only useful purpose that that enquiry had served was to prove that, on this occasion, Wilfred Crow had been telling the truth.

But, as Dave was quick to point out, it got us no further in the search for Bernie Pointer's killer.

Nine

Not having too much faith in the Immigration Service, I discussed the matter of the Dover connection with John Fielding at the National Investigation Service of Revenue and Customs. 'It's true what they say about container lorries, Harry,' he said. 'The best we can do is to work on intelligence. There's no way we can search over five hundred lorries a day. We don't have the staff and apart from anything else, we'd have a traffic jam of vehicles stretching all the way up the motorway to London waiting to get into the port while we messed about with those trying to get out. Anyway, this immigrant-smuggling thing's really down to Immigration.'

'So what do we do? Just let it go?'

Fielding laughed. 'Not bloody likely. I'll talk to our colleagues across the water. See if they can dig up anything. It's a start that you've got the name of this Ramo Aniç fellow, and as it looks likely that the route was through Salzburg, Stuttgart, Lyon and Dinard – although I doubt it is, any more –

we should be able to glean something. But it'll take time.'

'Ah, Mr Brock, I've been hoping to catch you.' The commander swanned into the interview room primping his top-pocket handkerchief.

At least he didn't say 'catch you *out*'.

'Yes, sir?'

'This immigrant-smuggling thing. Anything to do with the murders of, er, what were their names?'

'Gould and Pointer, sir.'

'Yes, they're the ones. Well?'

'There is definitely a connection between the smugglers and the murder of Pointer, sir. But Gould is a wild card at the moment.'

'A wild card?' The commander wrinkled his nose, his standard expression of distaste whenever I inserted slang into the conversation. He didn't think that senior officers should use slang, but then he didn't know detectives very well.

'There appears to be no connection between the murder of Spotter Gould and the immigrant smuggling, sir,' I said, spelling it out as clearly as I could without sounding too sarcastic. I chose not to mention that Darren Walters had been in possession of the murder weapons, or that he was shacked up with Mrs Gould, or had been. Nor did I expound on my theory that Gould had probably been shot by mistake. All of that would

146

complicate things too much for the commander.

'Going to take you long to get a result,
d'you think?' the commander asked airily as
he polished his spectacles.

I played my trump card. 'If I could have
authority to go to Bosnia, sir—'

I got no further.

'Out of the question, Mr Brock,' bristled
the commander. 'Out of the question. The
expense would be enormous and I'm sure
that the assistant commissioner would definitely draw the line at such a profligate
outlay. And for what purpose, pray?'

Excellent. I didn't want to go to Bosnia
anyway, but now I had a copper-bottomed
excuse for any delays that might occur as a
result of not going.

'It does rather mean a slowing down of the
enquiry, sir,' I said, contriving to sound
apologetic.

'Yes, well be that as it may, there is absolutely no question of you going off on
another of your foreign jollies.'

*God preserve us! If the commander thought
that a trip to Bosnia would be a jolly, he obviously didn't read too many newspapers.*

It's not often that one gets a stroke of luck in
the coppering game, but as a result of John
Fielding putting pressure on the customs
unit at Dover greater attention was paid to
coffins in transit.

And on the following Monday morning a phone call from Fielding proved that it had paid dividends.

'Harry, the guys at Dover opened a coffin that came off the six-thirty ferry from Calais.'

'Did they have a reason?'

Fielding laughed. 'Too right. The destination address on the documentation was the same florist shop as the one mentioned on the papers that accompanied the coffin we opened at Portsmouth.'

Shortly after the Portsmouth arrests, we'd asked the Birmingham police to make further enquiries about the florist whose address had appeared on the documents. The outcome was that the owner, an elderly and dedicated floriculturist, was clearly innocent of any involvement in immigrant smuggling.

'They're getting careless, John. So what happened next?'

'The coffin contained a dead body.'

'Well, that's a revelation, I must say.'

Fielding laughed. 'Yeah, but I don't think he was dead when he left Calais. Not unless the Bosnians dress their corpses in a black suit, complete with collar and black tie, and an overnight bag containing a spare shirt, underwear, a razor and a toothbrush.'

'You have a point there, John,' I said. 'So where do we go from here?'

'The Waterguard called the local police and I understand that there's a detective inspector from Dover nick looking into it.'

'Who are these Waterguard people, John?' I'd never heard of anything called the Waterguard.

'It's what the uniformed element of customs was called when I joined the service, Harry, but I think the "brains" at King's Beam House have probably changed it to something else now.'

'You don't send your guys to the Police College by any chance, do you, John?'

I decided against rushing down to Dover. At least not until I'd telephoned the police there.

The DI who had been lumbered with the dead body said that he was dealing with it as a suspicious death.

Well, that was a start.

'Have you arrested anyone?' I asked.

'Customs arrested the two guys who were accompanying the coffin and they're banged up here at Dover nick, now that we've taken them into our custody. Customs reckoned that importing a dead body in a coffin didn't seem to contravene any of the legislation for which they were responsible. Might contravene a few European Union regulations, though,' he added as an afterthought.

'Most things do,' I said. 'There were two guys, you said?'

'Yes, and they did it properly,' said the Dover DI. 'They were dressed in black suits, black ties and had the coffin in a flash hearse. The only things missing were black top hats with crêpe tied round 'em. Customs practically took the hearse apart, hoping they'd find drugs or whatever, but it was clean.'

'Any idea of the deceased's identity?'

'Not yet. We've done the usual: finger-prints, check in CRO, that sort of thing.'

'I doubt you'll find anything,' I said. 'If the job I've been investigating is anything to go by, your body will turn out to be a Bosnian illegal immigrant.'

I explained about the murder of Bernard Pointer and outlined my reasons for thinking that it was in some way connected with the immigrant-smuggling ring.

'D'you want to talk to the two we've got in custody?' asked the Kent inspector.

'Yes, I do. I'll be down there ASAP.'

By the time Dave and I reached Dover, it was four o'clock, and the post-mortem had already been carried out. The pathologist's opinion was that the deceased had probably died of a heart attack brought on by hyper-ventilation as a result of being confined in the coffin. A condition not helped by the fact that he also had a heart weakness.

'Pity, that,' I said. 'I'd've liked to talk to him.'

'I know a reliable medium in Clapham,' said Dave in an aside.

The Dover DI was not the first person to have trouble with Dave's sense of humour and shot him a sceptical look before continuing. 'These two admit that the guy was alive when they put him in the coffin just outside the port of Calais,' the DI said. 'So in view of the pathologist's findings, I'll charge them with manslaughter. The Crown Prosecution Service might even go for murder.'

'Or suicide,' said Dave, and was ignored by both of us.

'But as far as I'm concerned,' the Dover DI continued, 'the Immigration Service can deal with the charge of facilitating the entry of an illegal immigrant. Then it's up to the CPS. These guys are refusing to tell us who they are and where they live, which in my view makes them of no fixed abode. Not that it matters; we'll get a remand in custody anyway. And when the fingerprints are checked I'm damned sure we'll find they've got form.'

Despite their funereal attire, the two 'smugglers' were obviously villains, and pretty small fry at that.

Consequently, I didn't think it would do any good mentioning Ramo Aniç to either of them. If what Crow had said was true, Aniç kept the constituent elements of his operation in watertight compartments so that hardly anyone knew anyone else. I tried a different name.

'I get the impression that Wilfred Crow is not best pleased with you two,' I began.

'Never heard of him,' said one of the 'undertakers', but from the look of concern on the pair's faces, it was obvious that the name had registered with each of them.

Oh good! I was getting somewhere.

'I had a chat with him last Tuesday and he was grassing you two up a treat.' I didn't bother to mention that the interview had taken place in Brixton prison or that much of what I was about to say was fiction. 'He reckons this whole enterprise is down to you. He even told us the day this consignment would be coming in, where it would be arriving and at what time. That's why you got nicked. In fact, he said that you two are the brains behind it.'

'That's a bloody lie,' said one of them heatedly. 'Crow's the guy who runs things.'

'Perhaps he got the names wrong, then. Perhaps it was two other guys.'

'Must have been,' said the spokesman.

I looked pensive. 'But I'm not sure about that,' I said. 'You see he also suggested that you two were responsible for the murder of Bernie Pointer.'

'Christ, guv'nor, we never had nothing to do with that,' said one of the pair.

'I see you've heard about it, then.'

'Course we have. It was in all the papers and on the telly. Found on a golf course

152

somewhere, wasn't he?'

'But I still don't see why you couldn't have topped Bernie,' I observed mildly. 'After all, only this morning you were stopped by customs and found to be in possession of a dead body. Bit tricky that, and Her Majesty's judges tend to take a very dim view of that sort of thing.'

'That was an accident. We didn't know the stupid bastard was going to snuff it. That coffin was specially made, see. There's plenty of holes in it.'

'Bit like your story,' observed Dave mildly.

'Who makes these coffins?' I asked.

'Wilf Crow. He's got a place up the Smoke.'

I didn't think it worth telling the two 'pall-bearers' that Wilf had just gone out of business. For the time being it was more beneficial to let them think he was one of my best informants.

'Even so, it won't look good when the CPS comes to look at the report being prepared by the local police as I speak. Arriving with a stiff.' I shook my head. 'Probably contravenes all sorts of health-and-safety laws. And not ten minutes ago, the DI here was suggesting it probably falls foul of EU regulations as well. Bit difficult to explain that away,' I said. 'Anyway, Crow gave us names, so how do I know that he wasn't talking about you two?'

They practically fell over themselves to

reveal their identities.

'Charlie Steer,' said one.

'Fred Palmer,' said the other.

'Good,' said Dave. 'Now that we've got that cleared up, you can give me your dates of birth and where you live.'

Messrs Steer and Palmer hurriedly furnished Dave with their particulars. Both lived in the Limehouse area of London, not a million miles from Poplar, where Spotter Gould's widow had, until recently, shared a bed with her live-in lover. But that was probably a coincidence. Nevertheless, I floated it.

'Where's Darren Walters gone?' I asked.

Steer and Palmer looked at each other.

'Dunno,' said Steer eventually. Presumably some form of extra-sensory perception operated between these two. I found it difficult to believe that they didn't know Walters, or had at least heard of him.

'When did you last see him?' Dave took up the questioning again. It wasn't only Steer and Palmer who shared ESP.

Charlie Steer gave that some thought. ''Bout a month ago, I reckon,' he said eventually.

'Well,' I said, looking as though I was preparing to leave, 'your mate Wilf has put it firmly down to you. He definitely mentioned Steer and Palmer. Those were the names, weren't they?' I asked, glancing at Dave.

'Yes, sir,' said Dave. 'He definitely said

154

Steer and Palmer.'

Fred Palmer now decided it was time to put in his two-penn'orth. 'Might it help us out if we was to, like, give you a bit of info, guv'nor?'

'Depends,' I said.

'I reckon we're in shtook anyway, so we've got nothing to lose. Anyway, if Crow's grassing us up, I don't see why we shouldn't do the same for him.'

'I couldn't agree more. So tell me where you picked up this body.'

'Paris,' said Palmer without hesitation.

'Big place,' said Dave. 'Whereabouts in Paris?'

'Somewhere near the Eiffel Tower. Off of some road called something like … ' A frown furrowed Steer's forehead. 'Grenelle, I think it was, but I can't remember the exact address. It was in a warehouse at the back of an old building.'

'How did you find this place, then?' asked Dave.

'The bloke in Lyon' – Steer pronounced the name as though he was referring to one of the inmates of Whipsnade Zoo – 'give us a map, but we had to hand it over when we got to Paris. The geezer there said it was security, like.'

'Was he French, this "geezer"?' Dave kept pressing.

'Yeah.'

'Name?'

'Pierre. Least that's what he said.'

'I've no doubt the Paris police will find it, and him,' said Dave. 'They might even ask to have you extradited as you as good as killed the bloke in the coffin. Assuming it happened on the French side of the Channel, of course. Which seems likely from what the pathologist said.' The two prisoners became a touch agitated at that bald statement. 'They tell me the Santé prison's very nice at this time of year,' Dave continued. 'Lucky for you they've given up using the guillotine.' He paused. 'Well, I think they have.'

This piece of totally false information clearly discomfited our pair even further.

Palmer turned to me. 'Look, guv'nor,' he whined desperately, 'we've told you all we know.'

'Maybe,' I said doubtfully. 'As a matter of interest, how much were you going to get paid for this little trip?'

'A monkey apiece,' said Steer.

'Really?' I said. 'I somehow doubt that five hundred pounds will be appearing on each of your bank statements after this morning's little fiasco.'

'Oh, it wouldn't,' said Steer a little too quickly. 'We get cash in hand, see.'

'And who pays you?'

'Wilf Crow.'

'*If* you hadn't been turned over by customs, and *if* your passenger had survived the trip,' said Dave, 'what were you going to do

156

next?'

'As soon as we'd left the port, we were going to stop in a lay-by and let the guy out of the coffin so's he could sit in the hearse for the rest of the journey.'

'And then what?'

'We was going to take him to Wilf's place and hand him over and collect our money. Then we was done.'

'Well,' said Dave, 'you've been done a bit earlier than you expected.'

Armed with the pathetic scrap of information we had extracted from Messrs Steer and Palmer, we returned to London.

'We're getting much too involved in something that doesn't concern us, Dave,' I said. 'All we seem to be doing lately is to run about after illegal immigrants. This is all down to the Immigration Service.'

'The murders aren't, guv,' said Dave, as usual putting his finger on the nub of the matter. 'And all we've discovered so far is that the missing Darren Walters had the weapons stashed away in his garage. For all we know some hit man might have come over from Europe and done the job. He wouldn't want to get caught bringing in the weapons, and sure as hell he wouldn't want to get caught taking them out. It doesn't necessarily follow that these toppings are down to Walters. Could be he was just the armourer, so to speak.'

As usual, Dave had dissected the investigation that was occupying all our waking hours and come up with a credible reason for not charging Walters with murder. But if that was the case, it was going to be damned difficult, if not downright impossible, to get a result.

Fortunately, I had a friend in the Paris police who had assisted me on previous occasions.

I rang Inspecteur Henri Deshayes, and after the usual exchange of insults in which policemen indulge, I explained my problem.

'The tour Eiffel is not in my area, 'Arry,' he said, having his usual Gallic problem with aspirates, or lack of them, 'but I 'ave a friend in that *arrondissement* who will do the business. Now let me 'ave the details.' After taking a note of the vague address that Steer had given us, Deshayes asked, 'But what are you doing investigating illegal immigrants, 'Arry? I thought you were the murder expert. Big man at Scotland Yard, *non*?'

'Piss off, Henri,' I said, deliberately sounding the aitch in his name. 'But seriously, there are two murders involved.' And I went on to explain about Spotter Gould and Bernie Pointer, the finding of the firearms and, most importantly of all, mentioned the name of Ramo Aniç who almost certainly was masterminding the whole smuggling operation. And who had probably masterminded the murders too.

$\star$ $\star$ $\star$

The next morning brought good news.

It also brought with it the revelation that, even though the entire detective force of the United Kingdom can be conducting an assiduous nationwide search for what used to be called 'a fleeing felon', it is frequently a lowly constable who makes the arrest. More often than not, by accident.

'Darren Walters has been nicked, sir,' said Colin Wilberforce as I walked into the incident room.

'Excellent. Where?'

A grin spread over Colin's face. 'You're going to love this, sir. Walters was in a pub last night in Southwark. So was a guy with a dog. According to the report, this dog kept sniffing around Walters's ankles. First of all, Walters swore at the dog, but when the animal wouldn't give up he threw a glass of beer over it and then kicked it.'

'So how come he got nicked, Colin? With the state of the police today, I don't see a keen young constable rushing in waving his handcuffs.'

'The dog was a police dog and his handler was enjoying a quiet pint in the corner of the bar. He promptly nicked Walters and charged him with cruelty to an animal under the Protection of Animals Act of 1911.'

Dave had already read the report, but was still laughing. 'What's more, guv,' he said, 'the dog bit Walters on the leg.'

'Not surprised,' I said.

'I've suggested to the handler that he takes the dog to a vet, just in case it caught anything nasty,' said Dave.

Ten

I made sure that Dave and I arrived at Southwark police station before Walters was taken to court, and in time to charge him with the unlawful possession of firearms.

He limped into the interview room, his right trouser leg torn to reveal a bandage where he'd been savaged by the police dog he'd kicked. Dave had suggested proposing the dog for the Dickin Medal: the animal equivalent of the Victoria Cross.

I was in no mood to mess about and I told Dave to turn on the tape recorder and read the caution.

Reluctantly, I told Walters that he was entitled to a lawyer, but he declined. But, I later realized, that was because he thought he knew all the answers.

'On Friday the first of March we executed a search warrant on your premises at East India Dock Road,' I said.

'So?' Walters's response was surly and he slouched in his chair, his attitude radiating an air of indifference.

'We found an M16 carbine and a Walther P38 automatic pistol carefully wrapped in oilskin and secreted on the rafters.'

'Lucky you.'

'Those weapons have been examined by a ballistics officer and he is prepared to testify in court that they were the firearms that were used to murder Jimmy Gould and Bernie Pointer respectively.'

'Is that a fact?'

'So, for a start, you'll be charged with the unlawful possession of firearms.'

'I wasn't in possession of 'em, was I? You said you found 'em in my garage. And I wasn't there.'

'It's called constructive possession,' Dave pointed out.

'I don't know nothing about 'em. You must have planted 'em. Bloody typical, that is. And if you didn't, someone else must've. Easy to get into that place. Just a padlock. You could have banjoed it easy.'

'We did,' observed Dave mildly.

'And that,' I continued, disinclined to refute the standard defence allegation of planting evidence, 'is enough to charge you with the murders of both Gould and Pointer.' It was certainly good enough in my view but, I feared, not good enough for the CPS.

'Ain't our policemen wonderful?' said Walters sarcastically.

'Furthermore, the police in Blackpool wish to interview you with regard to an incident the following day – that's Saturday the second of March – when it's alleged you shot at several police officers while you were in possession of a stolen motor vehicle.'

'Never been to Blackpool.'

Unless the Lancashire officers could positively identify Walters as their assailant, the fact that his fingerprints were found in the stolen car didn't necessarily make him the shooter. It wouldn't be the first time that a vehicle had been stolen from someone who had himself stolen it. And it had been subsequently proved that some of the vehicles we found in Walters's garage had been stolen. All of which could make for a problem. But it was Blackpool's problem, not mine. If Walters were to be charged with the murders of Gould and Pointer, the attempted murder of a police officer would add but a few years to his sentence. And then only concurrently. But who cares about coppers getting shot at these days?

I was somewhat surprised that Walters didn't seem to be taking any of this seriously. His next few utterances made clear why.

'What was it your dusky mate said about saying something I later relied on in court?'

Dave just smiled. Racial slurs were nothing new to him, and he never rose to them. 'What I said was that it may harm your defence if you do not mention now something you later rely on in court.'

'Yeah, that's it. So I'd better mention it, hadn't I?'

I had a nasty feeling about this. 'I'd remind

you that this interview is being recorded,' I said, 'and that you're still under caution.'

'Great. That'll stop you putting the verbals on me, won't it? Right, mate, the score is this: the day that Spotter got topped, I was buying spares for a Ford Mondeo down in Maidstone. All legit *and* I got a receipt.'

'What time did you buy these spares?' I asked, mindful that Gould had been murdered at eight o'clock in the morning.

'Must've been just after nine,' said Walters. 'I left Poplar at about eight o'clock, stopped off for a cup of coffee on the way and got to this place just after they opened.'

All of which sounded much too convenient to be true because there was no way Walters could have been at Stone Mill prison at eight and in Maidstone by nine.

'And when Bernie Pointer got his—' Walters continued.

'How d'you know when Pointer was murdered?' asked Dave.

'It was on the TV and on the radio,' sneered Walters. 'Some bloke on the news said that you lot reckoned he'd been done in round about midnight on the eighth of February and dumped on a golf course. Right, am I? Anyway, before you butted in, I was going to tell you that I was shacked up with a bird up West.' He broke off to laugh. 'But for Christ's sake don't tell Terry Gould.'

'I don't think she'd be interested any more,' I said, 'but who was this woman?'

164

'Ah, that'd be telling.'

'In that case, I'll take it that she's a figment of your imagination.'

'Yeah, you do that, pal,' said Walters. 'But if you put me on the sheet for topping Pointer, my brief'll produce her in court.'

'And the receipt for these spares you were buying,' said Dave. 'Where's that?'

'At home down Poplar.'

'You mean at Gould's flat?'

'Yeah. Where else?'

'Let me just explain about alibis, Walters,' I said. 'Unless you produce the name of this woman you say you were sleeping with, and produce it now, it won't do you any good when you get to court. The judge will inform the jury that as you declined to reveal her identity to police when questioned it is likely that you'd subsequently concocted the alibi. And in all probability he'll direct the jury that it should, therefore, be regarded as suspect.'

Walters sat up straight and for a moment I thought I'd got him.

'Her name's Cindy Turner and she lives down Pimlico.'

'Where in Pimlico?' persisted Dave.

'Got a flat at 23 Purvis Street. Number 6.'

'A tom, is she?' Dave asked.

'No, she bleedin' ain't,' protested Walters.

But, as it turned out, he'd lied about that too.

* * *

Darren Walters appeared before the district judge at Southwark at half-past ten that morning. He was fined two hundred and fifty pounds for kicking a police dog and was ordered to pay the costs of his own treatment, which included several inoculations against tetanus and rabies, and the veterinary surgeon's examination of the police dog. I'd never met this dog, but I was beginning to like him.

After giving evidence of finding the firearms in Walters's garage, I outlined, as vaguely as I could get away with, the suggestion that other, more serious charges might follow. The district judge took the hint and remanded Walters in custody to appear before a Crown Court judge eight days hence.

He also gave permission for officers from Lancashire Constabulary to take Walters to Blackpool to take part in an identification parade, provided they returned him to Wandsworth prison immediately afterwards. I'd made a plea that Walters should not be remanded to Brixton, the same prison that presently housed Wilfred Crow. Prisoners tend to talk to each other when they meet, and I didn't want there to be any chance of those two lowlifes colluding. Such people have a nasty tendency to concoct all manner of disturbing stories.

Back at Curtis Green, I rang the Blackpool

police and told them that Darren Walters was in custody at Wandsworth prison and that they were free to take him back to Blackpool for an ID parade.

'When can we do that?' asked DCI Ray Lander, the Lancashire officer dealing with the case.

'Any time you like, Ray,' I said. 'He won't be appearing before the Crown Court for another eight days.' Although it was irrelevant I told him about the incident with the police dog, just for a laugh. 'But more importantly, Ray, I've charged him with unlawful possession of firearms. And I'll probably put him on the sheet for murder as well. Well, two murders actually.'

But as I said it, I had a suspicion that somehow or other, Walters was going to walk away from those two killings. And he might even wriggle out of possession of the murder weapons and the attempted murder of a Blackpool officer.

'These firearms ... ' began Lander.

'I know what you're thinking,' I said, 'but we seized those firearms *before* the incident in Blackpool involving your officers.'

'Sod it!' said the Blackpool DCI.

I was working on the assumption that Walters, having been arrested when he least expected it, was unlikely to have fixed himself up with an alibi in advance. But there again, being a devious bastard, he might just have done.

But I was determined to speak to Cindy Turner and check Walters's claim that he had been with her on the night of Pointer's murder. And in the meantime I sent DS Challis to Poplar with a warrant to search Terry Gould's flat for the receipt that Walters claimed he had obtained from a spares dealer in Maidstone.

It was a modern block of flats in Pimlico.

'Hi!' Cindy Turner put one hand on her hip and raised the other above her head to grasp the edge of the front door. She appraised Dave and me as though trying to assess the worth of our bank accounts by the quality of our suits. Had it been a competition I would definitely have come out the winner.

From the quality of the furnishings and Cindy's elegantly expensive appearance I deduced that she was quite a sophisticated woman. Until she opened her mouth enough to utter more than the single word with which she had greeted us. Then it became apparent that she was a home-grown gor-blimey cockney.

'Darren Walters? What about him?'

'He claimed that he slept with you on the night of the eighth and ninth of February.'

'Saucy bleedin' toe-rag.'

'Well, did he or didn't he?' I asked.

'I dunno. I don't keep a diary.'

'It was a Friday night, about four weeks ago.'

'Haven't a clue, mister,' said Cindy. 'He might've done.'

'Has he often slept with you?'

Cindy Turner, who, I had to admit, had a certain coarse sexual allure, did not seem at all offended that I was virtually accusing her of lax morals.

'Yeah, a few times. Anyway, why d'you wanna know?'

'Because he's a suspect in a case of murder,' I said. 'A murder that was committed that night.'

'Jesus Christ!' Cindy, colour draining from her face, looked aghast at both the possibility that she'd slept with a killer and the thought that he might return. 'Then the answer's no, mister. I definitely ain't seen him for months.'

This sort of response always puts the police in a difficult position. It was quite likely that Walters *had* spent the night with Cindy Turner, but then again, perhaps not. My immediate thoughts were that she did not want to get involved, a concept that in the circumstances seemed to me to be eminently reasonable. I imagine that being subpoenaed to attend the Old Bailey to give evidence on Walters's behalf did not appeal to this young woman.

'Are you absolutely sure about that, Miss Turner? It is *Miss* Turner, is it?'

'Yes, it is, and too bloody right I'm sure. He's nothing but trouble, that one.'

'How did you meet him?' asked Dave.

'Clubbing up West about a year ago,' was Cindy's terse answer. 'Yeah, sure we spent a few nights together, but that was a long time ago. And that's all it was: a quick screw. Nothing else to it. But I've moved up in the world since then. And I never had nothing to do with no murder.'

'I'm not suggesting that you did, Miss Turner,' I said, 'but Darren Walters put your name forward as an alibi for the night of the murder. Well, one of the murders, that is.'

'Bloody hell, you don't mean he done more than one, do you?'

'It's a possibility we're investigating,' I said.

By now, Cindy Turner was looking extremely distraught. 'Are you going to give me protection?' she asked.

'Why would you want protection?' Dave asked, contriving an uncharacteristic air of innocence.

But we both knew the answer to that. Whether or not Walters had spent the night with Cindy was immaterial, but if she refused to back his story, he was likely to cut up rough. And if he was not at liberty to do so, I was sure that he had several mates who would oblige.

'Walters is in custody at the moment,' I said, 'and unlikely to be granted bail. So I don't think you have anything to worry

170

about.'

'Says you.' Cindy clearly had the same faith in the justice system as I did.

'My sergeant will take a short statement from you to the effect that Darren Walters did not spend the night of the eighth and ninth of February with you, then,' I said.

And to my surprise she agreed to do so.

Dave produced the necessary stationery and began to write. 'What's your occupation, Miss Turner?' he asked.

'Prostitute. Well, call girl really.' Crossing her legs, Cindy placed her hands behind her head and stretched, thrusting her breasts against the delicate material of her silk dress. 'Wanna make something of it?'

Nevertheless, I was not convinced that her statement was true, apart from the bit about being a call girl, but that would be Walters's problem, and that of his counsel, not mine.

The unfortunate aspect of it, though, was that Walters might well have spent the night with her. And that would lead us in the wrong direction while the real killer was laughing like a drain. Perhaps.

It's always wise for a male officer to take a policewoman with him when he's searching premises occupied solely by a woman. All sorts of nasty allegations can be made, and often are. And in today's litigious society demands for outrageous sums of compensation usually follow. And occasionally succeed.

Consequently, DS Challis had taken DC Sheila Armitage with him to search Terry Gould's flat. Although Dave and I had already searched it, it had been but a cursory examination. At the time there was nothing particular that we were looking for.

But the two detectives found nothing of interest either, apart from a couple of forged vehicle logbooks that Challis promptly seized on behalf of the Stolen Vehicle Squad. It was Walters's bad luck that Challis had served on that squad prior to coming to the Serious Crime Group, and he could spot a bent logbook at a hundred yards.

He did, however, find the receipt that Walters claimed would cover him for the time of the Gould murder.

'Where was it, Tom?'

'In a drawer in the cabinet by the bed, guv.'

I was fairly sure that it hadn't been there when Dave and I had a look round, but it just might have been. 'Did you ask Terry Gould about it?' I asked.

'She reckoned she'd never seen it before, guv,' said Challis. 'So there's no telling how long it'd been there. I thought that one of Walters's mates might have dropped in and left it there for us to find, but she denied having had any visitors.' Challis smiled. ' "Apart from you bleedin' lot" is what she actually said. Not that I'd believe anything that cow told us. What d'you want me to do with it, guv?' he asked, waving the receipt.

'Go down to that spares place in Maidstone, Tom,' I said, 'and take Walters's mugshot with you. See if the assistant who issued the receipt can identify Walters as the guy who made this purchase. And when you get back do a check with the prison to see if Walters has had any visitors who might have done the business for him.'

DS Challis was back by early afternoon the following day.

'How did you get on, Tom?'

'Bit of a blow-out really, guv,' said Challis. 'This spares place is well set up, been there for ages apparently, and there's nothing shady about it. I spoke to the manager and he confirmed that the sale had taken place at eleven minutes past nine that day – that was on the receipt, of course – and that it was for a head gasket for a Ford Mondeo. But the assistant who dealt with the customer could not identify Walters from the photograph I showed him. He said they have hundreds of customers every day and he doesn't remember anyone looking like Walters because they all looked the same to him. Of course, that doesn't mean it wasn't him.'

'Did Walters use a credit card by any chance, Tom?'

'No such luck, guv. Whoever made the purchase paid cash.'

'And that could have been any one of his mates,' I mused. 'Assuming he's got any

173

mates. Looks like he's back in the frame.'

'In my book, guv,' said Dave, 'he was never out of it. And he's still got a lot of explaining to do as to how it was we found the murder weapons in his lock-up.'

'As you suggested, guv, I did a check with Wandsworth prison,' said Tom.

'More bad news, Tom?' I asked.

'Depends how you look at it, guv,' said Challis, 'but I wouldn't classify it as good. Walters hasn't had any visitors at all since he arrived at the nick.' And anticipating my next question, he added, 'And he hasn't had any post either. Mind you, there are ways and means of getting things out of the nick if you've got the right contacts. And I'm sure Walters has.'

Although I was convinced that Walters had not been the man who'd made the purchase at Maidstone, it looked as though I was going to have a damned hard job proving it.

But there were other matters occupying me at the moment and I decided to put the matter of Walters's receipt on the back burner. For the time being.

That afternoon Inspecteur Henri Deshayes rang from Paris with good news.

'I 'ave spoken with my colleague in the Fifteenth Arrondissement, 'Arry. Inspecteur Jules Fabien. There 'ave been whispers about this place your prisoners described and Fabien carried out a raid early this morning.

It was an old warehouse in an alley off the Boulevard de Grenelle.'

'Did he find anything, Henri?'

'Oh, yes. There were three coffins there, each 'aving special 'oles for ventilation. There were also two men, Alain Cocaud and Michel Solan, who 'e 'as arrested.'

'Did they say anything, these two?' I asked.

Deshayes chuckled. 'Not yet, 'Arry, but Jules Fabien can be very persuasive. I will let you know what 'appens. Oh, by the way, these men did say that the coffins 'ad been delivered only the previous night from England. I don't know if that 'elps, but maybe you can do some checking.'

'Thanks, Henri. I owe you one.'

'That's right. When you come to Paris next, you buy me a drink, *non*?'

'You're on, Henri.'

'What am I on, 'Arry?'

I set DI Frank Mead the task of checking on those heavy goods vehicles that had left Portsmouth for St-Malo and Le Havre on the day prior to Fabien finding them, but predictably he got nowhere.

'Without the index mark, Harry, there's no way the guys down there can identify a vehicle carrying empty coffins, not unless they're listed on the manifest. And sure as hell, they won't be. But apart from that, the vehicle could have travelled via Dover to Calais. Anyway, there are hundreds of them.'

Which was exactly what John Fielding had said.

I was annoyed that we had not yet discovered the mysterious long-distance driver who delivered coffins; not that I thought he was anything other than a pawn, but I do like to tie up all the loose ends.

Eleven

I'd no sooner put down the phone following my conversation with Henri Deshayes than DCI Lander rang from Blackpool.

'We've had to row Walters out of this shooting, Harry,' he said, sounding very dispirited.

'What went wrong, Ray?'

'We put him on an ID parade with eight other guys but the two PCs in the patrol car couldn't identify him. Understandable, I suppose. It was dark at the time, and in view of the fact that this maniac was loosing off rounds at them, they were a bit busy taking cover. Anyway, he's on his way back to Wandsworth prison as I speak.'

'But what about the fingerprint evidence, Ray?' I asked.

'Personally I'd've given it a run, but the CPS doesn't want to know,' said Lander. 'They reckon that although the fingerprints prove that Walters was in the car at some time, it doesn't prove he was the guy who shot at our officers. So, I hope you can screw the bastard for those two murders of yours.'

'So do I,' I said, 'but frankly it's not looking

good at the moment. I'll let you know.'

There was an ironic laugh from the other end. 'If he gets away with it, we can always stick him on for nicking a car, Harry. I reckon the fingerprint evidence will at least be good enough for that.'

'Oh, sure,' I said, matching the Lancashire copper's cynicism, 'but don't put money on it. Half the social services will turn up at court to say he was abused as a kid.'

'I'm more interested in abusing the bastard now,' rejoined Lander.

Once again my enquiry had ground to a standstill, and I decided to combine business with pleasure.

I rang Gail. 'How d'you fancy lunch tomorrow?' I asked.

'Great. What time shall I meet you?'

'I'll pick you up at home at half-past seven.'

'*Half seven!* I thought you said lunch, not dinner.'

'Half-past seven in the morning, darling. We're having lunch in Paris,' I said smugly.

Gail was dressed in her black leather coat, boots and fur hat, and her long blonde hair was flowing free down her back. I attracted some envious glances as I escorted her down the escalator to the Eurostar terminal at Waterloo: admiring from the men, somewhat catty from the women. The check-in was already open and a half-hour later we were aboard the train and quaffing champagne.

My decision to lash out and take Gail for lunch in Paris was partly driven by the fact that a face-to-face meeting with Henri Deshayes might just push things along. But I didn't tell Gail that. I mean, how can you suggest a romantic lunch for two in Paris when you have an ulterior motive? Like talking shop with a colleague.

I'd telephoned Henri and asked him to join us at the Terminus Nord, a splendid brasserie immediately opposite the Gare du Nord. And being in a generous mood, I'd suggested he brought his wife with him. Over the years he'd done me a few favours and I reckoned I owed him a lunch.

Henri is about my own age, and a typically suave Frenchman. And his wife Gabrielle was a real beauty. Henri made a great fuss of Gail, bowing low and kissing her hand, and paying her fulsome compliments in his beguilingly accented English. It seemed to beguile Gail anyway. Gabrielle, standing behind her husband, shot a conspiratorial glance at Gail, shrugged and raised her eyebrows. It's funny how often policemen's cynicism rubs off on their wives and girlfriends.

There was something else too. It's one of life's enigmas that even though you can go out with a girl for quite a while there's always something new to learn about her. And it was at this point I discovered that Gail spoke

179

perfect French.

In no time at all she and Gabrielle were engaged in animated conversation about the latest fashions and, worse still, the best couturiers in Paris at which to buy them. Or so I later learned; I hadn't understood a word of their rapid exchanges. And as if that wasn't bad enough, it turned out that Gabrielle had been a dancer too. In the famous Folies Bergères. I had a feeling that we would be visiting Paris far more often in the future.

In the circumstances I didn't feel so bad about discussing the people smuggling with Henri.

'These two men that Jules Fabien arrested, 'Arry. Cocaud and Solan.' Henri shot a glance at his wife and lowered his voice. I doubt that he was worried that she might overhear confidential information; rather that she would disapprove of him talking about police work.

'What about them?' I asked.

'They know nothing. Jules gave them a good talking to—' Henri broke off to chuckle sadistically. 'But it seems that they don't know who runs this racket. They told Jules that they get a phone call – they don't know who from – and turn up at the warehouse in the alley near the Boulevard de Grenelle when they're told to. A delivery is made of the man who is to go to England. They keep him there until a courier arrives and takes

180

this man away. That is all they know.'

'Did they say what they get paid and, more to the point, how they get paid?'

'A hundred and forty euro each,' said Henri.

'A hundred and forty euro,' I repeated, attempting to work out in my head what that was in real money.

But Gail, who had overheard that part of the conversation, turned and said, 'About a hundred pounds, darling,' before continuing her discussion with Gabrielle.

'And they are paid in cash by the courier who collects the passenger. So there are no bank accounts or cards that can be traced,' Henri said.

'Was your colleague able to find out anything about the delivery of the coffins?'

'*Non!* It seems that they are delivered while there is no one in the warehouse. Whoever brings them 'as a key. As I told you before, there were three coffins there already but they arrived the night before Jules raided the place. Cocaud got a telephone call to say that they were there. Jules tried the usual trace on the telephone call, but got nowhere.'

'So Cocaud and Solan don't know who brings them.'

'Alas, *non*.' With Gallic eloquence, Henri shrugged his shoulders and spread his hands.

'I don't understand why the coffins are

delivered to Paris, Henri,' I said. 'Surely they don't put their passenger into one there.'

'*Non*. It seems they arrive in an 'earse. The immigrant travels in it as a passenger and then is put in the casket somewhere near Dinard.'

'Is that a guess?'

'Only the last bit. Cocaud and Solan only know about the man sitting in the 'earse when he leaves, nothing more. But I guess that that is what 'appens.'

'Yes, probably, Henri. There may be no suitable place in Dinard to keep the coffins, although I have heard that there is. However, the source of that information might not be reliable.'

Henri glanced at his watch. 'What time is your train, 'Arry?' he asked.

'We need to be at the Gare du Nord at about a quarter past five.'

'Good. Time for a cognac. On me.' The waiter was there in an instant. I presumed he was aware that Henri was a Paris detective, but on the other hand, it may have been that there were two extremely attractive women at our table.

The party eventually broke up at about four thirty with handshakes, embraces and kisses.

'If anything else 'appens, 'Arry, I'll telephone you straight away,' said Henri. 'And I 'ope you 'ave an 'appy ending to your murders.'

'So do I,' I said.

Having waved goodbye to Henri and Gabrielle, I was about to escort Gail across the road to the railway station when she placed a hand on my arm.

'We're not going home, darling,' she said.

'What d'you mean, not going home?'

'We're staying the night in Paris.'

'But ... I mean—'

'When you rang last night and told me we were coming to Paris for lunch, I booked a room. So, no arguments.' And with that, Gail gave rapid instructions to a taxi driver.

'But I'm supposed to be at the office in the morning,' I said as the taxi pulled away.

'Well, you'll be back there by lunchtime. Why don't you ring them and tell them you've eaten a bad oyster or something?' Gail leaned back against the cushions and smiled. 'That'll teach you to bring me to Paris and then talk shop with your friend.' She paused. 'Henri's a very nice man, isn't he?' she added.

I came to the conclusion that it had been a mistake to allow her to meet Henri and Gabrielle. And particularly Gabrielle.

Just in case the commander asked where I was, I telephoned Dave early the next morning from Paris and told him to say that I'd gone direct to Shepherds Bush on an enquiry.

I got to Curtis Green at about midday and

Frank Mead followed me into my office with an interesting snippet of news.

'Gavrilo Lemez has escaped, Harry.'

'Where from?'

'An overflow secure-detention facility at Hounslow.'

'Doesn't sound very secure to me. And what was he doing there, anyway? Wasn't he supposed to be up for extradition or deportation or something?'

'That was the game plan, Harry, and he was being held there while his case was sorted out,' said Frank, settling himself in my only armchair. 'But according to the CPS there's a bit of a problem with extradition.'

'Thought there might be,' I commented. 'Like what?'

'For starters there's no red-corner circular from Bosnia, which doesn't surprise me. Neither have the Bosnians made an official request for his extradition. The information about Lemez being wanted in Bosnia was the result of the enquiries that Dave Poole instigated through his mate at Interpol. Sort of semi-official, you see. The immigration people reckon the best course of action is to go for straightforward deportation.'

'Terrific!' I said. 'So how come he escapes from this so-called secure accommodation?'

Frank smiled. 'According to the Squad—'

'The Flying Squad?'

'Who else?' said Frank with a grin. 'According to the DI who's dealing with the job, a team of about three hoods turned up at two in the morning, well tooled up, and took the security guys totally by surprise. They tied them up, sprang Lemez and went on their merry way in a van. All over in about five minutes.'

'Wonderful! And I don't suppose any by-stander happened to notice this van, or its index mark?'

'Oh, come off it, Harry. That doesn't happen at midday, let alone at two in the morning.'

'I know,' I said. 'I was just being facetious.'

'Doesn't make any difference, anyway. The van that was thought to have been used was found burned out on the outskirts of Slough. Nicked four days ago from there. The CSEs are giving it the once-over, but they're not very hopeful.'

'Sounds like a professional job,' I said. 'But I wonder why they were so keen to spring Lemez. Or someone who set it up was.'

'Maybe they want a cut of the money he screwed this Bosnian bank for,' said Frank. 'If it's true, of course.'

'No, I think there's more to it than that. Unless they know where the cash is. But somehow I doubt it's in the UK. Could be anywhere: the States, Switzerland or even the Cayman Islands. I think it's more than likely something to do with people smuggling. But what? Incidentally, how did the Flying Squad get involved?'

'This facility is in an old barracks and initially it was thought that a heist to obtain firearms was going down. First messages were a bit garbled, but the minute mention was made of "barracks at Hounslow", the place was flooded with the Old Bill: armed-response vehicles, Territorial Support Group, half a dozen area cars and the Flying Squad. It was probably the usual cock-up and everyone started thinking of terrorism, particularly given the close proximity of the airport. The Squad must've been disappointed to find it was only a kidnapping. Not that I think it's as simple as that, and neither do they now, but they've been lumbered with the enquiry.'

'Isn't there a special squad that deals with kidnapping, Frank?' I asked.

'Not as far as I know, Harry.'

'Very remiss of the boy superintendents up at the Yard. I reckon there soon will be.'

'By the way, Harry,' said Frank, 'I was at Kingston Crown Court this morning. Remand hearing of Wilfred Crow.'

'I didn't think that was until next month.'

'Should have been, but his brief had him brought up on a bail application.'

'What happened?'

'He got bailed. The judge said that he didn't think he was justified in keeping him in custody. I'm afraid our brief from the CPS didn't do a very good job. I whispered in his ear about the possibility of conspiracy to

186

murder. But when our counsel propped that, the judge said it was too tenuous.'

'But that's bloody ridiculous.'

'Yeah, I know,' said Frank, 'but Crow's brief more or less demanded that we put up or shut up, and the judge agreed. If Crow was actually charged with conspiracy to murder, then he said he'd reconsider.'

I'd only been away from the office for a day and a half, and during that time, Gavrilo Lemez had been snatched from custody by an armed gang, and Crow had been released on bail.

Frank Mead read my thoughts. 'Shouldn't have taken the day off, Harry,' he said.

'How did you know I did?'

'I'm a detective,' said Frank.

I had a word with the Flying Squad DI who was dealing with the 'liberation' of Lemez, and told him in detail what I knew about the people-smuggling racket. For his part, the DI was able only to tell me what I already knew, and then muttered something about it not being a job for the Squad anyway. And, he added, the scientific examination of the burned-out van used by the kidnappers had drawn a blank.

The Squad had already put Gavrilo Lemez' name on the PNC, but I didn't think it would do any good. We only had Lemez' word that Lemez was his name, and given the twists and turns of my murder enquiry, I was by no means sure that he was who he said he was.

And it took me no nearer finding who'd killed Gould and Pointer.

John Fielding, however, had made a little progress through the customs network.

'It's about the address in Lyon that you gave me, Harry. The French customs raided it this morning.'

'Any joy?'

'Yes and no. They found two guys there and a Citroën car.'

'Is that it?'

'They also found some narcotics ... cocaine, I think. Anyway, whatever it was it was enough to hold them on. They were questioned about the people smuggling, but claimed they didn't know it was illegal.'

'A likely story,' I said.

'It gets better, Harry,' said Fielding. 'They were told it was some sort of race, and that the guys involved were doing it for a bet. They had to get from France to London without being caught.'

I laughed. 'Surely the French customs didn't swallow that, did they, John?'

'No, of course not, but it might just have been what Ramo Aniç told them, or told them to say if they got nicked. These two guys are none too bright, according to my source in Lyon. But it makes me think that whoever's running this racket is into drug smuggling as well.'

'So what's happening next?'

'They're being kept in custody and PAF – the Police de l'Air et des Frontières – are getting involved. They deal with immigration matters. The customs chief has promised to keep me posted. I'll let you know of any developments.'

'Anything from Austria or beyond, John?'

'Not yet, Harry, but if this guy Aniç is as smart as he's been so far, I suspect the answer will be the same. In other words, if the customs in Salzburg and Stuttgart are lucky enough to find anyone who's involved, they'll know no more than we've discovered already. Which is zilch,' he added.

'What about Portsmouth–Le Havre and Portsmouth–St-Malo, John?'

'What about them?'

'It's possible that the empty coffins are being taken out that way and then delivered to Lyon, or God knows where else, by a heavy goods vehicle.'

'I'll have a word with the chaps at Portsmouth, and get them to liaise with those two French ports, but I doubt that empty coffins will be shown on the vehicle manifest. If that is the route, the chances are that they're secreted beneath an innocuous load. But I'll give it a try.'

On Tuesday morning, one week after Walters's arrest, Dave and I were due at Southwark Crown Court. And fortunately we fared better there than Frank Mead had done at Kingston.

As the court was close to the south side of the River Thames, and London traffic more chaotic than ever despite the wondrous congestion charge, we cadged a lift from Thames Division. Or Marine Support Unit as it is now known, courtesy of the 'new names and total confusion squad' at Scotland Yard.

A panic-stricken young barrister was standing on tiptoe in the vast entrance hall, peering in all directions and frequently looking at his watch. I knew him and I knew he was our brief, but he obviously hadn't remembered me.

Out of sheer devilment, we spent a few moments watching this quivering mass of indecision before introducing ourselves.

I put him out of his misery. 'I take it you're appearing for the CPS?' I asked. 'Case of Walters?'

'Oh, thank God,' said the lawyer, fanning himself with his very white wig. 'I thought you weren't going to turn up.'

'Never one to miss a pantomime,' said Dave in an aside. 'Especially when the principal boy's from the Crown Prosecution Service.'

'Counsel for Walters's defence is making a strong application for bail, Mr Brock,' said the barrister, dropping his brief and picking it up again. 'I don't think we'll be able to resist it.'

'That's no problem,' I said. 'In the unlikely event that Walters gets bail, I'll re-arrest him for murder.'

'What possible grounds d'you have for—?' But our lawyer's shocked response was interrupted by an usher calling our case.

I don't know why our brief was bobbing and weaving. After all, it was up to me to refute any suggestion that the odious Darren Walters should be released on bail. Or, as we say in the trade, released in order to run away and commit more crime.

Walters's counsel did indeed make an impassioned plea for bail, citing the fact that his client's only previous convictions were of a minor nature.

The judge nodded at our barrister. 'Well?' he demanded tersely.

'I call Detective Chief Inspector Brock, Your Honour.'

Dispensing with the need for our barrister to take any part in the proceedings, the judge decided to question me himself. 'Well, Mr Brock?' he asked, once I'd reached the witness box.

'The charge is one of unlawful possession of firearms, Your Honour. The firearms were found secreted in a garage in East India Dock Road, the sole lessee of which is the accused. Subsequent ballistics examination has shown that the weapons were used in two murders that are still under investigation. Insofar as Darren Walters himself is concerned, further charges may ensue.'

The judge got the message, made a sour face and stared at defence counsel. 'Seems pretty pointless your applying for bail,' he said. 'Remanded in custody to reappear one month from today.'

Twelve

When Dave and I got back from court, there was a further surprise waiting for us.

'Somehow or another, sir,' said Colin Wilberforce, 'the military police in Bosnia – our military police, that is – have managed to get hold of a photograph of Ramo Anič.'

For a moment or two I stared in disbelief at the print. 'Bloody hell, I don't believe it!' The face was that of the man who had claimed to be Dr Gavrilo Lemez. I handed the print to Dave. 'Lemez and Anič are one and the same,' I said. 'And thanks to the Immigration Service, he's slipped through our fingers, and is now on the loose somewhere in the United Kingdom. Perhaps. I suppose it's possible that his escape from Hounslow was engineered so that he could go back to Bosnia. But if that was the case, why did he come here in the first place?'

'It certainly wasn't to kill Pointer,' said Dave, 'because Pointer was murdered before Anič arrived here.'

'Maybe,' I said thoughtfully. 'But it might not have been his first visit to this country. A guy as devious as Anič could have been here

193

before. Probably strode confidently through Heathrow Airport on a duff passport.'

'If so, guv, why come here in a coffin this time, pretending to be Dr Lemez?'

'Perhaps he wanted to test the route, Dave.' But even as I said it, I realized that it was an unlikely explanation.

'More likely that the heat was on in Bosnia for Aniç alias Lemez,' said Dave. 'And if Lemez was wanted for bank fraud – as it's said he is – it's possible that he had to do a runner a bit quick. And what better place than here to avoid justice,' he added cynically. 'After all, he wouldn't have wanted to present his passport to an immigration official on his way out of deepest Bosnia.'

'I doubt he'd've wanted to risk facing British immigration either,' I said. 'For all he knows there could be an international arrest warrant out for him.'

But whatever the reason for Aniç's bizarre mode of travel this time, it merely served to muddy the waters even more. One thing however was certain: we had to find him. And I said as much to Dave.

'If he's still here, guv. Frankly I can't see him running about the country constantly in fear of being knocked off. I reckon he's long gone.'

As usual, Dave's perceptive analysis had crushed my theory. But this time he'd got it wrong.

★　★　★

There was, however, a piece of cheering news from the DCI in Blackpool.

'Harry, we've got the bastard,' were Ray Lander's opening words when I picked up the phone.

'How so?'

'There's a golf course just north of Lytham, and yesterday afternoon the groundsman was out mowing a bit of the rough.'

'Is this going somewhere, Ray?' I asked, wondering what the groundsman of a golf course in Lytham had to do with anything. It seemed that golf courses were featuring just a touch too much in my enquiries.

'His mower hit something metal and took a chunk out of one of the blades. Bit pissed off about it, he was. Anyway, it turned out to be a handgun. And guess what? It had Walters's fingerprints all over it. And ballistics have matched it to the rounds found at the scene of the shooting. Walters must have dumped it when he legged it after we'd stopped him with the stinger, and he'd taken a few pot-shots at our officers.'

'And what do the CPS think about that?' I asked.

'They said we're to go for it.'

'Congratulations. I'm seeing him this afternoon because I've got something else that'll cheer him up. D'you want me to break the good news to him?'

'Be my guest, Harry,' said Lander. 'Be my guest.'

195

'What d'you want to do? Have him back there and charge him?'

'Wouldn't give him the pleasure of another trip to the Golden Mile, Harry. We don't have to question him because I'm satisfied we've got him bang to rights. So if I send a report down there perhaps you'd get one of your chaps to charge him. It's only a formality, after all.'

'They'll probably tack it on to my indictment for unlawful possession of the firearms we found in his garage,' I said.

'That's what our CPS up here is suggesting,' said Lander. 'But if you screw him for your murders as well it'll be a long time before he sees the light of day.' And with a wicked laugh, he replaced the receiver.

'I ain't got nothing to say,' said Darren Walters when he was brought to the interview room at Wandsworth prison that afternoon.

Dave frowned at such desecration of the English language, but said nothing.

I imagined that Walters's defence counsel had buoyed his hopes to the extent that he thought he'd be walking away from the Old Bailey that morning promptly to disappear into Greater London or the environs thereof.

Consequently he wasn't quite so surly, although he still lounged in his chair. But that was undoubtedly an attempt at bravado.

'I've something to say, though,' I said, and noted that Walters was none too pleased at that. 'The Blackpool police have decided to charge you with the attempted murder of several of their officers.'

Walters scoffed, and opening a battered St Julien tobacco tin began to roll a slender cigarette. 'I told you last time, copper, I've never been to no Blackpool,' he said, licking the gummed edge of the cigarette paper.

I shrugged. 'It's nothing to do with me,' I said. 'But I'm assured by the police up there that they have adequate evidence to secure a conviction, and the Crown Prosecution Service agrees with them.' I had no intention of telling him exactly what that evidence was. Time enough when the prosecution was obliged to tell the defence.

'In their dreams,' said Walters, lighting his thin cigarette.

'I see you've learned the cons' way of doing a roll-up,' Dave commented, pointing at Walters's cigarette. 'Just as well. You're going to be here for a long time. Here or Dartmoor,' he added, naming the grim penal establishment in the wilds of Devon.

'And I've got some more good news for you, Walters,' I said. I would have liked to tell him that Cindy Turner had declined to provide him with an alibi, but I suspected that to do so might well put her life in danger.

'Oh yeah.'

'Yes, indeed. Ramo Aniç is here in England.'

'*What?*' Unable to disguise his shock at this revelation, Walters sat up sharply, the slouching attitude giving way to one of acute nervous tension.

'Now why should that alarm you so much, Darren?' I asked.

'Who says it did?' demanded Walters, slowly relaxing as he recovered from the nasty jolt that my news had given him.

I laughed. 'You're not that good an actor,' I said. Then I put forward an entirely spurious theory that, even so, might just be the true reason for Aniç's arrival. 'Word is that he was not best pleased with the way in which Bernie Pointer was topped, and that he's come here to do some sorting out. I mean to say, it was a bit public to leave an obviously murdered body on a golf course for anyone to find, wasn't it? I dare say that Mr Aniç would have liked the body disposed of in such a way that no one would ever have found it. After all, there are still some motorway bridges being built. It's just as well you didn't get bail this morning, because he's probably looking for you.'

'That job was nothing to do with me,' protested Walters, once more trotting out one of his favourite expressions. But he seemed nowhere near as confident as hitherto, and I thought that maybe I'd got close to the truth. 'I don't know no Bernie Pointer.'

'Then you've nothing to worry about, have you?' Dave and I stood up to leave. 'But if anything does occur to you that might help me to find Aniç, you'll be sure to let me know, won't you, Darren?'

'You mean you don't know where he is?' What little confidence Walters had still possessed ebbed even further.

'Not at the moment. For all I know, he might even be banged up here in Wandsworth nick. Under an assumed name, of course. But somehow I doubt it. I dare say he's searching the country for you, Darren.' I paused and turned to Dave. 'Perhaps we shouldn't object to bail next time Mr Walters applies for it,' I said pointedly.

'I don't want no bleedin' bail,' said Walters with more feeling than he'd ever displayed before.

Dave and I got back to Curtis Green at just after five.

'The commander wants to see you, sir,' said Colin Wilberforce.

'Wonderful! I suppose he wants to be brought up to speed on an enquiry that's going at a snail's pace.'

'He didn't say, sir,' said Colin diplomatically.

I tapped on the commander's door. 'You wanted me, sir?'

'Ah, Mr Brock, come in. Sit down.'

That was ominous.

199

The commander toyed with a few pieces of paper until he found the one he was looking for. 'Detective Inspector Mead.'

'What about him, sir?'

'He's starting a course on Monday.'

'But we're in the middle of a complex murder enquiry, sir,' I protested. Strange how administration always manages to bugger up the operational side of police work. And it was a well-known fact that when the Metropolitan Police training school was full its numbers were equal to the third largest police force in the country. I thought they could have managed without Frank for a while.

'I appreciate that,' said the commander smoothly, 'but then we always are in the middle of something complex here in SCG.'

Well, I might be, but I can't speak for you, guv'nor.

'However, the order comes from on high,' continued the commander, as ever impressed by superior authority.

'What's that all about, then?' I asked, fairly certain that some lowly clerk in Human Resources had signed the memorandum that had so impressed the commander.

'It's a promotion course, Mr Brock.' The commander beamed at me.

I knew that Frank Mead had been selected for promotion to DCI some time ago, but I'd put it to the back of my mind. In the Metropolitan Police these things always seem to take forever and a day to come to fruition, and when they do crop up it's always at the most inopportune moment.

'How long's this course, sir?'

'The length is immaterial, Mr Brock,' the commander said loftily. 'The point is, he won't be coming back. He'll be posted in his new rank when the course finishes.'

'But I can't manage without a DI, sir. Frank's in charge of the legwork team, and there are enquiries coming up all the time. It'll be very difficult right now losing a DI who knows what's going on.'

'Which reminds me,' said the commander, ignoring my protests. 'How is your enquiry going?'

I summarized my progress as succinctly as I could. Not that it would have taken any longer had I explained it in full. The commander nodded wisely from time to time.

'So you can see that I really do need a DI, sir,' I said, hammering home the point yet again.

'That has been catered for,' the commander said as he plucked another piece of paper from his pending-tray. 'Detective Inspector Ebdon is being posted to SCG West on Monday. On promotion from the Flying Squad.' The commander did not seem very happy about that. Not having been a detective himself, he harboured grave reservations about the Squad, was unhappy about its methods, and regarded any officer with a

201

Squad background as being some sort of loose cannon.

'*Kate* Ebdon, sir?'

The commander resorted to his precious memorandum once more. 'Yes, Kate Ebdon.' He looked up. 'You know her?'

'Yes, sir. You may recall she was attached to us recently to help out in an enquiry involving an Australian. She is an Australian.'

'Oh!' said the commander, a worried expression on his face. '*That* Ebdon.'

'Yes, sir,' I said, 'that Ebdon.'

Frank Mead was in the incident room.

'You're a crafty bugger, Frank,' I said. 'You'll do anything to escape a bit of hard work.' It was light-hearted. Frank Mead was one of the best and most assiduous officers with whom I'd ever had the pleasure of working.

'Came out of the blue, Harry. I didn't think I was due to be made for another month at least.' Most officers who had been selected for the next rank could tell you, almost to the day, when they were likely to be promoted.

'Any idea where you're going at the end of this fabulous course?'

'There's a whisper that I've been marked up for a vacancy on the Fraud Squad,' said Frank.

'D'you know anything about fraud or accountancy?'

'Not a thing,' said Frank with a laugh.

'You're an obvious choice, then,' I said. 'Mind you, I'm surprised you're not being sent to Traffic Division.'

'It's not called Traffic Division any more, sir,' volunteered Colin Wilberforce.

'Don't you bloody start,' I said, and turned back to Frank. 'Same thing happened to me. I got posted to the Fraud Squad when I was a sergeant. Knew nothing about it, but I soon picked it up. However, I look forward to your farewell do. It'll be on Friday, I suppose.'

'Yes. I hope you can make it, Harry.'

'Wouldn't miss it,' I said, 'but right now I'm interested in speaking to Wilfred Crow again. I want to see his reaction when I tell him that Ramo Aniç is on the loose. What address did he give when he was bailed?'

Frank thumbed open his pocketbook. 'Battersea,' he said. 'Number 55 Gillen Street. Want me to come with you?'

'No, I'll take Dave. I dare say you've got a lot of loose ends to tidy up before you go.'

Early the following morning Dave and I made our way to Battersea. As we attempted to turn into Gillen Street, which lies in that maze of roads to the west of Queenstown Road, we were confronted by a sign that said 'Road Closed', a forest of blue lights and blue and white tape strung out across the road. And a policeman.

The PC approached our car. 'Can you read that?' he demanded officiously as he pointed to the sign.

'Yes,' said Dave, thrusting his warrant card in the policeman's face. 'Can you read *this*?'

'Oh, sorry, Skip.'

'Yeah, well next time you want to flex your vocal muscles find out who you're talking to before you get all puffed up with piss and importance.'

'What's going on?' I asked leaning across Dave.

'There's been a murder,' said the PC and then, playing it safe, added, 'Sir.'

'Don't tell me, it's at 55.'

'Yes, sir.' The PC looked surprised, but then he didn't know what I knew. Which was that the victim was bound to be Wilfred Crow and that, before the day was out, I'd be lumbered with the investigation. But I did have one advantage: I had a gut feeling that the murder of Crow was down to Ramo Aniç.

DCI Colin Marsh and I went back a long way. As far back as a detective training course when we were both DCs.

'Harry, what brings you here?' asked Marsh.

'Intuition, Colin,' I said, and introduced Dave Poole. 'Your victim is one Wilfred Crow, and any minute now I'm about to tell you who topped him.'

'How the hell d'you know that?'

I explained about the people-smuggling racket and dropped in the name of Ramo Aniç. I started to tell him about Gavrilo Lemez and the way in which he'd been sprung from Hounslow, but he already knew. In fact, I should think that everyone in the Metropolitan Police knew about that. Then I told him that Ramo Aniç and Lemez were the same person.

'Christ, that's what I call a bit of a dog's dinner,' said Marsh.

'Don't worry about it, Colin,' I said, 'because I'd bet serious money on my commander putting this little lot firmly on my plate.'

'You'd better have a look at the scene, then,' said Marsh. He looked as though a great weight had been lifted from his shoulders.

Crow had occupied a bedsit on the first floor of the house. The body was lying on its side in the centre of the room, arms thrown out. Close to the victim's head a small puddle of blood had seeped into the worn carpet.

We stood on the threshold of the room while the CSEs got on with their task of seeking fingerprints and other evidence, and photographing the scene.

The senior CSE, a man called Mason, walked towards us, and Colin Marsh introduced Dave and me, explaining that I'd probably be taking over the enquiry.

'We're done here, Mr Brock, if you want to

take a closer look,' said Mason.

I followed him across the room to Crow's body.

'It looks very much like a close-quarter killing.' Mason took out a pen, knelt down and pointed at the back of Crow's head. 'This is what we call a contact wound. You'll see that the entry area is split, and the hairs around it are scorched and slightly black-ened. And what you can see there' – he sketched a small circle in the air with the pen – 'are probably particles of burned powder.' Pocketing his pen and standing up, he said, 'But there's no exit wound. At a guess, I'd say the victim was sitting down when he was shot and fell forward on to the floor. From the size of the entry wound, I'd hazard a guess at it being a point-two-two pistol plac-ed against the back of the head, but the pathologist may be able to tell you more. From my experience, though, I doubt that you'll be able to get anything from the round when the pathologist gets it out.'

'How so?' I asked, somewhat perturbed by this piece of information.

'When a two-two enters the skull it doesn't just stop, it loses force and bounces off the inside of the cranium. In most of the cases I've dealt with the bullet is so damaged that it's useless from an evidential point of view, but you might get lucky.' Mason paused and smiled. 'Just one other thing: one of my guys found a fibre on the doorpost of the room.

It's possible that the killer brushed against it on his way in or out. But don't hold your breath.'

I thanked Mason and turned to Colin. 'What puzzles me is how Aniç, if this *is* down to him, managed to get behind Crow in order to kill him. Crow knew he was a dangerous man and I'd've thought he would have kept him well in sight all the while he was here.'

'Maybe Crow didn't suspect he was armed, Harry,' said Colin. 'For that matter, he might not even have known it was Aniç. On the other hand, I suppose the murderer could have lulled him into a false sense of security. Telling him what a good job he's done and offering him more money. But who knows?'

'I don't suppose we'll ever know now,' I mused. 'But come to think of it, you're right about him not knowing it was Aniç. When I interviewed Crow he told me he'd never met the guy; only ever spoken to him on the phone. He knew him as Lemez, because Crow was nicked at Portsmouth when Lemez was brought in.'

Marsh laughed. 'Looks like a can of worms, Harry.'

'And some,' I said. 'Do we know who owns this place?'

'A West Indian guy called Errol Wilkinson. One of my skippers is taking a statement from him right now. He said that he was out most of yesterday evening and got back late, after midnight apparently. He always goes out first thing in the morning to get cigarettes, and buys a copy of the *Daily Mail* for Crow at the same time. When he took the paper up at about half seven this morning, this is what he found.' Marsh gestured at the body.

'Pathologist been?' I asked.

'Yes. He took a cockshy at death having occurred at about ten o'clock last night, but he'll be more positive once he's done the post-mortem.'

'I'd better have a word with Mr Wilkinson, then.'

'D'you really think this is down to this Ramo Aniç, then, Harry?' asked Marsh as we went back downstairs.

'I'm bloody sure of it, Colin. But as I said just now, the problem is that he's on the run somewhere, and for all I know he might be back in Bosnia.' I glanced at my watch. 'If he'd taken off straight after the killing last night, he could be sitting in a cafe in Sarajevo having breakfast as we speak.'

Errol Wilkinson, a man of about fifty with frizzy grey hair and a small goatee beard, was clearly shaken at what had taken place upstairs.

'Mr Wilkinson, I'm Detective Chief Inspector Brock of the Serious Crime Group West, and this is Detective Sergeant Poole.'

Wilkinson glanced at Dave, apparently

relieved to see what he must have regarded as a friendly black face. On the other hand, there are still a lot of people of West Indian origin who regard any of their kin who are policemen as suspect in some way. 'Uncle Tom' was the derogatory term they used, and Dave had been called that on more than one occasion.

'Have a chat, Dave,' I said quietly.

'I know you've already told Mr Marsh what happened, Mr Wilkinson,' said Dave, indicating Colin, 'but perhaps you'd just run through it again for the benefit of my guv'nor.'

'Yes, sir. I was out at a party last night. I left here at about seven o'clock. As a matter of fact, I met Mr Crow who was on his way in. He told me he'd just been out for a breath of fresh air. I never got back here until, oh, it must have been one o'clock this morning.' Wilkinson grinned. 'It was a good party, man. I never heard nothing from upstairs and I thought that Wilfred had gone to bed. But this morning I took his newspaper up to him as usual, and there he was. Dead. Who would want to do that to him? He was a nice man. You know, we played chess together once or twice.' He shook his head as though unable to grasp that Crow had been killed and, even less, why it had occurred. 'I asked him if he wanted to come to the party last night, but he said no. If only he had, this wouldn't have happened.'

Perhaps not, I thought, but it would only have succeeded in delaying Crow's murder, of that I was certain.

'Was there any sign that the front door had been forced, Mr Wilkinson?' asked Dave. 'When you came in last night.'

We had given the front door a cursory examination as we came in, and there was no sign of a break-in. But Dave is a thorough detective.

'No, definitely not. I came in with my key, as usual, and there was no problem.'

'What about the windows? Any indication that someone might have come in that way?'

'No, sir. I'm very particular about security. I read all the crime-prevention stuff and we're Neighbourhood Watch round here. I always make sure all the downstairs windows are locked before I go out.'

'Oh well, Colin,' I said, once we were in the street again, 'all we have to do now is find Ramo Aniç.'

It turned out that Mason was right about the bullet that had killed Crow. When the pathologist extracted it from Crow's head it was a misshapen lump of metal.

The ballistics expert at the laboratory sighed when he saw it and shook his head.

'It *could* be a two-two, Harry,' he said, 'but I'm not prepared to go further than that. As for comparing it with anything fired by the murder weapon, well, forget it.'

As it happened, it didn't matter. We never found the weapon. It looked as though everything would hinge on the fibre that Mason's man had found on the doorpost of Crow's room. And that gave me little hope.

Thirteen

Frank Mead's farewell do was held on Friday evening in a private upstairs room of a friendly pub in Westminster. By 'friendly' I mean a pub where we pay the licensee in full for what we have, and who expects no 'favours' from the police.

Every member of the Group who was off duty, and one or two who weren't, turned up because Frank was what is known in the Job as 'a good guv'nor', and there was genuine regret at his departure. The turnout at such functions is not always a gauge of an officer's popularity; in fact, it is sometimes the opposite. An unpopular officer will often find that a vast horde of his colleagues will attend, and out of spite do their best to consume as much beer as possible knowing that he'll be picking up the tab.

But that was not the case with Frank Mead, and the value of his leaving present showed it. Apart from the usual inscribed tankard – and we've all got at least a half-dozen of those – the men and women of his team gave him a gold fountain pen and pencil set.

'The idea, guv,' said Tom Challis when he presented it, "is that it'll be an incentive for you to learn to write.' Frank's appalling handwriting had been a standing joke on the Group from the day he'd arrived. 'Which should come in handy on the Fraud Squad.'

The rest of the evening was naturally spent in drinking, and a raucous singsong to the accompaniment of Dave Poole who, I belatedly discovered, was both an accomplished pianist and a fair singer.

'I didn't know you played the piano, Dave,' I said during a lull in the entertainment.

'Of course, guv. My wife's a ballet dancer,' said Dave enigmatically.

Although Alan Cleaver, the detective chief superintendent, had never been known to miss a farewell party, there was one exception to the muster of those attending. True to form, the commander had made an excuse of a prior engagement, but scuttlebutt had it that Mrs Commander gave him hell if he was late home from the office. It was as well that he wasn't there because the usual suspects got legless and had to be poured into taxis.

At half-past eight on Monday morning, the newly promoted Detective Inspector Kate Ebdon appeared in my office.

'G'day, guv,' she said.

I stood up and shook hands. 'Welcome to the madhouse,' I said.

'What have you done to deserve all this?' She waved a hand as if to encompass the entire Group.

'Deserve what?'

'An Australian DI and a black sergeant,' Kate said mischievously.

I laughed. 'I'll get by.'

'What's first up?' Kate sat down in my only armchair.

'For a start, report to the commander when he gets in at ten o'clock.'

'Ten!'

'He observes strict office hours, does the commander: ten to six.'

'Lucky him,' said Kate, 'and after I've seen him?'

'After that there are three unsolved murders to sort out.' And I gave her a rundown on the killing of Gould, Pointer and Crow. As I had predicted, the commander had directed me to take over the enquiry into the Wilfred Crow topping, but I only had myself to blame for that. I'd told him that I was sure it was down to Ramo Aniç and, in his naivety, the commander had suggested that Crow's murder would, therefore, be easily solved. I think he reads too many detective novels.

'Is there a warrant out for Aniç, guv?' Kate asked.

'Yes, of course.' And I went on to tell her about the armed raid at Hounslow that had resulted in his escape.

'Yeah, I know about that. The Squad was lumbered with it.'

'Are they getting anywhere?'

'Not really. They've been out and about, chatting up their favourite snouts. Bit like casting bread on the waters, if you know what I mean. They hope that a message in a bottle will come drifting in.' Kate gave a coarse laugh.

Dave kicked open my door and came in with three cups of coffee on a tray.

'Good morning, *ma'am*,' he said with a straight face, and handed Kate a cup of coffee.

'Don't take the piss, *Sergeant*,' said Kate with a grin. And after a pause, '"Guv" will do.'

For the next hour, mainly for Kate's benefit, we reviewed the evidence in the triple murders that we were doing our desperate best to solve. But despite all our theorizing, we knew that progress depended on finding the errant Aniç. And that could prove to be very difficult. If Aniç were as clever as I thought, he would probably have a network of accomplices in London prepared to hide him and, if necessary, get him out of the country again. And, as I'd suggested to Colin Marsh, he might already have gone.

And leaving the country would not present too many difficulties. The Immigration Service was not particularly vigilant when it came to examining outbound passengers

and even when its officers did exert themselves, they tended to concentrate on travel-
lers of Middle Eastern appearance.

On the stroke of ten, I heard footsteps in
the corridor followed by a door banging.

'The guv'nor's arrived,' I said, standing up.
'Let's go and see him.'

The commander's office was immaculate,
but then I've never seen it any other way.
The carpet was of a quality superior to that
which the rest of us slaves enjoyed, and the
commander-sized desk was devoid of paper.
All three correspondence trays were empty,
and the telephone was lined up with the
edge of the desk, as were several pens and a
letter-opener. On a filing cabinet was a
photograph of a harridan who I took to be
Mrs Commander. His raincoat, on a hanger
of course, hung on the hatstand in the
corner. Next to it was an umbrella. A belt
and braces man is the commander.

I didn't need to be there because Kate was
quite capable of introducing herself. But I
was dying to see how the commander would
react to the arrival on his staff of this attractive flame-haired Australian woman, attired
in jeans and a man's white shirt that, far
from disguising her figure, served to emphasize her curves.

Taking the initiative, as she always did,
Kate strode aggressively across the room and
thrust out her hand. 'G'day, sir,' she said.
'And may I say what a great honour it is to

have been posted to this prestigious outfit.'

Opening round to Kate.

'Oh, er, yes.' The commander struggled to his feet, not helped by the fact that his chair was too close to his desk, and shook hands cautiously, as though he was being led into a trap. 'Welcome to Serious Crime Group West, Miss Ebdon. Do take a seat. You too, Mr Brock.'

We sat down in the group of chairs in the corner of the office, but the commander remained behind his desk, a remote and authoritative figure. At least, *he* thought so. For a moment or two, he played with his letter-opener, spinning it this way and that.

'We have a very good clear-up record here, Miss Ebdon,' he said, deigning eventually to look up. 'And we want to keep it that way. I'm sure that Mr Brock has explained to you the difficult triple-murder enquiry that he's dealing with at the moment, and it is a truism to say that he needs all the help he can get.'

'No worries, guv'nor,' said Kate, grinning cheekily and deliberately sharpening her Australian accent. 'He can definitely stand on me for that. And so can you.'

'Er, yes, of course.' The commander wrinkled his nose and played with the top button of his waistcoat, a garment he wore in summer as well as in winter. I suppose he thought it added to his perceived status.

'As a matter of interest, guv, are you get-
217

ting your hands dirty with these murders? I mean to say it's a pretty big job.'

'Getting my hands dirty?'

'Yeah, you know, hands on.'

The commander blinked and peered at Kate over his glasses. 'My role here is more one of administrative oversight, Miss Ebdon. To give support and er ... ' He glanced briefly at me, but immediately glanced away when I smiled. 'And, er, advice when needed. I presume the commander of the Flying Squad does much the same.'

'No chance,' said Kate. 'The guv'nor there likes to get in amongst the muck and bullets, if you know what I mean. Always out and about, chatting up his snouts.'

'Mmm! Yes, well things are rather different here.' The commander glanced at me again. 'Well, I won't hold you up, Mr Brock. No doubt you want to brief Miss Ebdon on the progress of your enquiries to date.'

But before I had a chance to reply, Kate chipped in. 'No worries,' she said again. 'Mr Brock gave me an in-depth briefing at half eight this morning. Before you got in, sir.' And with another cheeky grin, Kate stood up.

As she left the office, the commander spoke again. 'One moment, Mr Brock, if you please. And close the door.'

'Yes, sir?'

'Perhaps you'd speak to Miss Ebdon about her appearance, Mr Brock.'

I affected innocence. 'What's wrong with it, sir?'

'I don't really think that jeans and a man's shirt are suitable attire for a detective inspector. Perhaps a dark suit, eh? Jacket and skirt, white blouse, court shoes. That sort of thing.'

'I'll try, sir, but we have to be careful these days,' I said, deliberately winding him up. 'There is a strong women police association in the Job, encouraged by the Commissioner I may say, and its members may regard such an observation as a form of sexual discrimination. After all, some of our male officers dress in jeans and a shirt.'

'They're not inspectors, though.' The commander was clearly determined to have the last word.

But so was I. 'I'll offer her words of advice, sir,' I said, deploying the standard disciplinary formula, 'but if it comes to giving her an order, I think it would best come from you.'

Sure as hell, I wasn't going to mention anything to Kate about the way she dressed. Anyway, I liked the way she looked, and as far as I was concerned it was her ability as a detective that was important. I knew that the commander wouldn't have the balls to take her on, so that would be an end of the matter.

As it was Monday morning, the team was assembled in the incident room, ready for the weekly briefing. I briefed them most mornings, but Monday was the day when we tended to review the whole case from start to what we hoped would be the finish.

'Some of you will have met DI Ebdon before,' I began. 'She was here a while ago, helping us out with an enquiry. But now she's here permanently and is taking Mr Mead's place as leader of the legwork team.'

'Good to have you with us, guv,' said DS Tom Challis.

'Good to be here, Tom,' said Kate, and evinced a glance of surprise from Challis that she'd remembered his name. But there was a further surprise in store. 'Last Wednesday, as you know, Wilfred Crow was murdered in his bedsit at 55 Gillen Street, Battersea. The front runner for that topping, as of now, is Ramo Aniç alias Gavrilo Lemez, a Bosnian who was sprung from Hounslow in the early hours of Friday the fifteenth.'

There were looks of amazement that the new DI had grasped the intricacies of the enquiry when she'd only been here five minutes. I was surprised too, but I was to learn in the days and weeks to come that Kate Ebdon was a very capable detective.

And she hadn't finished yet.

'So the priority, mates, is to get out and find this loser Aniç. Talk to your snouts, keep your ears to the ground and come up with some answers, because until we've got this no-hoper in the bin we ain't going any further forward.' Kate turned to me. 'Anything else, guv?'

'No, Kate, that's it.'

She nodded to her team. 'That'll be right, then. Go for it.'

'What are you going to do now, Kate?' I asked as her team made for the door.

'I'm getting out there too, guv,' she said. 'I've got a few snouts who are going to have their arms twisted.'

And I had no doubt that when Kate Ebdon said that, there would be some informants who were about to wish they were some other place.

The chief CSE's report into the Crow murder arrived that afternoon. But it contained only a scintilla of useful evidence.

No fingerprints had been found in Crow's bedsit other than those of Crow himself and Errol Wilkinson, the landlord. But that was no more than I expected. If Aniç had been the killer he wouldn't have left a fingerprint. Even a search of the dustbins at 55 Gillen Street, and the surrounding area, had been searched to no avail. Criminals are sometimes stupid enough to leave rubber gloves near the scene, and fingerprints had been obtained from the inside on more than one occasion.

Thus the only telling find was the fibre that the CSEs had found adhering to the frame of the door to Crow's room.

In itself it meant very little. But if it were later proved to have come from Aniç's clothing, he would have some explaining to do. On the down side, it could equally have come from something that either Crow or Wilkinson had been wearing, and that was now being checked.

The CSEs had also confirmed our original assumption that there had been no forced entry to the house. That meant that our friend Aniç, if indeed he *was* the killer, had been admitted by Crow. Or had somehow acquired a key, but I thought that unlikely.

Before he'd left the Group, Frank Mead had organized house-to-house enquiries in Gillen Street, but none of the neighbours had seen anyone loitering near number 55 in the days leading up to Crow's murder. Not that that meant there hadn't been anyone. In my experience neighbours only emerged *after* the event, peering around for the nearest camera in the hope of appearing on the evening television news. But even that hadn't happened this time.

The conclusion was that the murderer had waited until Wilkinson was out of the house before knocking at the door. On the other hand, he may have been prepared to murder Wilkinson, or anyone else who got in his way, without a second thought. And that having killed Crow, he rushed out as fast as he could and collided with the doorpost, thus leaving the fibre.

All of that was academic, however. Or as Dave succinctly put it, pie in the sky. Until we found the garment to which the fibre could be matched, we were no further forward.

The pathologist's report confirmed what Mason, the chief CSE, had suggested: that the round with which Crow had been killed had been fired in close proximity to the back of the victim's head. But, as the ballistics expert had already said, the misshapen lump of metal was useless in terms of determining the calibre, and even less in identifying the weapon.

Finally, there was a report from the laboratory, and that was interesting too. At least it appeared to be.

The scientist who had signed it began by apologizing for the delay, but then went on to report that the army discharge book found at Bernie Pointer's address in Shepherds Bush had been examined. The name beneath the whitening was that of Geoffrey Morrison.

'Who the hell's Geoffrey Morrison, I wonder?' I said. I was beginning to get confused.

'Bernie Pointer's brother-in-law, sir,' said Dave in a tone of voice that implied that I'd lost the plot. 'The guy we interviewed down at Merton Park. Remember?'

'Oh, *that* Geoffrey Morrison,' I said. Dave stared pointedly at the ceiling.

I rang Morrison's number and his wife

Karen answered the phone. 'He should be in at about six, Mr Brock,' she said. 'Is there anything I can do?'

'Not really,' I said. 'We'll come and see him this evening.'

'You were in the army,' I said, when Dave and I were settled in the front room of the Morrisons' house in Merton Park.

Geoffrey Morrison raised his eyebrows in surprise. 'How on earth did you know that?' he asked. 'Have you been checking up on me?'

'Why should we want to check up on you, Mr Morrison?' I countered. 'No, I was wondering when you last saw your army discharge book.'

'Good God, I haven't a clue,' said Morrison. 'Must be years. Why, is it important? Hang on, I'll see if I can find it.' And before I had a chance to tell him that it was already in police possession, he rose and left the room.

When he returned five minutes later, there was a look of bewilderment on his face. 'I don't understand it,' he said. 'It's always in a drawer along with things like our birth certificates, marriage certificate, passports, and so on. But it's not there.'

'That's because it was found in a room in Shepherds Bush, Mr Morrison,' I said.

'What the hell was it doing there?'

'The address was one where your late

224

brother-in-law Bernie lived prior to his conviction for embezzlement. And your discharge book was found there a week or two ago by officers who were searching the premises.'

'Well, I'll be damned. Mind you, I've never had cause to look for it. I chucked it in there the day I was demobbed and to be honest, I've never looked at it since.'

'When were you demobbed, Mr Morrison?' asked Dave.

'It must be ten years ago now.'

'What regiment were you in?' Dave knew that, of course. It had been in the discharge book.

'The Royal Logistic Corps.' Morrison grinned. 'It was known as the Really Large Corps ... from the initials. I was a clerk for twelve years. Twelve wasted years. Got as far as corporal. Big deal, eh?' Then he asked a question that I thought he should have asked at the beginning of our conversation. 'What was Pointer doing with it, anyway?'

'He'd used Tipp-Ex to cover up your name and write his own over it,' I said. 'Well, not his name, the name of Salter. Robert Salter. It was an alias he was using at the time. Does that name mean anything to you?'

'No, it doesn't,' said Morrison. 'The little bastard must've nicked it when he was here once.'

'I thought you discouraged his visits,' observed Dave.

'Yes, I did. I never trusted him, even before he was arrested. I don't know what he got up to, but he never seemed to hold down a job for long. Always round here trying to borrow money. But he was my wife's brother, after all.' Morrison paused. 'What would he want my discharge book for, anyway?'

'We were originally told he used it as a reference to get a job,' I said, 'but there's some doubt about that now. The man he worked for, a funeral director, has since been found murdered.'

'Was that the guy who was killed in Battersea last week some time?'

'That's him,' I said.

'Bloody hell! What was that all about?'

'That's something we're trying to find out,' I said.

'Strikes me nobody's safe these days,' said Morrison. 'I don't know what the world's coming to. I get worried about the boys, you know. You read about kids being snatched off the streets, raped and strangled. It's a bloody awful world, Mr Brock. In more ways than one.'

'More ways than one?' echoed Dave, raising an eyebrow.

Morrison gave a bitter smile. 'It's all right for you chaps,' he said. 'You've got steady careers. But I'm looking for a job right now. Funny thing, but when I left the army, everyone told me that there was plenty of work on the outside. D'you know, I must have had eight or nine jobs since I came out of the Kate, but none of them ever lasted very long. Perhaps I should've soldiered on.'

'Must make for difficulties with the mortgage,' said Dave, who in common with most young coppers was no stranger to financial strictures himself.

'Fortunately Karen's got a good job with a building society,' said Morrison, 'and because of that she's got a preferential rate of interest.' He glanced at his watch. 'She should be home anytime now.'

Fourteen

Some time ago, I had imposed upon our own Foreign and Commonwealth Office to make a formal request to the Embassy of Bosnia-Hercegovina for information about Ramo Aniç. But we had heard nothing.

When Wilfred Crow had been murdered we repeated our request, on this occasion saying that we wished to interview Ramo Aniç in connection with this crime. We further added that we would be grateful for any information regarding his present whereabouts. We thought it politic not to mention that he had once been in custody but had escaped.

The second request did elicit a response.

I received a telephone call from a young man who sounded terribly precious.

'Chief Inspector Brock?'

'Speaking.'

'Oh, er, this is the, um, Foreign Office.'

'Yes?'

'It's about your enquiry concerning a man named, er, Ramo Aniç.'

'Oh, at last,' I said.

'Yes, well these things take time,' said the

effete one. 'But there is a man in London, a Bosnian police official called Mr Djork, who is willing to talk to you about this, um, Ramo Aniç.'

'Is he at the Bosnian Embassy?'

'No, he's nothing to do with their embassy, but we have checked his bona fides, so to speak, and you may talk freely to him.'

'What is he, a spy?'

'Good heavens no,' said the young man quickly enough to make me think that his disavowal was suspect.

'Where do I find this Mr Djork, then?'

'He has an office over a shop in Piccadilly.' And the Foreign Office official reeled off an address and telephone number.

This all sounded highly suspicious and I asked the young man for his name. Somewhat reluctantly, I thought, he gave it to me and I rang him back via the Foreign Office main switchboard.

'Just checking,' I said when eventually I was put through to his extension.

I telephoned Mr Djork and made an appointment to see him.

On Tuesday morning at precisely ten minutes past ten, the time that Mr Djork had specified, Dave and I presented ourselves at the Piccadilly address the Foreign Office official had given us.

Having regarded us somewhat suspiciously, an assistant pointed out a door at the rear of the shop. We mounted a rickety staircase to be confronted by a hatchet-faced woman who invited us to take a seat.

After a wait of half an hour we were shown into an office that barely had space for a desk and two chairs. It all looked rather temporary and I wondered if Djork had come to England especially to talk about Aniç.

'Ah, Mr Brock, I am Mr Djork. I do most sincerely apologize for keeping you waiting,' said the man in perfect English as he rose from behind the desk, but gave no reason for the delay. He was a small, square, bullet-headed man, immaculately dressed in a dark suit that I suspected came from Savile Row rather than some Sarajevo tailor. 'Please take a seat. My secretary will bring refreshments.'

During the six minutes it took for coffee and some strange-looking little cakes to arrive, we waited in silence, a silence broken only by Djork's fingers playing an incessant tattoo on his desktop.

'Good,' said Djork, handing us small cups that were only half full of some murky liquid. 'Now to business.' He paused. 'But first...' He took a scrap of paper from his pocket and showed it to me. 'As you are a London policeman, Mr Brock, perhaps you can tell me if this is a good club to go to. There are girls, perhaps? Some strippers?'

'Most unlikely, Mr Djork,' I said, having leaned across to read the name. 'The Garrick Club is a gentlemen's club and membership is very difficult to come by. There certainly won't be a floor show *there*.'

'Oh! Pity,' said Mr Djork, screwing up the paper and tossing it into a wastepaper basket. 'Well now, Ramo Aniç. What is it you wish to know about this man?'

I explained in some detail how Aniç had come to our notice and what we had learned about the immigrant-smuggling scam in which he had been involved. Finally, I hinted to Djork that Aniç might well have been responsible for the murder of Wilfred Crow.

'You will appreciate, Mr Djork, as one policeman to another, that we are by no means sure of this man's guilt. Although the evidence we have acquired so far seems to point to it, I doubt if it is sufficient for a conviction.'

Djork nodded gravely. 'Of course he did it,' he said adamantly, as though lack of evidence was a minor impediment to securing a conviction. 'The man Aniç is a criminal.' He selected a piece of paper from among a pile on his desk and briefly scanned it. 'Last year he stole several thousand US dollars by swindling a bank in Sarajevo.'

'Was he using the name Gavrilo Lemez at that time?' I asked.

Djork looked up sharply. 'I have not heard that name before. What makes you think he might have called himself Lemez, Mr Brock?'

I wondered what sort of game Djork was

playing. When Gavrilo Lemez' fingerprints had been sent to Bosnia, they had been identified as those of Lemez. And, we had been told, Lemez was wanted for the fraud that Djork had just attributed to Aniç. Furthermore, the name Lemez had been included in the information I'd sent to our Foreign Office. It was possible, I suppose, that Djork was just badly informed. Or was taking a backhander from someone involved in the scam we were investigating and was making up his responses as he went along.

'That was the name he gave when he arrived in this country. In a coffin,' I added with a smile. 'But we later found out that he was Ramo Aniç.'

'In a *coffin*?' Djork raised his bushy eyebrows. 'He was dead?'

'No, very much alive. He's an illegal immigrant.'

'Interesting,' said Djork, and made a note on his pad. 'We would like to speak with this man.'

'So would I,' I said, and explained how an armed gang had helped Aniç to escape from Hounslow.

Djork shook his head. 'There are many bad men in Bosnia-Hercegovina, Mr Brock.' He sat back in his chair and folded his hands across his stomach. 'Now, let me see. What can I tell you?' Suddenly he shot forward again. 'I can tell you this, Mr Brock,' he said, leaning on one elbow and wagging a podgy forefinger. 'We, that is the police, know that Aniç was responsible for at least seven robberies both in Sarajevo and in Mostar. And probably elsewhere too.' He spread his hands in a gesture of resignation. 'Aniç was the leader of a gang that has killed several people, policemen among them. We want to have him returned to Bosnia-Hercegovina as soon as possible.'

'That rather depends on my government, Mr Djork,' I said. 'You see, if Aniç was responsible for this murder he will stand trial here and if he's convicted will be sent to prison for life. Only after that will he be deported.' But as I said it, I knew it was but a pious hope.

'Pah!' exclaimed Djork with a derisive snort. 'You send him back to us, Mr Brock, and we'll hang him,' he said.

I had to admit that Djork's suggestion was an appealing one. Unfortunately I had a problem with that: the English judicial system.

Despite the correspondence that had passed between the Metropolitan Police and the Foreign Office, our visit to Mr Djork had benefited us little. He had not told us much that we didn't already know. But on reflection, he probably didn't know any more, and I got the feeling that we'd told him more than he'd told us. I certainly placed little faith in his final offer: that he would make enquiries on our behalf among the Bosnian community in London in an attempt to trace Aniç.

One of the perverse facts about the coppering game is that intensive enquiries can be made throughout the country in the search for a wanted man. Highly qualified and highly paid detectives spend incredible amounts of time and money in trying to track down a particular criminal, only to find that he is arrested by a patrolling constable whose interest lies far from the fields of high-powered international criminal investigation.

So it was with Ramo Aniç. Well, very nearly.

And I heard about it on the day following our visit to Mr Djork.

I was sitting in my office wondering where to go next. Not physically, but in terms of my so far abortive investigation.

Dave Poole appeared in the doorway. 'Aniç's been nicked, guv,' he announced.

'Where, when and how?' I asked.

'By a checkout assistant in a supermarket in Kensington, would you believe?'

I laughed. 'Come on, Dave, what's the true story?'

'It's kosher, guv.'

'When was this, Dave?'

'Yesterday morning, funnily enough while we were talking to Djork, Aniç tried to buy a bottle of vodka with a duff credit card. But the checkout woman didn't like the look of his signature, which was nothing like the one on the card, so she rang the alarm under her till. Next thing that happens is a couple of heavies in fancy uniforms, claiming to be security, turn up and have Aniç away for a stressful interview with the manager. And probably more stressful for the manager than for Aniç. Anyway, whatever, the local Old Bill was called, chummy was knocked off and carted down to the nick. When they got him in the custody suite, they searched him and, would you believe, the prat had got a few more stolen credit cards on him, and a driving licence in someone else's name.'

'But surely he didn't hold his hands up to being Aniç, did he?'

'No chance.'

'So what happened?'

'When the DS at Kensington fronted Lemez stroke Aniç with being an illegal immigrant, the bastard had the cheek to say that he was a Bosnian and asked for political asylum. He said that if he went back to Bosnia he'd be killed.'

'He's probably right about that,' I said, recalling what Djork had said.

'Anyway, on the basis of that, the DS at Kensington had him fingerprinted and got a hurry-up done with the search. Aware that Ramo Aniç was also a Bosnian, and was wanted for murder, he suggested that the fingerprint officer went straight for the set of

Lemez' dabs they'd got on record. And lo and behold, he got a match.'

'So where is he now, Dave?'

'Still in a cell at Kensington.'

'Excellent. Get him brought up to Charing Cross nick and tell the custody sergeant that if he loses him I'll have his stripes. Oh, and arrange for an interpreter to be there.'

'But he speaks perfect English, guv,' said Dave. 'We know that from when we talked to him at Portsmouth.'

'Yes, I know, but he might just change his mind about that. And tell whoever sets up these things that I want a police officer to interpret, not a civilian. We must have an officer somewhere in the Job who speaks Aniç's lingo.'

It was about three that afternoon that I got a call to say that Aniç was now detained at Charing Cross police station, and Dave and I went straight there.

But it was a very different Lemez to the one we had questioned at Portsmouth. Different in the sense that he was now revealed as a hardened criminal, and that from the word go he was going to be as unhelpful as possible.

The interpreter was a PC from a traffic unit in Catford. No, don't ask. He assured me that as well as being a Class One motor-cyclist – *this I needed to know?* – he also spoke Aniç's language fluently on account of having a Bosnian wife whom he had married while serving there in the army. Well, it takes all sorts, I suppose.

Dave set the tape recorder going and cautioned Aniç in both his names. And just for good measure I got the interpreter to translate it. It evinced no response, not even a change in expression.

'Ramo Aniç,' I began, 'I wish to question you about your movements on the evening of Tuesday the nineteenth of March.'

'My name is Gavrilo Lemez and I have nothing to say,' Aniç replied in English, and continued to use that language for the remainder of the interview. The motorcyclist interpreter looked disappointed.

'It was during the course of that evening that Wilfred Crow was murdered at his house in Battersea.'

'I do not know anyone called Wilfred Crow.'

'Really?' I said, affecting an air of perplexity. 'He knew you. In fact he told me that you were responsible for the murder of Bernard Pointer, a man who worked for you to bring illegal immigrants into this country.' That was not quite true, of course, but the gist of it was. Aniç's reaction was predictable.

'Then he is telling untruths. I do not know anyone called Bernard Pointer.'

'Do you still maintain that your name is Gavrilo Lemez?' asked Dave.

'Yes, that is so.'

'In that case, you can tell us the names of the men who carried out a raid on the Immigration Detention Centre at Hounslow and secured your release.'

'I have nothing to say.'

'Where did you get these from?' I asked, producing the three or four credit cards and the driving licence that he'd had on him when he was arrested.

'I have nothing to say.'

'Where d'you live?'

'I have nothing to say.'

'You told an officer at this police station that you are claiming political asylum,' said Dave, leaning forward.

'That is correct.'

'Pity, that,' Dave commented, closed his pocketbook and stood up. 'I'm afraid you're as good as on your way home, pal.'

'What do you mean by that?' For the first time since the interview had begun Aniç showed some emotion, a frisson of fear crossing his face. 'My life is in danger if I return to Bosnia,' he said, a note of desperation creeping into his voice. 'I will be killed if I am sent back there.'

'Oh well, that's different,' said Dave, affecting an artificial air of sympathy. 'There's only one problem, though.'

'And what is that?'

'Unless you tell us where you've been living, we can't possibly put your application forward to the Home Office. They don't like blank spaces on their forms. Very particular about that sort of thing is the Home Office.'

It was obvious from his expression that Aniç realized he was being led into a trap, but there was nothing he could do about it. We held all the cards and he knew it.

Reluctantly, he gave us an address in Willesden. 'Can I go now?' he asked.

'No,' I said. 'You will be charged with forging or stealing these credit cards and driving licence, and attempted theft by deception.'

Aniç half rose from his chair, but then slumped back again. 'You have deceived me,' he protested.

'Must be an odd experience for you to find that the boot's on the other foot,' said Dave.

'Boots? Why are you talking to me about boots? I know nothing of any boots. This is harassment.'

We took the full team of crime-scene examiners with us to Aniç's address, but left them outside until we'd spoken to the owner.

The house was in one of the seedier parts of Willesden – a purely comparative term, you'll understand – and was probably Victorian or Edwardian, I should think but, as I've probably mentioned before, I'm not too good at architecture. In common with most coppers I tend only to learn about things when I need to know them for the purposes of an enquiry.

Three storeys high with a basement area, the property was in a bad state of repair. In places chunks of the concrete cladding had come away from the walls to reveal the brickwork. It appeared that the owner had so far resisted the blandishments of double-glazing salesmen, and the paint on the wooden window frames was peeling badly.

Carefully avoiding the overflowing black rubbish sacks that festooned the steps leading to the front door, we rang the bell.

The girl who answered was probably no more than twenty. Her long blonde hair was braided into pigtails, and hung down the front of her body past the top of an off-the-shoulder blouse cut so low that were it to fall another millimetre in public it would undoubtedly cause a breach of the peace. An excess of make-up, principally rouge, gave her face the appearance of a wooden doll, and her skirt was so brief that I wondered momentarily if it was actually a scarf worn around the waist.

'Yes, please? You want room?' The girl smiled seductively.

I had a feeling that this was perhaps some sort of coded invitation.

'No, I want to speak to the owner. Is that you?' I asked. Well, you never know these days. Prostitutes can earn good money, and this girl looked as though she was in the trade.

'No, I not owner. I get him.'

A few minutes later a middle-aged man with wavy iron-grey hair appeared at the door. He wore a red and black check shirt, a neckerchief, jeans with a thick leather belt and calf-high boots, and looked as though he'd escaped from a low-budget Western film.

'What you want?' the man demanded.

'Police,' said Dave. 'We have a warrant to search these premises. What's your name?'

Somewhat grudgingly the man identified himself as Mico Babiç.

'Are you a Bosnian?' asked Dave.

'Yes. But why you want to search? There no criminal here. No terrorists.' Babiç showed a marked unwillingness to admit us. 'No al-Qa'eda,' he added, presumably as an earnest of his good faith and total reliability.

'That *is* good news,' said Dave as we pushed past Babiç into the hall.

'Why you want search?' asked Babiç again, raising his arms in an attitude of extreme agitation. 'There nothing here.'

'Does Ramo Aniç, otherwise known as Gavrilo Lemez, live here?' I asked for starters.

'He upstairs, first door on right,' said Babiç without hesitation. Loyalty to fellow nationals was clearly not his strong suit.

'Not any more he isn't,' said Dave.

We mounted the staircase and found Aniç's room. The bed was unmade, the

241

wardrobe door hung open and the only table in the room bore a small television set, a jar of hair gel, a bottle of what looked like cheap aftershave lotion and several newspapers. Obviously the exorbitant rent that Babiç undoubtedly charged his unfortunate tenants did not include the services of a chambermaid. At least, not chambermaid services in the conventional sense.

'Give Linda and her team a shout, Dave,' I said, being careful to remain on the threshold of Aniç's room.

It took the CSEs an hour to search the room thoroughly. They lifted a number of fingerprints – not that they were likely to prove anything – but found little of evidential value.

Until they got to the wardrobe.

'Looks as though we could be in luck, Mr Brock,' said Linda Mitchell. She waved a latex-gloved hand at a green loden overcoat.

We both knew what she meant by that. If the fibre found on the doorpost of Crow's room at 55 Gillen Street, Battersea, matched the fibres on this coat, I reckon I'd be justified in charging Aniç with Crow's murder. Whether it would achieve a conviction was, of course, another matter.

Linda lifted the coat from its hanger and inspected the inside. 'The label says Fischer Stuttgart. But there's no name.' She glanced at me. 'You know, like the owner's name.'

'I wonder whether that's the manufacturer

or the shop where he bought it,' I mused.

'Or where he nicked it,' said Dave.

But as I've said many times before, Dave is rarely prepared to see the good in people.

'Anything else, Linda?' I asked.

She shook her head. 'There's not a scrap of corres anywhere.'

'Corres' is police shorthand for correspondence, but doesn't only include letters. Anything on paper, like bank statements, building-society books, diaries, cheque stubs, travel tickets and receipts, comes into that category as well. Even anything on a computer these days, not that I know much about computers.

But Aniç was obviously a careful man and had left nothing that might have been of help to us. Not even an aforementioned computer.

'I'll get this across to the lab ASAP, Mr Brock,' Linda said, having supervised the packing of the overcoat in a plastic evidence bag. She signed the label that was attached to the bag and replaced her pen in her pocket. 'Anything else?'

'No, that's it, Linda, thank you. I doubt if the fingerprints will tell us anything, but you never know. How long for the examination of the overcoat?'

Linda glanced at her watch. 'If they start work on it first thing tomorrow morning,' she said, 'they should be able to give you an answer by midday.'

243

* * *

The next morning, while I was waiting for the lab report on the coat, I rang the police in Stuttgart.

One of the advantages of having had a German wife – in Helga's case the only advantage – was that I had learned to speak the language fluently. It certainly cut corners whenever I needed an enquiry done in Germany.

Kommissar Haas at the headquarters of the Stuttgart CID assured me that Fischer of Stuttgart was a department store. Without my asking, he offered to make enquiries there to see if the store could recall having sold such a coat to either a Ramo Aniç or a Gavrilo Lemez. I thanked him, but thought that it would be discourteous to suggest that he would probably be wasting his time. It wouldn't prove anything.

Neither did I complicate matters by mentioning the immigrant smuggling, even though we believed that Stuttgart played a significant part as a staging post. But I only withheld that information because I was aware that John Fielding was making enquiries through his customs network.

Which reminded me: I must give him a call.

Fifteen

Next morning, I rang John Fielding, but the result was disappointing. He told me that he had put out feelers, as he called them, with his opposite numbers in Austria, Germany and France, but with such sparse information as he was able to give them they'd been unable to track down any of the immigrant smugglers. The customs service in those countries had discovered some of the premises that had been used, but they'd been abandoned, and a scientific examination had provided nothing in the way of evidence. Which proved what we already knew: that usually Aniç was a careful man. It was still out of character, on the basis of what we knew already, that he had been caught out trying to buy a bottle of vodka with a dodgy credit card.

More worrying was the strong indication that the network had been alerted to the arrests that had been made in London, Portsmouth and Dover. All of which proved that there was still someone out there running the operation, but the route they were now employing was open to conjecture.

As for Fielding's tentative enquiries of the

Bosnian Customs Service, they had apparently been met with ironical laughter. While sympathizing, a Sarajevo official had told Fielding that immigrant smuggling was going on all the time to the extent that it was almost a national sport. *But out of Bosnia, not in.* And somewhat unprofessionally he had added that the more troublemakers they got rid of the better. Yes, he had heard of Ramo Aniç, he said, but who hadn't?

At about eleven thirty, the forensic-science laboratory report arrived. The fibre found on the doorpost at Crow's bedsit matched the green loden overcoat taken from Aniç's room in Willesden. Hooray!

I walked through to the incident room. 'Any news on what's happened to Aniç yet, Colin?' I asked DS Wilberforce.

'Yes, sir.' Colin referred to his daybook. 'Miss Ebdon —'

'Miss Ebdon's here,' said Kate from the doorway. 'Aniç appeared before the Horseferry Road district judge this morning, charged with theft and attempted theft by deception. He had a TP brief but?'

'A what, Kate?'

'A taxpayers' solicitor, guv. We always called them TP briefs on the Squad. You know, the sort you and I pay for. Didn't do him any good, though. I had a quiet word in the ear of the CPS counsel and told him that Aniç was certainly implicated in the conspiracy that effected his escape from Hounslow and that enquiries were continuing. I also pointed out that there was a question mark hanging over Aniç with regard to his status as an illegal immigrant. I have to say that the CPS guy was good. He put all that to the district judge. Despite a clever bit of tap-dancing by Aniç's brief, the beak remanded him in custody to Brixton prison pending a remand appearance at the Bailey.'

'Good. In that case, Dave and I will pay him a visit and charge him with murder.'

Ramo Aniç was still in an uncommunicative mood. If anything, even more so than the last time we'd talked to him. Furthermore he'd had the services of a solicitor who had undoubtedly told him to say nothing to anyone. I think he was also feeling furious with himself that he, the master criminal, had been caught out by, of all people, a checkout assistant in a supermarket. It was fortunate that he hadn't been carrying a weapon when he was arrested; knowing what we did about him, he might have been tempted to shoot his way out of trouble. God knows what would have happened then.

'I have nothing to say,' he said before I'd spoken a word.

'You don't have to,' I said. 'Ramo Aniç, I am charging you with the murder of Wilfred Crow at 55 Gillen Street, Battersea on or about Tuesday the nineteenth of March this year. Dave ... '

Before Aniç had a chance to respond, Dave reeled off the caution.

'I have already told you that I do not know this person Crow,' Aniç said, 'nor have I ever heard of this Battersea place of which you speak.' And then, as an apparent after-thought, he added, 'Better men than you have tried to put me in prison, Mr Police-man.' He might have been regretting the cause of his incarceration, but his arrogance had not diminished since the last time we spoke to him.

I imagined that Aniç was well versed in fencing with the police, especially those much tougher than we were allowed to be. I certainly had no intention of telling him about the fibre that had come from the over-coat we'd found at his Battersea bedsit, because I feared that that alone would not hold up in court. We needed more and Aniç would know that. I could visualize the defence already: 'Of course a fibre was found, members of the jury. My client was a friend of Mr Crow and frequently visited his home. They often played chess together.' But I dismissed that immediately. If Aniç's counsel knew what he was about, he would be unlikely to put forward a proposition that contradicted his client's avowal that he didn't know Crow. And Aniç had denied it.

However, bearing in mind how long it takes the CPS to make a decision, I hoped that more substantial evidence would be forthcoming before they decided to throw out the case and send Aniç back to Bosnia. And if that did happen, I'd be straight on the phone to Mr Djork, the mysterious 'police official' whose office over the shop in Piccadilly Dave and I had visited.

When we got back to Curtis Green, I received a telephone call from Kommissar Haas in Stuttgart.

'I have made enquiries at the shop Fischer of Stuttgart, Herr Brock, but I regret to tell you that they have no record of the coat you describe having been sold to either a Ramo Aniç or a Gavrilo Lemez. Is there anything else I can do for you, Herr Chief Inspector?'

'Thank you for your efforts, Herr Kommissar,' I said, 'but further enquiries won't be necessary.'

It would have been useful if Haas had been able to confirm Aniç's purchase of the coat; it would have negated any claim by Aniç that he'd never seen it before. And would also have negated the usual defence claim that it had been planted by the wicked police. But I realized that I had wasted not only my time but also that of Kommissar Haas. All Aniç would have to say was that it had been stolen from him.

'I've been doing a few follow-up enquiries, guv,' said Kate Ebdon as she wandered into my office and sat down uninvited. For a moment or two she shuffled through the sheaf of paper she had brought with her.

'Find anything interesting?' I asked.

'Sort of. I decided to set the team to doing house-to-house enquiries again opposite Stone Mill prison, and they turned up this joker who saw something.'

'But Frank Mead didn't find anyone who saw anything,' I said.

'Yeah, but he was demob-happy,' said Kate, shooting me one of her wicked grins.

'He hasn't left the Job. He went to the Fraud Squad.'

'Same thing,' said Kate dismissively, but then laughed. 'It wasn't his fault, guv. This witness, James Roper he's called, lives bang opposite the prison, but he wasn't there when the team made enquiries.'

'Have you interviewed him yourself?'

'Too right. But don't get excited because there's probably nothing in it. Anyway, at the time of the shooting, he was leaving his house to go the airport. He was off to Prague on a business trip and didn't get back till two days later, on the Friday. That was the eighth of February. Which is why Frank didn't get to interview him.'

'Go on,' I said, leaning forward.

'Roper was waiting for a taxi, but at the crucial moment this bloody great goods vehicle stopped right outside his house so he had to walk along the road a bit to find the cab.'

'Did he see the shooting? Or hear anything?'

'No, the lorry blocked his view and the noise of the traffic at that time of the morning would have been loud enough to wake the dead, I reckon. Except for Gould,' she added with a laugh. 'Roper was too busy looking for his taxi to notice anything else, apart from the fact that the lorry seemed to have stopped for no good reason. There was nothing to hold it up, so he said, because he looked in front of it for his taxi, and then walked back to the rear of it.'

'I don't suppose he got the number of this lorry, did he?'

'You suppose right,' said Kate with a grin. 'Nobody ever does.'

'Did he see the driver?'

'No. Whoever was driving it was too high up and on the offside of the cab, obviously. But apart from anything else, it was pouring with rain and Roper had got his umbrella up.'

'A description of the lorry, then.'

'Yeah, for what it's worth,' said Kate, glancing down at her notes again. 'Big!' She looked up and laughed again. 'It was an articulated rig, black and red with solid sides. He thinks there might have been a name on the side but he didn't notice what it was.'

'So it's just possible that the driver of this vehicle was the shooter,' I mused.

251

'It's a possibility, I suppose,' said Kate. 'Of course if our witness had looked in the back and found a coffin, I reckon that would have clinched it.'

'Yeah, thanks, Kate,' I said.

'I put out a note on the PNC asking if any street coppers see a black-and-red rig, they are to take the number and let us know. Nothing else. We don't want some dim copper trying to solve our case all on his own. The only drawback is that there's bound to be hundreds of them and it'll probably mean one hell of a lot of work, but it might just pay off.'

'Yes,' I agreed, 'but send a message to the ports of Dover and Portsmouth asking them to pay special attention. Give the Special Branch blokes there something to do.'

'We could ask customs to take a quick look in the backs of outgoing vehicles that fit the description, guv. Never know, they might find a coffin or two.'

I telephoned John Fielding at customs and told him of Kate's discovery. He promised to get the local customs officers to keep their eyes open. But he held out little hope of success. Neither did I.

The result of Kate's initiative was that we received thousands of vehicle-index numbers of lorries that vaguely fitted the description James Roper had given. The sightings stretched from Land's End through to John

O'Groat's, and there were even one or two from Northern Ireland. And the Garda Siochana, bless them, spotted a couple in Dublin.

There were so many that six members of Kate's team were fully engaged in identifying the owners of these lorries, but none of the names meant anything, and we eventually abandoned the idea as being too cumbersome and time-consuming to contribute much to our enquiry.

The following morning, Kate Ebdon came bouncing into my office.

'A mate of mine on the Squad has nicked a guy called Ben Dixon, guv,' she said excitedly.

'Should this be of interest to me, Kate?' I asked.

'Very much so. Brad Naylor, a DI out of the Lea Bridge Road base, got wind from a snout of his that Dixon was involved in springing Ramo Aniç. Brad said that the guy's a reliable informant and reckoned that there weren't many villains who could handle a job like the Hounslow one. Anyway, the Squad spun Dixon's drum at five o'clock this morning and had him away.'

'So what's happening now?'

'They've got him at Hackney nick for a cosy little chat. Brad Naylor's lads know who Dixon usually runs with and they're out picking them up now.'

★ ★ ★

By the time that Kate, Dave and I got to Hackney police station, two more of Dixon's little team had been arrested.

Brad Naylor, a snappily dressed, typical Flying Squad detective inspector, shook hands.

'I gather from Kate that you've got an interest in this lot, guv,' he said. 'And she said you fancy this Aniç finger for the Crow murder.'

'Yes, I do,' I said. I explained about the three murders I was investigating and told Naylor about the fibre found at Gillen Street. 'What's the SP on the three you've nicked?'

'One of my snouts whispered that word was out about some guy in this Hounslow place wanting out. The fee on offer was twenty-five big ones. A couple of days later, he rang me and said that Ben Dixon had taken the bait. We knew his running mates were "Taffy" Eldridge and Sid Hawkes and so this morning we nicked them as well. But Dixon's well pissed off about the whole thing. In fact they all are.'

'Have they coughed to it, then?' I asked.

'Dixon has, more or less. He's doing some bargaining at the moment, but whether the CPS will wear it is another thing. Want to have a chat with him?'

'Yes, indeed.'

Dixon was a typical London villain. He

254

had a broken nose and a cauliflower ear, and looked as though he might have been quite a useful boxer in his youth.

I decided to catch him wrong-footed. 'I'm investigating three murders,' I began.

'Here, hold on, guv'nor. I don't do no toppings. I'll hold me hands up to having done a few armed robberies in the past, but topping's definitely not my scene.'

'All right. Tell me about Gavrilo Lemez.' I had decided to keep with Aniç's alias to avoid confusing Dixon.

Dixon licked his lips and looked suspiciously at Kate Ebdon. 'If I give you chapter and verse on this, guv'nor, is it going to get me some consideration?'

'Depends what you have to say. But let me lay it on the line for you. Lemez, who we now know to be Ramo Aniç, was seized from Hounslow at gunpoint, and several of the guards claim to have been assaulted. That's worth a few penn'orth in the nick before we go any further.'

'Yeah, I s'pose.' Dixon did not look happy at the prospect and from what Naylor had told me, I knew he was not unfamiliar with the inside of Her Majesty's prisons. 'All right, I'll have to trust you, I s'pose. This is the SP. Word was out that this geezer Lemez wanted liberating from this place out at Hounslow, see. Some detention centre it was. The asking price was twenty-five grand. I sussed the place out a couple of times, and it seemed a handsome handful of gelt for an easy enough little tickle, so I went for it.'

'Along with Taffy Eldridge and Sid Hawkes,' I said.

'I ain't grassing on anyone, Mr Brock. You'll have to work that out for yourself.'

'I already did,' put in Naylor. 'I nicked them a couple of hours ago.'

'Oh!' said Dixon, and lapsed into momentary silence. 'Well, like I said, the fee was good, so we went for it. It was a pushover, but no one got worked over. If anyone said they was done over, they're blowing smoke up yer arse, Mr Brock. That's the God's honest truth.'

'Who was the inside man?' asked Kate, her Australian accent rasping through the temporary silence of the interview room.

'There weren't no inside man,' Dixon protested.

'Come off it.' Kate grinned at the prisoner. 'Of course there was. And as a matter of fact he's next door singing like a canary. Put you well in the frame, he has.' She told the lie without compunction.

Dixon shook his head in disbelief. 'I knew we shouldn't never have trusted that bastard Jack Lynn. No wonder he's known as Vera.'

'Does he usually run with your team?' asked Brad Naylor, clearly keen to do some more arresting.

'No, he bloody don't,' said Dixon. 'He was given us as the contact.'

'So,' I continued, 'you may as well tell us the whole story.'

'I was approached.'

'Who by?'

'Dunno, but someone had obviously propped us for a job like that and this geezer come in my local boozer one evening.'

'And you don't know his name?'

'Nah. Anyhow he put this job on offer and give me a grand as down payment when I said I'd go for it.'

'That was a small payment considering the fee was twenty-five,' I said. 'You usually go for half down and half when the job's done.'

Dixon shook his head mournfully. 'Yeah, but times is hard, Mr Brock. Anyhow, this finger said he'd be back once we'd sprung Lemez and he'd pay us the rest. Well, we done the job, all neat and tidy. We'd nicked a van from Slough and we was in and out in about five minutes. And like I said no one got hurt. We waved a few imitation pistols about and the security guys just give up this geezer without a murmur. All done and dusted. If anyone said they got duffed up they're telling you bleedin' lies, Mr Brock.' Dixon was at pains to emphasize that violence had not been used, well knowing that it could add to the sentence he was already resigned to receiving.

'Where did you take Lemez after you'd liberated him?' Dave asked.

Dixon laughed. 'Dumped him at an all-night bus stop on the Bath Road. I thought he was having a laugh at first, but that's where he said he wanted to go. So we did just that. Then we drove the van back to Slough where we'd nicked it from and set fire to it. We'd got a motor waiting there, and that was it. We buggered off home and emptied a bottle of Scotch to celebrate.'

'And when did you get the rest of the money?'

'That's the point, guv'nor, we never did. This geezer what set it up said as how he'd be in the same boozer two days later at ten o'clock sharp, but he never showed, the bastard.'

'Could sue him, I suppose,' said Dave quietly.

'It ain't funny, guv,' said Dixon.

'I think you probably didn't get paid because the go-between had to get the money from Lemez,' I said, 'and unfortunately for you Lemez got nicked himself a few days later.'

'That's his problem, guv'nor,' said Dixon angrily. 'A promise to pay's a promise to pay. Know what I mean? I'm no grass, but we ain't got our money, so anything I can tell you about him's on the house, and he can have that with me. Anyway, I'm bloody sure the bleedin' middleman could have come up with the folding stuff. If he never had it in his hand, he's stark staring bonkers to go about making arrangements without having the readies in his pocket. I wouldn't mind betting he's had it away on his dancers with our twenty-four grand. I can tell you, guv, that go-between's life's in definite danger. This is serious money we're talking about.'

'This guy who met you in the pub, you say you don't know his name.'

'No, guv. It don't do to ask questions like that in this game,' said Dixon. 'Anyway he'd only have given us a duff moniker.'

'Would you know him again?'

'Too bloody right I would,' said Dixon vehemently, 'and if I see him before you feel his collar he's likely to suffer some serious damage.'

'A description, then?' asked Dave, pocketbook at the ready.

Dixon thought carefully about that and eventually gave us a description that could have fitted a hundred men. Unfortunately that's always the way of things.

'An E-fit might be a good idea, guv,' said Dave, and aware that I was not familiar with such clever devices, added, 'It's a piece of equipment that enables the operator to build a computer-aided likeness from a description given by the witness ... sir.'

'Thank you, Dave,' I said.

We tried, but it was obvious that the man who had approached Dixon in his local pub had been at pains to disguise himself sufficiently to prevent a useful description being compiled, electronically or otherwise.

259

Dixon volunteered the information that Lemez' contact man had been wearing a donkey jacket, a baseball cap, pulled well down, sunglasses – even though it was early March – and a muffler around his neck. Dixon had not found this at all unusual, and nor did I. Men who approach villains in smoky East London pubs offering substantial sums of money for an illegal enterprise generally do not want to be remembered. But Dixon swore he'd know the man's voice if he ever heard it again.

Just before we left Dixon to Brad Naylor, he asked one more question, casually as though it was unimportant.

'What nick's this Lemez in, guv'nor?' he asked. 'I s'pose he got a lay down.'

'I don't know,' I lied. If Dixon was thinking what I think he was thinking, our Mr Aniç was likely to suffer some serious impairment to his health. A big man in Bosnia he might have been, but he'd be no match for a handful of hardened East London villains with a few years in the nick behind them.

We interviewed Eldridge and Hawkes but, apart from admitting their involvement in Aniç's escape, neither was able to add anything to the information, sparse though it was, that Dixon had given us.

Thanks to Ben Dixon, though, we now had the name of the inside man at Hounslow. And I determined that before long 'Vera' Lynn would be interviewed.

Sixteen

I sent Kate Ebdon with DI Brad Naylor to the Hounslow detention centre that afternoon.

At three thirty she rang to say that Jack 'Vera' Lynn was in custody at the local police station.

'This Lynn's a wimp, guv,' said Kate when Dave and I arrived. 'I reckon he's a pushover.'

But first we sat in on DI Naylor's interview with Lynn's shift supervisor. Clearly at pains to distance himself from the unsavoury events that culminated in Aniç's release, he almost fell over himself to tell Naylor as much as he knew about Lynn. He said that the security guard, who was twenty-eight years of age, had only been taken on a week prior to the raid. And then only temporarily because they were short-staffed. He went on to say that Lynn lived in Hounslow, was married with two children, had a crippling mortgage and topped-up credit cards. Preening himself, the supervisor added that he knew about the mortgage because he made it his business to find out about such things.

All of which, doubtless, created a motive for Lynn's involvement.

It was interesting that the shift supervisor denied having informed his superiors about this obvious security risk and it briefly crossed my mind that he might have benefited financially by turning a blind eye. It was a bit of a coincidence that there happened to have been a vacancy for a temporary security guard at just the right time. I decided to rattle his bars.

'Where were you when this raid occurred?' I asked.

There was a moment of suspicious hesitation. 'I was out in the mess-room making a cup of tea for the lads when I heard all this shouting, see, guv'nor. Well, I went out to see what was going on. There was these three geezers there with them balaclavas on, like what the IRA wear, and they was waving guns about, and Jack Lynn was getting a bit of a beating and so was the other lads.'

'I was told that none of them showed any signs of having been assaulted,' I said, 'but go on.'

'Well, then we got tied up, except for Jack Lynn. Then one of these blokes stuck a gun in Jack's back, like he was going to shoot him, and made him show 'em where this Lemez bloke was. The next minute they was away with him. I heard a motor starting up and that was that. Jack undone our ropes and I rang the police. That was my job, see, being shift supervisor.'

'I can't somehow see you getting the Queen's Gallantry Medal,' said Dave drily.

Ben Dixon had denied tying up the guards and oddly enough I believed him. He, I'd decided, was an honest villain, whereas the shift supervisor was definitely dodgy.

Ben Dixon had told Brad Naylor that they were going to give Lynn two thousand pounds for his part in the Great Escape and divide the remainder between themselves. As it turned out, none of them was getting anything. Apart, that is, from a few years in prison.

Having cleared it with Naylor, I interviewed the 'inside man' in the plot to free Aniç.

Dave and I sat down in the sparsely furnished room and gazed at the miserable specimen opposite us.

Jack Lynn was as thin as a beanpole and, I discovered almost immediately, would break just as easily. He wore cheap wire-rimmed spectacles through which he blinked all the time, and his flashy uniform hung on him as though it had been made for someone larger.

'I'm Detective Chief Inspector Brock of the Serious Crime Group,' I said, 'and I'm investigating three murders. It's likely that one of them wouldn't have been committed if Gavrilo Lemez, also known as Ramo Aniç, hadn't escaped. And that, Jack, puts you in an invidious position.'

It was obviously a mistake to have said that.

Lynn blinked even faster. 'Puts me in a what?'

'It means that as a result of your involvement in all this, the Crown Prosecution Service may well regard you as a co-conspirator in a case of murder. That of course could mean life imprisonment.' *Fat chance!*

Lynn went ashen white and for a moment I thought he was going to faint. 'But I never—' he said and then lapsed into silence, presumably while he thought over the implications of what I had just said.

'Now then,' I said, 'tell me about this man who approached you.' It was a wild guess, but I knew that someone must have put him in place.

'What man?'

'The man who suggested you got a job at the Hounslow detention centre thereby being in a position to let in the three men who snatched Lemez.'

'How did you know about that?' asked Lynn, surprise registering on his pasty face.

'Because I'm a detective,' I said.

Lynn ran his tongue round his lips. 'Yeah, well, I got a phone call.'

'Where were you when you got this phone call?'

'At home. This bloke said that it would be

to my advantage to get a job at the centre. So I asked him what it was all about, but he said to do it and that there'd be a nice little earner in it for me.'

There was something not quite right about all this, and I was beginning to think that Lynn was not the pushover that Kate had suggested he was. Either that or he was scared witless of his mysterious caller.

'Just hold it right there,' I said. 'Are you telling me that a man you'd never heard of rang you up at home and told you to get a job as a security guard at the Hounslow facility? Is that it?'

'But that's what happened.'

'Well, I'm not buying it,' I said.

'What job did you have before you became a security guard?' asked Dave suddenly.

Lynn shot Dave a nervous glance. 'I never had one,' he said, a little too hurriedly.

'Are you telling me that at the age of twenty-eight you've never had a job before this one?'

'Not since I came out of the army, no.'

Dave leaned closer to the emaciated soon-to-be-ex-security guard. 'And what did you do in the army?'

'I was a clerk.'

'And what regiment were you in?'

'The Royal Logistic Corps.'

Suddenly I realized that Dave might just be getting somewhere, but I tried not to read too much into what Lynn had said. After all, it was known as the Really Large Corps because it was really large.

'When did you leave the army, Jack?' Dave continued to press Lynn.

'About a year ago.'

'Why?'

A furtive look settled on Lynn's face and for a few moments he stared down at the table. 'I was chucked out,' he said eventually. 'After ten years,' he added bitterly.

'And why did the army throw you out?'

There was another long pause before Lynn answered. 'I nicked some money.'

'Oh dear! And that was to buy drugs with, was it?'

'How did you know that?'

'I've only got to look at you to see you're on drugs, and I know that the army doesn't approve of drug addicts in its ranks.' Dave leaned back, smiled and glanced at me. It was an indication that he wanted me to take back the questioning.

'How well did you know Bernie Pointer, Jack?' I asked. It was an irrelevant question, but the fact that Pointer had been convicted of embezzlement might just provide a connection. All right, so there was nothing to make me think that but, believe me, crimes have been solved before with that sort of slender guesswork.

Lynn frowned. 'I don't know anyone of that name,' he said.

'He was murdered on a golf course very

close to where you live,' I said. 'You must have read about it in the paper.'

'Oh that,' said Lynn. 'Yeah, well I heard about it, but I never knew him.'

And I believed him. There was little chance that this weakling opposite me was capable of murdering anyone.

I tried another tack. 'How about Geoffrey Morrison? He was in the RLC too, as a clerk.'

'No, I've never heard of him. It's a very big regiment. There are thousands of squaddies in it.'

But a brief expression had crossed Lynn's face, sufficient to tell me that Morrison's name did mean something to him.

We left it there. That I'd believed Lynn had recognized Morrison's name gave me cause to have more enquiries made about Bernie Pointer's brother-in-law. They had both been in the same regiment, but as Lynn had said, it was a very big regiment and the likelihood of them having met each other was remote. In fact, it was probably impossible because Morrison had claimed to have left the army ten years ago. And that was about the time that Lynn would have enlisted.

Kate Ebdon had volunteered to 'put the arm' on the military, and I couldn't think of a better detective to do it. If she was unable to prise information out of them about Geoffrey Morrison and Jack Lynn, I

267

doubted that anyone could.

Late that afternoon she returned in triumph.

'You're going to love this, guv,' she said, settling in my armchair. 'For a start, Morrison didn't leave the army ten years ago. It was five. But this is the interesting part: he enlisted in an infantry regiment and rose to be a sergeant. He was then seconded to "special forces". They wouldn't tell me which one, but I guess it was probably the Special Air Service. And he was an instructor in small arms specializing in training snipers.'

'But the discharge book that Pointer stole from him showed that he was in the Royal Logistic Corps,' I said. 'If Pointer did steal it, that is.'

'Yes, he was in the RLC, but only for the last year of his service. According to the army he was injured during some special operation abroad, but they said it was his own fault; he was reckless, apparently, and endangered the men under his command. As a result he was reduced in rank to corporal and transferred to the RLC. When he got to the end of his engagement, he threw in the towel. Complained that he was bored out of his skull and was going to try his luck in civvy street. And two more things: at one stage he was in the same unit as Jack Lynn *and* he served in Bosnia. I reckon Morrison probably met up with Ramo Aniç while he was there and they hatched a nice little plot that would earn them a fair amount of money. And I wouldn't mind betting that Morrison recruited his brother-in-law, Bernie Pointer. And it's a racing certainty that he would have made it his business to know where Lynn was living.'

I got a search warrant just before the court rose for the Easter weekend. The next day, Good Friday, we hit the Morrisons' house at Capstick Road, Merton Park at half-past five in the morning.

After a great deal of knocking, Karen Morrison eventually opened the door. She was wearing a dressing gown and was rubbing the sleep from her eyes.

'Whatever's wrong?' she asked, moving a lock of hair away from her forehead. 'Has something happened to Geoff?'

'Isn't he here, then?'

'No, he's working.'

'What, on Good Friday?' This was bad news. 'I thought he was looking for work,' I said. 'Isn't he unemployed?'

Karen Morrison appeared surprised at my comment. 'I don't know what gave you that idea,' she said. And then, finally, it occurred to her to ask what the hell we were doing on her doorstep at half-past five on a Good Friday morning.

'I have a warrant to search your house, Mrs Morrison,' I said.

'Search? Whatever for?'

'I think it might be better if we came in, don't you? And then I'll explain.'

'If you like to come into the kitchen, I'll make some tea.'

We followed the woman and she put on a kettle and began to set out some mugs with silly slogans on them. She turned and leaned against the worktop. 'I still don't understand why you want to search my house,' she said. 'Is it something to do with Bernie?'

'Only indirectly,' I said, but wondered why she should have come to that conclusion. 'Tell me, Mrs Morrison, what exactly does your husband do for a living?'

'He's a long-distance lorry driver. Has been ever since he came out of the army.'

I hoped that I'd managed to conceal my excitement at this revelation. 'And how long ago was that?' I asked mildly, as though it was of but passing interest.

Karen turned as the kettle boiled, threw some teabags into the teapot and poured on hot water. 'About five years ago, I suppose,' she said over her shoulder.

'You met when he was in the army, then?'

'Yes, we did.' Karen turned again, a puzzled expression on her face. 'But why d'you want to know all that? Has Geoff done something wrong?'

'I certainly need to talk to him,' I said, deflecting her question. 'One or two things have come up in the course of my investigation into your brother's death that need to be clarified, and your husband may be able to help us.'

I had come rapidly to the conclusion that if Geoffrey Morrison had been involved in the deaths of Jimmy Gould and Bernie Pointer, then Karen knew nothing of it.

'Yes, we met when he was in the army,' said Karen. 'I was living in Aldershot at the time. Well, that's where I was born. I used to go to army dances, a lot of the girls did, and that's where I met Geoff. He used to look really great in his uniform. He was a corporal then, but he got made sergeant just after we were married. That was when he got posted to Hereford.'

Interesting. Hereford was the depot of the Special Air Service.

'It was a good life,' continued Karen. 'There was always something going on in the sergeants' mess, almost every night. Dances and tombola, fancy-dress parties. It was really good.' She stood for a moment, a dreamy expression on her face as she recalled those far-off days, but then remembered that she should be pouring the tea. 'D'you take milk and sugar?' Her gaze took in Kate, Dave and me.

'Have you any idea when your husband will be back?' I asked.

Karen glanced at the kitchen clock. 'He should be in at about six this evening,' she said. 'D'you want me to tell him that you'd like to see him?'

I smiled. 'I don't think so,' I said, 'but we'll just have a look round, if you don't mind. We won't disturb your sons.' I didn't think it necessary to alienate this woman too much by telling her that we were going to search the place anyway. But I held out little hope of finding anything incriminating. Not if Morrison was as cunning as I thought he was.

And that proved to be true. We went through the few papers that were in the house: bills for utilities, telephone accounts and a statement from the building society. But there was nothing that pointed to Morrison being engaged in any nefarious activity. I came to the conclusion that anything that would lead us to believe he was on Aniç's payroll would be kept somewhere else. And somewhere where his wife would not find it.

And that led to my next question.

'Is your husband self-employed, Mrs Morrison? Does he own his own rig?'

'Yes, he started up when he came out of the army.'

'And where does he park this lorry of his?'

'I don't know. He always comes home in his car, so I suppose he leaves the car where he keeps the rig and swaps over when he's finished work.'

'Does he ever go to the Continent?' asked Dave.

Mrs Morrison gave that some thought. 'It's

possible, I suppose. He never talks much about his work. Always says it's boring, just driving mile after mile. But now I come to think of it, he did ring me from France a couple of times. And I'd ring him, but always on his mobile, so I never knew for sure where he was. He did bring me some perfume from France once,' she added, presumably believing that to be helpful.

We left it there and returned to our car.

Kate Ebdon rang Colin Wilberforce, who had just taken over from Gavin Creasey, the night-duty incident-room manager, and instructed him to get a couple of her team out to Merton Park ASAP, complete with a nondescript observation van.

'You two are to keep discreet observation on number 27,' said Kate when John Appleby and Sheila Armitage arrived. 'Geoffrey Morrison is due back here at about six this evening. As soon as he shows, ring the guv'nor.' She indicated me with a wave of the hand. 'We'll not be far away.'

But by ten o'clock that evening there had been no sign of Geoffrey Morrison. The inevitable conclusion was that Karen Morrison, probably in all innocence, had telephoned her husband and told him of our call.

There was little else we could do but put Geoffrey Morrison's name on the PNC as someone I wished to question. But as we didn't know where he kept his rig and we didn't know the index mark of the vehicle, the chances of him being found, if he didn't want to be found, were remote.

On Saturday morning I made a decision, a rare occurrence for me, and determined to go to Dinard.

I knew that the commander wouldn't give me permission to go at the Job's expense, not again, so I booked next Tuesday as a leave day. That would give me nearly four days: the rest of today, Easter Sunday, Easter Monday and Tuesday. And as I would be paying for the trip there was no reason why I shouldn't take Gail with me.

My thinking was that if Geoffrey Morrison had taken flight, at least from his home, he might still have some outstanding obligations to Aniç to deliver empty coffins to France. But at the back of my mind was the thought that he was more important to the operation than merely driving a lorry. Someone had tipped off Walters and Aniç and it was just possible that it was Morrison. All of this, I told myself, was pure supposition and merely an excuse to carry Gail off for the weekend. Well, why not? But I did explain to her that I would be working for some of the time that we were there.

I telephoned Jacques Bloyet, the Maréchal des Logis chef in Dinard, explained why I was coming and asked him to recommend somewhere for us to stay.

We arrived at half-past two. I left Gail at the Crystal, a hotel that overlooked the wide expanse of beach, and made my way to the gendarmerie in Rue Gardiner for a chat with Jacques Bloyet.

'I 'ave 'ad a word with Odette Gouret, 'Arry, and she is keeping a lookout for coffins. You remember Odette?'

'Yes, indeed.' I would not easily forget the elegant and attractive officer in charge of customs at the airport.

'If one arrives,' Bloyet continued, 'she will call me and I will telephone you. You 'ave a portable telephone?'

'Yes,' I said, and gave him the number of my mobile. 'But I don't know if it'll work that easily. It's on a British network.' I didn't know whether it made any difference but mobile phones, like computers, are a complete mystery to me. I can just about use one but the finer points, like sending a text message, are beyond me. Despite Gail having shown me on several occasions how to do it.

'*Alors!*' Bloyet took a two-way radio from a rack on the wall and handed it to me. 'There you are, 'Arry. That is easier, *non*? But don't forget to give it back before you go 'ome.' He laughed. 'Otherwise I shall be court-martialled.'

And that seemed to be that. There was no point in hanging around the airport for hours on end, and Jacques Bloyet had obviously got everything buttoned up. My interest was not so much any movement of coffins, but more of whether Morrison would be in the vicinity keeping a watch. I had been certain all along that someone had witnessed the arrests at Portsmouth and had alerted other members of the team. The more I thought about it, the more I was convinced that Morrison was the lookout man. If he was now seen at Dinard Airport that would clinch it in my book.

I was happy to leave it all to Jacques Bloyet and Odette Gouret. And by six o'clock that evening Gail and I were sitting on the balcony of our room, gazing out at the sea and drinking champagne.

'I know you said you'd be working some of the time we're here, darling,' Gail said, holding out her glass for a refill, 'but why exactly *are* we here?'

I decided to tell her the whole story of the investigation and why Dinard played such an important part in the enquiry. I think she was quite disappointed at how mundane it all sounded, but I've found over the years that people who watch cop shows on television are often disillusioned when the real stuff doesn't come up to their dramatic expectations. But that's police work for you: ninety-nine per cent hard work and one per cent luck.

* * *

Apart from restaurants, Dinard closed down on Easter Sunday and we spent the day lazing around and going for the occasional walk interspersed by frequent stops at cafes for a drink.

Easter Monday morning was much livelier and I left Gail to wander around the small town, no doubt to spend some money, while I renewed my acquaintance with Odette Gouret at the airport, and dropped in, once more, to the gendarmerie. But there was nothing new to be learned.

As I had arranged to meet Gail for lunch, I promised Jacques Bloyet that I would buy him dinner that evening. But he declined, and with a throaty laugh and a broad wink said that he didn't want to impose on my romantic weekend. Had he met Gail, however, I'm sure he'd've changed his mind.

The afternoon revealed another aspect of Gail's character that I'd not witnessed before: insanity.

'I'm going for a swim, darling,' she announced. 'Are you coming with me?'

'Are you raving mad, woman?' I asked. 'The water will be freezing.'

Gail gave me the sort of pitying glance that implied a condemnation of my lack of courage. 'Up to you,' she said, 'but I'm going anyway.'

'But you didn't bring a swimsuit, did you?'

'No, but I bought one this morning.'

We descended the steps that led from the hotel directly on to the deserted beach.

Once there, Gail shed the complimentary towelling robe that she had found in the bathroom and plunged into the icy waves.

I sat on her towel, huddled in my Barbour waterproof, and drew some comfort from the fact that it was not only Easter Monday, but also April Fool's Day.

Seventeen

First thing on Tuesday morning, I paid a last visit to Odette Gouret at the airport and called in at the gendarmerie to return the two-way radio Jacques Bloyet had loaned me.

It was something of a disappointment that during our stay in Dinard nothing had happened that had helped to advance my investigation. I had thought that the Easter weekend would have been a good time to export a coffin, but it seemed I was wrong. I'd taken the view that holiday traffic would have taken up all the time of port officials despite the abolition of frontier controls. The increase in international terrorism had added the burdens of luggage screening and zealous examination of passports to the other routine problems like drug smuggling.

I returned to the hotel to pack prior to taking Gail out to lunch later on, and was attempting to dissuade my strong-minded girlfriend from going swimming again when the telephone rang.

"Arry, it's Jacques. Can you come to the airport straight away? I think there is something 'ere to interest you.'

'A coffin?' I asked.

'Yes. Odette is asking all sorts of difficult questions, so it won't be leaving 'ere for some time.' Jacques chuckled. 'If at all.'

'I'll grab a taxi,' I said.

'Don't bother, 'Arry,' said Jacques, 'there is a gendarmerie car outside your hotel now. He will take you.'

Pausing only to give Gail a perfunctory kiss and to warn her once again not to go swimming, I raced down to the street.

'M'sieur Brock?' The driver of the gendarmerie car, its blue light lazily revolving, leaned across and opened the door.

'Yes, that's me.'

'Ah, *bon*. The *marêchal* 'as told me to take you to the airport *toute de suite*,' said the gendarme. ''Op in,' he added, grinning broadly.

With a total disregard for other road users, a feature of police drivers in France it seemed, we sped through the streets of Dinard and out towards the airport. Despite the constant blare of the siren we had several near misses, and each time my driver leaned on his horn, swore volubly and waved his fist.

Three men were being questioned in the customs area: a Bosnian 'illegal', who had been in the coffin, and the two men who were to accompany it to England.

Leaving Bloyet and Odette Gouret to get on with the paperwork that goes with any sort of investigation anywhere in the world, I walked quickly around the small concourse. I went into the toilets and looked carefully at the people in telephone booths. I wandered into the restaurant and glanced into the boutiques. But of Morrison there was no sign. I had to admit, however, that if he had been there at all he would have disappeared the moment he realized that Odette's customs officers had started to take an interest in the bogus undertakers. If I'd been in his shoes, I'd certainly have done a runner in the circumstances.

'What are you going to do about this little lot?' I asked Odette when I returned to the customs post. By now she and Jacques Bloyet had been joined by two officers of the Police de l'Air et des Frontières, and I gathered from the heated exchange that was taking place between the four of them that there was some argument about jurisdiction.

'One of two things, 'Arry,' said Odette. 'The PAF' – she indicated the two officers with a deprecating sweep of her hand – ''ave said that they can deal with them 'ere, or let them go and you can 'ave them for your collection in England.' And she gave me a captivating smile.

Sensing that the French were trying to lumber me with a tricky job, I explained that immigrant smuggling was not a police matter in Britain and that as far as I was concerned, the Republic of France was welcome

281

to keep them, lock them up or throw them away.

'I thought you would say that, 'Arry.' Odette translated my comments for the benefit of the PAF officers and laughed. The PAF officers did not laugh.

'May I use your phone?' I asked.

'Of course.' Odette conducted me to her small office.

I rang the incident room at Curtis Green and told Colin Wilberforce to alert Southampton Airport to the fact that someone there might be awaiting the arrival of a coffin on the next flight from Dinard. I mentioned also that there might be someone keeping watch from a distance. And that that someone might just be Geoffrey Morrison.

'What d'you want done if they spot anybody, sir?' asked Colin.

'Tell them to nick anyone who looks in the slightest bit suspicious, or who makes any enquiries about the arrival of a coffin. Oh, and if there's a hearse hanging around outside tell Special Branch to detain it and its crew. And just in case there are no SB officers there, alert the local nick.' I glanced at my watch. 'With any luck, I should be there by about three o'clock.'

My gendarmerie driver took me back to the hotel, driving with the same urgency as before, and waited while I raced up to my room. There was no sign of Gail.

I went out on to the balcony and looked

down. She was trudging across the sand towards the hotel in her swimsuit, the towelling robe loose around her shoulders. I whistled – not a sexy whistle but an imperative one – and she looked up.

'Hurry up, Gail,' I shouted. 'We're on the move.'

She began to run and seconds later crashed into the room, breathless.

'I've got to have a shower, darling,' she protested, shedding her robe and her swimsuit.

'No time,' I said as I threw the rest of our belongings into the grip we'd brought with us.

'I'll catch the next flight, then,' said Gail, by now muttering and complaining.

I could see problems with that. 'No you won't,' I said masterfully.

Minutes later we were speeding back to the airport. Gail was still protesting about having wet hair, but I think she was impressed at having a ride in a French police car, even if the driver was mad.

By the time we arrived at Southampton, the local Special Branch had detained two hoods they had discovered waiting in a hearse in the cargo area.

'Where are they?' I asked.

'In the police room, sir,' said one of the detectives. 'This way.'

Having been obliged to cut short our long

weekend, although not by much, and infuriating Gail by depriving her of a shower, I was in no frame of mind to mess about.

'Right,' I said to the two prisoners. 'For a start your illegal immigrant has been arrested in Dinard along with the two idiots who were with him. Where's Morrison?'

'Who?' asked one of the prisoners, clearly the spokesman.

'Geoff Morrison. Where is he?' I slapped the table with the flat of my hand. It wasn't play-acting; I was in a very bad mood.

'I've never heard of him,' said the spokesman, shifting back in his chair.

'You were told that someone would be here.' By now I had become familiar with the pattern of the operation. 'Where were you supposed to meet him?'

'We weren't told nothing like that, guv'nor, honest. We was just told that we'd be contacted.'

'Who told you?'

'Dunno. I got a phone call on me mobile.'

'When?'

'This morning.'

'Where were you supposed to take the coffin you were waiting for?' I demanded.

'Dunno,' said the spokesman again. 'We was told we'd be contacted when it got here and someone would tell us where to take it.'

'How were you to be contacted?'

'On the mobile. That's what the bloke said.'

And that, I suspected, was the truth. Whoever was running the operation in Ramo
Aniç's absence was taking no chances. And I
was in no doubt that the call would come
from somewhere within Southampton
Airport, and that the caller would almost
certainly be Morrison.

If Aniç, in his guise as Gavrilo Lemez, had
told us the truth, a fee of twenty-five thousand pounds per trip meant that it was
worth keeping such a lucrative operation
going, despite the risks involved. And at that
price, the immigrant-smuggling ring could
afford to lose a few consignments along the
way. The immigrants would have paid 'up
front', and even if they were intercepted they
wouldn't be able to tell the authorities anything, because they didn't know anything.
Aniç's careful security measures ensured
that the integrity of the scam remained
intact, and he wouldn't have been bothered
in the slightest how many of his mercenaries
were arrested. They didn't know anything
either.

I gave up. I wasn't interested in the small
fry. Morrison was the man I was now after.
But I still had a nagging suspicion that he
would have a complete answer to the
charges. I just hoped that that answer would
be 'Guilty'. *Some hopes!*

'What d'you want done with this pair, sir?'
asked the Special Branch sergeant who had
made the arrests.

'That's up to you, Sergeant,' I said. 'They are of no interest to me. I suggest you have a word with your guv'nor and with Immigration.'

I caught up with Gail in the cafe, now on her third cup of coffee.

'I'm sorry about all that, darling,' I said. 'I'll make it up to you with a slap-up dinner somewhere this evening.'

'Not until I've had a hot shower,' said Gail, somewhat tersely, I thought.

The next morning the commander demanded an up-to-date briefing on the progress of my enquiries.

'I spent the weekend in Dinard, sir,' I said, and started to tell him what I'd discovered there. But I was promptly interrupted.

'By whose authority did you go to Dinard, Mr Brock?' The commander's face was always a picture of his thoughts, and I could see that right now he was thinking 'discipline'. 'Just because you're investigating a murder you can't just—'

'I took leave, sir,' I said quietly, 'and went at my own expense. It was a brief holiday really, but I took the opportunity to do some work while I was there.' And that, I think, almost certainly put a few more plus points on the chart that determined my suitability for promotion.

'Ah, I see.' The commander nodded approvingly. 'Well, I have to say, Mr Brock, that

286

that sort of devotion to duty does you credit.'

'The job has to be done, sir, one way or another,' I said, snivelling bastard that I am. 'And I had a lot of assistance from the gendarmerie, even to the extent of providing me with transport.'

But I didn't get away with it altogether. 'It's as well you weren't injured, Mr Brock. There could have been all manner of problems with reports and so on. Supposing this car you were travelling in was involved in an accident.'

'In that event, sir, I'd've put myself on duty immediately.' It was as well that the commander hadn't witnessed my driver's roadcraft. Or lack of it.

'Mmm!' The commander thought about that. 'Of course you *were* in a foreign country,' he said. 'Without authority.' He was obviously far more concerned about interpreting the regulations than he was about what I'd learned in Dinard. In fact, I hadn't learned much, but I wasn't going to tell him that.

'So this man Morrison is your leading target criminal, is he?' asked the commander, abandoning his administrative objections, and switching to a useful phrase he'd obviously picked up somewhere. Probably from television.

'He's certainly someone I need to interview, sir. Sooner rather than later.'

'Good, good. Well, efforts must be intensified, Mr Brock. Leave no stone unturned.' The commander nodded again and withdrew before the conversation became too technical.

I threw the whole weight of law enforcement into finding Geoffrey Morrison.

Firstly, I obtained a warrant for his arrest from the Horseferry Road district judge; not that I needed one, but now that the Metropolitan Police is obsessed with administration one needs all the bits of paper it's possible to lay one's hands on.

The next thing I did was to amend Morrison's entry on the Police National Computer to take note of the fact that he was now to be arrested on suspicion of murder. I also added the word 'urgent', and for good measure included the caveat that he might be armed and dangerous.

It was on Friday that 'a confluence of agencies', as the buzzword kings at the Yard would undoubtedly have called it, came unwittingly to my assistance.

I was just contemplating going out for lunch when a DCI rang me from the Hampshire Constabulary's headquarters at Winchester and told me an intriguing tale.

That morning the Hampshire police had set up a roadblock somewhere on the southbound A3 road between Petersfield and Portsmouth. Together with representatives

288

of the Vehicle and Operator Services Agency, the Driver and Vehicle Licensing Agency and Customs and Excise, they were checking all heavy goods vehicles to ensure that their drivers were complying with the multifarious regulations that govern their use.

But British lorry drivers are not as well organized as their American counterparts who warn each other of the presence on the road of 'Smoky Bears', as truckers in the States call their highway patrols.

Although Morrison's wife Karen had undoubtedly warned him that a Scotland Yard detective had visited their home in Merton Park on the outskirts of London, Morrison did not for one moment imagine that a traffic policeman in the wilds of Hampshire would present any threat to his freedom.

Mistake!

As a result, Geoffrey Morrison thought he was safe and drove straight into the trap.

He knew that his red-and-black rig complied with every regulation enshrined in the multiplicity of traffic law, and he also knew that there was no illegal red diesel fuel in his tank. Furthermore his tachograph would show that he was well within the time limit for lawful driving. After all, when one is engaged in a lucrative bit of immigrant smuggling, which I'm sure he was, one does not want to be caught out for some peccadillo.

A white-capped policeman had stepped

into the road and indicated that Morrison should pull into the lay-by. As he did so another officer, seated in a patrol car, ran a check on the licence plate. The check showed that the registered owner was a Geoffrey Morrison. And a Geoffrey Morrison was on the wanted list. *For murder.* Even before Morrison's vehicle had stopped, the second policeman was out of his car like a dose of salts.

And that's when things started happening.

As Morrison stepped down from his cab he was suddenly seized and found himself face down on the ground and handcuffed.

The cargo area of his lorry was searched and three empty coffins were found, each with carefully disguised ventilation slits.

Twenty minutes later he was in a cell at Portsmouth Central police station. And two and a half hours later still he was in a slightly larger cell at Charing Cross police station in central London.

The helpful Hampshire traffic officers had also undertaken to deliver Morrison's rig to the Metropolitan Police driving school at Hendon, which, I'd decided, was a convenient place for it to undergo a detailed scientific examination.

Beyond satisfying themselves as to Morrison's identity, the Hampshire officers had asked no other questions. But I had plenty to ask him.

'Why on earth have I been arrested, Mr Brock?' Far from adopting an air of hostility, Morrison posed the question as though he were the innocent victim of some terrible case of mistaken identity.

'Why did you have three empty coffins on your lorry?' I asked, countering his question with one of my own.

'I was taking them to France.'

'Where exactly in France?'

'Le Havre. To a warehouse near the port.'

'And who was the consignee?

'Alain Bouron. He's an undertaker.'

'Would be, I suppose,' commented Dave in an aside.

'Why did they have special vents in them, Mr Morrison?' I asked.

'Did they? I didn't look at them. I just loaded them.'

'And where did you pick them up?'

'I didn't. They were delivered to the place where I leave the rig overnight.'

We now knew where Morrison kept his lorry: it was registered to a lock-up in Mitcham. And Detective Inspector Ebdon and Linda Mitchell's team of CSEs were searching it at this very moment.

'Who was the man who delivered them?' This was beginning to be a tortuous interrogation.

'I don't know. I didn't see him. In fact I don't even know him. He has a key and lets himself in during the night.'

'This is a regular run, then, is it?'

'Not that regular. Perhaps five or six times a year.'

'Why should a French undertaker want coffins from England?' I asked. 'Don't they make coffins in France?'

Morrison gave me a pitiful look. 'I'm only the driver,' he said.

For a few moments I said nothing, but leaned back in my chair and gazed at him in silence. It had the desired effect: Morrison began to get twitchy.

'Is it all right if I smoke?' he asked.

'By all means.' But apart from those brief words of consent, I remained silent.

'Is there something wrong with all this?' Morrison asked eventually. 'I've got a manifest and everything. It's all in order. I just don't know why I've been arrested.'

'You told me that you'd left the army ten years ago, Mr Morrison.'

'Yes ... ' He drew out the word, as though puzzling why I'd asked it. But the fact that I had asked it clearly disconcerted him.

'But you didn't, did you? According to the army, it was nearer five years ago.'

'It was a long time ago,' said Morrison lamely, but didn't question why we should have made enquiries of the army.

'And you were only in the Royal Logistic Corps for the last year of your service. Before that you were a sergeant specializing in sniper training. Which means that you were a highly qualified marksman. And you were in the SAS.' That was a guess, but not much of one; Morrison's wife had mentioned that they'd lived at Hereford after his promotion to sergeant.

'Everyone had to do infantry training whatever mob they were in.' Morrison was starting to wriggle now. *Good!*

'Darren Walters has been arrested,' I said.

'I don't know anyone of that name.'

'And so has Ramo Aniç.'

'I don't know why you're telling me about these people. I don't know any of them.'

'Let me refresh your memory then, Mr Morrison. Aniç is a guy you met when you were serving in Bosnia with the army. You formed a conspiracy with him to bring rich Bosnians to this country as illegal immigrants.' I was way out on a limb with this line of questioning, even though my instinct told me I was right.

I had to admire Morrison's reserve. He leaned back in his chair and laughed. 'I think you're mixing me up with someone else, Mr Brock,' he said. 'I get stopped by the police somewhere in Hampshire for a routine vehicle check, and suddenly I'm in a police station in London being accused of all sorts of ridiculous things. I'll say it again: I don't know these people and I don't know what you're talking about.'

'In that case I'll tell you what I'm going to do next,' I said. 'I'm going to telephone the

French police in Le Havre and have them arrest this Alain Bouron. And we'll see what he has to say. The French police can be very persuasive.'

'You must do what you think,' said Morrison with a shrug.

We were going to need more. If Morrison had been in the SAS he would undoubtedly have undergone a course of counter-interrogation training. He was certainly proving a hard nut to crack.

'Ever used an M16 carbine?' I asked.

'Of course. I was in the army.'

'We found one in Darren Walters's garage in East India Dock Road, together with a Walther P38. The M16 had been used to murder James Gould outside Stone Mill prison, and the P38 to kill Bernie Pointer. I hope you're not going to tell me that you didn't know Pointer, your brother-in-law.'

A tired smile crossed Morrison's face. 'If you don't mind my saying so, Mr Brock, I think you're running out of sensible questions. Why don't you admit that you've made a mistake and that you've got the wrong man?'

I took another gamble. 'Your rig was seen outside Stone Mill prison on the morning of Wednesday the sixth of February. It was stationary for no good reason.'

'I was nowhere near that place. In fact if you care to examine my records you will see I was somewhere else.'

'Where exactly?'

'Good heavens, I don't know. But I do know I was nowhere near any prison on that morning. Or for that matter on any other morning.'

'That's about to change,' said Dave, a comment that did little to comfort Morrison.

But I knew that we'd have to do better than we'd done already. It was evident that Morrison was not going to make any admissions of guilt. All we had were the two firearms that the ballistics check proved had been used in the murders. There were no fingerprints on either of them, and the fact that they had been found in Walters's possession didn't mean that he was the killer.

It was time to play both ends against the middle.

Eighteen

Darren Walters was not due for his next remand hearing at the Crown Court until the nineteenth of April. Consequently he was still languishing in Wandsworth prison and I decided that Dave and I should pay him a visit.

'I've got nothing to say to you.' Walters's incarceration had obviously done nothing to diminish his bloody-minded attitude.

'Why did you agree to see me, then?' It was a remand prisoner's inalienable right not to be interviewed by police unless he was so inclined.

'Makes a break, dunnit?' Walters, slouching in his chair, lit a half-smoked cigarette. 'So what's the weather like out there?'

'Geoffrey Morrison was arrested yesterday morning.'

'So?'

'You obviously know who he is.'

'Never heard of him.'

'Well, he's heard of you.' Now was the time to do a bit of creative interrogation. 'In fact he told us that you murdered Spotter Gould, better known as the whispering grass, and

Bernie Pointer.'

'The lying bastard.'

'So you have heard of him.'

'I ain't saying nothing.'

'Well, that makes my job much easier. As I told you before, Darren, when we searched your lock-up on the East India Dock Road we found the two firearms used to commit those murders. Consequently I take the view that they're down to you. And I'm sure the Crown Prosecution Service will agree with me.'

'Now just you bloody hold on, mate.' For the first time in any of our meetings Walters became seriously animated. He shot forward in his chair and thumped on the table. 'I ain't taking the rap for what someone else done.'

'I don't blame you,' said Dave, deciding to join in. 'So who's the "someone else" of whom you speak?'

Walters sneered, presumably at Dave's correct sentence construction. But Walters didn't know Dave was a graduate in English. Not that he'd've cared anyway.

'Well?' Dave prompted.

But still Walters remained silent.

'There are a few things I forgot to tell you, Darren,' I said. 'Apart from Geoff Morrison, Ramo Aniç has been arrested and Wilf Crow's been murdered. Oh and Jack Lynn's been knocked off too. I presume you know that Crow is dead.' I guessed he'd heard about that, the prison grapevine being what it is, but the fact that Aniç was also in custody may just loosen Walters's tongue. 'And the strange thing is that all the survivors are pointing a finger at you for the Gould and Pointer toppings.'

'Well, fuck that for a game of soldiers,' Walters protested vehemently. 'I'm not taking that on me own.'

'So speak, Darren.' I leaned back and waited.

'It was Morrison what done for Spotter and Bernie.'

'Oh really?'

'Yes, mate, really. Morrison was in the SAS, you know. Reckoned he was a sniper. He done for Spotter and he topped Bernie. And then he lumbered me with looking after the shooters.'

'Why did you hang on to them? Why didn't you dump them in the river? That's what any self-respecting villain would've done.'

'Morrison said as how he might need 'em again. I never thought anyone'd find 'em.'

'So why did Morrison murder those two?'

'It was orders.'

'Stop pissing about, Walters,' said Dave. 'What's the SP?'

Walters gazed at Dave in evident surprise; one moment my sergeant was speaking correct English, the next he was lapsing into the sort of argot that villains understood.

'Aniç.'

'I hope you're going to give us more than that,' said Dave.

Walters sighed, lit another cigarette from the butt of the first and leaned back in his chair. 'Ramo Aniç's the geezer behind it all. And Morrison's his sidekick. Bernie Pointer upset Aniç?'

'How?' Although I had heard a version from the late Wilfred Crow, he was now in no position to give evidence.

'Dunno. Some argument.'

'You can do better than that,' said Dave.

'Pointer wanted more money and he might have got it, but on the next run the prat dumped one of the imports on the beach at Dinard and then shoots his mouth off the French law. Stupid bastard. Anyhow, Aniç said Pointer had got to be rubbed out.'

'Who did he tell?

'Wilf Crow. Wilf passed it on to me and I told Morrison.'

'And where did Morrison get the weapons from?'

Walters gave me a pathetic glance, as though doubting my abilities as a detective. 'Leave it out, mate. If you want a shooter and you know where to go, you can pick one up just like that.' And he gave a flick of his fingers.

'Why was Gould murdered, Darren?' I asked. 'Was he involved in this immigrant-smuggling scam?'

'What, Spotter?' Walters gave a derisory

laugh. 'Course not. He were in the nick, weren't he? Can't say that Morrison didn't do me a favour, though. I'd been shafting Spotter's missus ever since he was captured, and I reckoned there'd've been a bit of punch-up when he got home and found out. He was a nasty bastard was Spotter, and he had a few mates who'd've done for me just for old times' sake.'

'So you added his name to the list you passed on to Morrison, is that it?'

'Never thought of it, otherwise I might've done. Nah, it was a mistake. See, we'd had the word that Bernie Pointer was being let out that morning. Eight o'clock on the dot. Ex-cons are always let out at eight.'

'You'd know about that, I suppose,' observed Dave.

Walters gave Dave a withering glance and continued. 'So Morrison goes up there in his bloody great lorry, sees Spotter coming out and lets him have it thinking it was Bernie. He never knew that Spotter was coming out the same time as Bernie, in fact he never knew Spotter, so he takes a potshot and pisses off a bit sharpish. Hard luck on old Spotter really but, like I said, he done me a favour.'

'Aniç's been charged with Crow's murder,' I said.

'Serve him right,' said Walters. 'What d'you want me to do about it?'

'It means that he's likely to be in prison for

300

a very long time, so you can tell me how this immigrant-smuggling business went down.'

'Nothing to it. Aniç made the contacts in Bosnia and fixed up for the marks to be taken to Dinard. A couple of guys there'd bung him in a coffin, fly him over to Southampton and let him go. End of story. Well, it was till bloody Pointer cocked it up by grassing to the local law in Froggyland.'

'And what did you get out of it?'

'Five grand for everyone who was brought in. But I never got anything if it all went pear-shaped.'

'And did it? Often, I mean.'

'Yeah, sometimes. Usually when your blokes stuck their bleedin' noses in.'

'And when that happened, who blew the whistle?'

'Morrison, of course. He'd always be hanging around to make sure it all went all right. If it never, he'd let Wilf Crow know, and Crow'd tell the others. Sometimes he'd ring me direct.'

'And who were the main players in all this?'

'Aniç, obviously, and then there was Morrison and Crow. Bernie Pointer got too greedy so he was written off.' Walters broke off to cackle. 'Don't do to upset Aniç. Never seen a bloke get so arsey as him when things went bottoms up.'

'So you knew Aniç.'

'Met him a couple of times. When he was

over here, like.'

So Aniç had been in the country before. Well, that was no surprise.

'So why did Crow get topped?'

'Easy, mate. Somehow Aniç heard you was poking about in Dinard. So Aniç got himself brought over in a coffin to sort out the geezers who'd put him in the frame. But the bleedin' customs had set traps and he got himself nicked in the warehouse at Pompey. He reckoned Crow'd gone bent on him and tipped the customs off, and he was going to square him up for that. But when the Pompey knock-offs went down Morrison give me the heads up, and I split. Once Aniç started thrashing about, no one was safe, I can tell you.'

'Not very clever going up to Blackpool and taking a few potshots at the Old Bill, then, was it?'

'Nothing to do with me.' Despite the very strong evidence that Walters had been involved in that incident, he was obviously not going to hold up his hands to it. He probably realized that, even these days, there are still one or two judges left who take a dim view of criminals who go about shooting at policemen. Thank God!

'Where did Aniç get the shooter that he topped Crow with?' asked Dave.

'Search me, mate. I dunno where it came from, and I dunno where Morrison got the two you found in my lock-up. All I know is

302

he asked me to look after 'em.'

I now asked the big question. 'Are you willing to give evidence against Aniç and Morrison at the Old Bailey, Darren?'

Walters scoffed. 'What, me grass?' He paused as it occurred to him that to do so might reduce the sentence he would inevitably receive. 'Too bloody right, mate,' he said.

'OK,' said Dave. 'Now you can write it all down.'

I decided this was not the moment to tell Walters that, in addition to the firearms-possession charge, he would also be indicted for conspiring with Aniç, Morrison and the deceased Crow to murder Gould and Pointer.

Time was running out. Morrison would have to be charged before his twenty-four hours in custody expired. Or we'd have to obtain a superintendent's authority to hold him for a further twelve. After that I would have to convince a district judge of the need to extend the period further.

'Geoffrey Morrison, I am about to charge you with the murders of James Gould and Bernard Pointer on or about the sixth and ninth of February respectively.' I nodded to Dave and he reeled off the caution.

'Don't be daft,' said Morrison.

'I have to tell you that Darren Walters has made a statement implicating you in those murders and further alleging that you then gave him the weapons for safekeeping.' I handed him a copy of Walters's statement, something that the law obliged me to do.

'I've never heard of this man Walters you keep talking about,' said Morrison, fingering the statement and then tossing it to one side.

'In that case I'll have the pleasure of introducing him to you at the Old Bailey,' said Dave. 'Now, d'you wish to make a statement?'

'No,' said Morrison. 'And I've nothing to say until my solicitor is present.'

'You can send for him by all means,' I said, 'but we shan't be here. You see, Morrison, I have sufficient evidence to support two charges of murder against you.'

'In your dreams,' said Morrison, finally abandoning his pose of injured innocence.

Unfortunately I knew he was right. The evidence of one co-conspirator against another doesn't count for much. We needed to obtain some scientific evidence that would negate Morrison's denial.

Nevertheless, I was quite happy that when Morrison appeared at court tomorrow morning, the district judge would be justified in refusing bail.

However, that afternoon Kate Ebdon and Linda Mitchell came up with some of the answers I'd been seeking.

'We searched Morrison's lock-up garage at

Mitcham, guv.' Kate was grinning like the proverbial Cheshire cat. 'There was a whole load of stuff that we're going through at the moment. Paperwork dealing with the transit of the coffins, telephone bills that are being checked out and bank statements showing substantial sums of money paid in. Incidentally the bank statements are in the name of Salter ... ' She broke off to laugh at that. 'But I've no doubt that they'll prove to be down to Morrison when we check with the bank. The statements also show hefty withdrawals at dates we'll probably find coincide with the arrival of illegals, and they were probably made to Darren Walters and Wilfred Crow. One of them certainly tallies with the arrival of Aniç at Portsmouth. Funny that, when you think about it. But all in all it demonstrates that Morrison's a bit of a prat, keeping all that stuff.'

'So he's the paymaster as well,' I mused. 'Well done, Kate. That should put him well in the frame for smuggling immigrants, but we're no nearer proving that he committed the murders. All the evidence we've got at the moment is circumstantial.'

'Oh no it's not,' said Kate, still finding it difficult to contain her jubilation. 'I went with Linda and her CSEs to Hendon and searched Morrison's rig. Well, he's either careless or overconfident. The cab was a tip; typical long-distance lorry driver, I should think. It was littered with polystyrene coffee cups, plastic sandwich packets, sweet wrappers and old newspapers. And caught up in the carpet under the driver's seat were two shell cases. According to Linda, one was definitely a 5.56-millimetre and the other one a 9-millimetre. The ballistics guy at the lab is checking them as we speak, but with any luck they'll turn out to be a match for the two weapons seized from Walters's garage.'

And so it proved to be. I don't know precisely how it's done, but the ballistics expert identified the marks on the cartridge cases as being identical with those left on the test firings of the weapons we had seized at Walters's garage.

Later that afternoon Dave and I journeyed to Brixton prison to break the bad news to Ramo Aniç. I didn't want Aniç to think himself too important so I let Dave do the talking. There is nothing quite so guaranteed to deflate a self-important villain than to think he only warrants being interviewed by a detective sergeant.

'In addition to the charge against you of murdering Wilfred Crow,' Dave said, 'you will also be charged with conspiring with others, namely Darren Walters, Geoffrey Morrison and Wilfred Crow, to murder James Gould and Bernard Pointer.'

Aniç seemed unimpressed by this portentous announcement, but he did make a mild protest.

'I had nothing to do with the murder of the man Gould,' said Aniç. 'That fool Walters made a mess of things, and so did Morrison. They were not told to murder Gould. He was nothing to do with it. They are fools, all of them.'

Give it a run, Brock, I said to myself. 'But you did order the murder of Pointer.'

'Yes.' Aniç paused. 'Er, no.'

'Too late,' I said. 'It's on the tape.'

'Is that why you came over here to murder Crow?' asked Dave. 'Because he'd made a mess of things.'

Suddenly Aniç appeared to tire of the whole charade. Perhaps he thought he would be going back to Bosnia after all, and had decided that a few years in an English prison would be preferable to what the Bosnian authorities might have in store for him. And knowing the CPS, there was likely to be a fifty-fifty chance of him escaping justice altogether. I was glad I'd kept Mr Djork's telephone number. I'm bloody sure that the Bosnian police wouldn't bother to go through all this rigmarole.

'The man Crow was a cretin. It was his fault that you people found me in the coffin at Southampton. And that meant I had to go the expense of arranging for my release.' Aniç seemed very annoyed that Crow's apparent ineptitude had cost him money.

I inserted a wedge between him and

Morrison. 'The men who got you out of Hounslow are not best pleased with you and Morrison,' I said. 'They didn't get their money, apart from a thousand pounds, so I reckon that Morrison's defrauded you.'

Aniç's face went black with rage when I told him that. 'Morrison is a useless fool,' he said. 'I tell Crow to give him a simple instruction but what does Morrison do? I tell you. First of all, he murders the wrong man in broad daylight, outside a prison of all places. And then when Morrison does get around to killing Pointer, what does he do? He leaves the damned body in the middle of a golf course.' Aniç shook his head at the sheer stupidity of the men he had hired and, by all accounts, paid well. 'Morrison was supposed to be a good soldier. An SAS man, he said. But I see your army in Bosnia. Useless. How did you ever beat the Germans?'

I have to admit that I sometimes wondered about that myself. I suppose in a way it was similar to the way the British police caught the baddies. There was no doubt in my mind that Aniç thought we'd be a walkover after the nasty bastards who comprise police forces in the Balkans. But we blunder on, hoping it'll all come right in the end. And it usually does.

Gail had declined to have dinner with me when we had eventually returned from Dinard. It was only yesterday but it seemed ages ago. She had muttered something about going home and having a long hot bath. 'As I was not allowed to have a shower before we left France,' she had said, 'and had to travel home with wet hair.' *Ouch!*

She was however in a more equable mood today and agreed to hop on a train and come to London.

'Well, was it worth it?' she asked once we were seated in our favourite restaurant.

'Was what worth what?' I asked.

'Our trip to Dinard, of course, darling.' Gail spoke the words slowly as though talking to a halfwit.

'As a matter of fact it was,' I said, and went on to tell her that we had all but buttoned up our triple-murder enquiry.

'That's good.' And that was all that Gail said about it. She took a sip of her gin and tonic and beamed at a passing waiter.

The young man skidded to a halt. 'Madam?' he purred, trying to pretend he was not looking down Gail's cleavage.

We ordered our food and spent longer than we should in eating and chatting and drinking.

It was very nearly midnight by the time we got back to Surbiton.

'Are you going to stay the night?' asked Gail when we reached her front door.

Obviously I'd been forgiven.

I decided I was justified in turning up late at

Curtis Green the following morning but, in any case, I had to call in at my flat for a change of clothing.

'Good morning, Mr Brock.'

Oh God! Gladys Gurney.

'Good morning, Gladys.'

My lady cleaner was standing in the middle of the sitting room, hands on hips, gazing around at my domestic detritus and humming some unrecognizable tune.

'It won't do, Mr Brock. It won't do at all, you know.'

'What won't do, Gladys?' I asked innocently. But I knew perfectly well what she thought wouldn't do. I also had a nasty suspicion that it was Mrs Gurney who wouldn't be 'doing' for very much longer. Not unless I mended my ways.

'I do my best, Mr Brock, I really do,' said Gladys plaintively, 'but every time I come round here the place is in a mess. I don't know what that nice young lady would think. The one who stays here sometimes.'

'How d'you know about her?' I asked, somewhat alarmed that I appeared to have no secrets from Gladys.

'I've got eyes in me head, Mr Brock, and I've noticed things in the bathroom. I have to say she's got a very expensive taste in cosmetics has that young lady. And that bra she left in your bedroom must have cost a fortune. So you ought to take more care to hold on to her otherwise you'll find she'll have upped sticks and gone. I certainly wouldn't stand for it if I was in her shoes.' Mrs Gurney did not seem at all offended at discovering that Gail had been sleeping with me.

'I'm sorry, Gladys, but I've been rather busy solving three murders, and travelling back and forth to France. I've been on the go all the time.'

Mrs Gurney was unimpressed by this major effort of criminal investigation. 'Yes, well, be that as it may, Mr Brock,' she said, hands still on hips, 'it's just as easy to hang your clothes up as it is to throw them on the floor. And just as easy to put your newspapers in the dustbin as it is to leave them all over the place.' She emphasized her point with a sweep of her arm that encompassed the chaos that was my living room.

There was only one thing for it: admit defeat. I took a fifty-pound note from my wallet. 'I'm sorry, Gladys,' I said. 'I'll try to do better in future. In the meantime, I'd like you and Mr Gurney to go out and have a meal at my expense.'

Gladys Gurney took the money and tucked it into her apron pocket. 'Very kind, I'm sure, Mr Brock,' she said.

But as I walked through into the bedroom, I heard her mutter 'Men!' under her breath. Just before she switched on the Hoover.

I seemed to have done rather well at upsetting the women in my life just lately. What with Gail's wet-haired trip home and Mrs Gurney's dissatisfaction with the state of my flat, it was costing me quite a lot of money.

Nineteen

The trials were spread over several months. Geoffrey Morrison was tried separately from his co-conspirators, much to the satisfaction of his defence counsel. In response to the indictment of having murdered James Gould and Bernard Pointer, he pleaded not guilty. Well, why not?

At the outset, prosecuting counsel made the mistake of advising the judge that most of the evidence in the case would be 'forensic'. The judge spent the next few minutes delivering a little homily about the misuse of the English language, and pointing out that the word 'forensic' meant 'pertaining to the court' and nothing else. Presumably, he observed acidly, prosecuting counsel meant that most of the evidence was scientific.

At least Dave was pleased.

Argument and counter-argument criss-crossed the courtroom, much of it about the evidence that the prosecution proposed should be given by Darren Walters. But these arguments were conducted in the absence of the jury, whose members wouldn't have understood it anyway. Finally, however, they were sent to the jury room to consider their verdict.

It took them three days, but eventually they found Morrison guilty. The judge wasted no time in sentencing him to life imprisonment. Twice.

A week later we were back there again for the trial of Darren Walters.

For starters, his counsel complained bitterly that Cindy Turner, the prostitute with whom Walters claimed to have spent the night of Pointer's murder, had lied in the statement she'd made to police. Walters was adamant that he *had* spent the night with the girl. Strangely enough I believed that he had.

With a view to examining Cindy Turner in court, counsel had obtained a subpoena, but she'd failed to appear.

The judge drily pointed out that Walters was not charged with Pointer's *murder*, but merely *conspiracy* to murder him and it didn't really matter where he was on the night that Pointer met his death.

However, Walters's brief made such an issue of it that the judge issued a bench warrant for Cindy's arrest, largely I suspect to shut him up. And probably because His Honour had worked out that counsel was trying to lay down a smokescreen that would confuse the jury.

But Cindy Turner was never found. At least not before the trial ended. Not that any of it mattered; in his summing up the judge pointed out that Cindy Turner's evidence would have been totally irrelevant to the conspiracy indictment anyway.

At the end of the trial, Walters received twelve years' imprisonment for conspiring with Aniç, Morrison and the late Wilfred Crow to murder Gould and Pointer, and ten years concurrent for having the audacity to shoot at policemen in Blackpool. The judge seemed to attach more gravity to the latter than the former. The indictment of unlawful possession of firearms was considered to be an intrinsic part of the conspiracy and was left on file, as the legal eagles say. In case, Heaven forfend, that Walters had his convictions overturned on appeal, I suppose.

I later learned that during the afternoon of the day Walters was sent down, police were called to 37 New Labour House, Walloch Street, Poplar, following complaints that a demented woman, subsequently identified as a Mrs Terry Gould, was throwing Walters's belongings off the balcony to the detriment of the passers-by below.

At the next trial, Dixon, Eldridge, Hawkes and Lynn were convicted of the raid on the detention centre at Hounslow that culminated in the release of Aniç, and received sentences of ten, nine, eight and seven years respectively. Presumably the judge liked symmetry in her sentencing pattern.

Somewhere along the way, the B team – the mercenaries involved in fetching and

carrying at Portsmouth and Southampton –
were weighed off for their part in the immigrant-smuggling scam. The Dover two,
Charlie Steer and Fred Palmer, who had had
the misfortune to import a dead body,
received six years apiece for manslaughter,
despite their protests that they hadn't actually put the man in the coffin. That he'd climbed in unaided seemed not to carry any sway
with the judge.

Finally we came to the pièce de résistance:
the trial of Ramo Aniç.

I still had no idea where Aniç had acquired
the weapon with which I was sure he'd
murdered Wilfred Crow, and even less of an
idea where it was now. I suspected that it was
at the bottom of the River Thames, somewhere along the two hundred and fifteen
miles between its source near Cirencester
and its mouth at the Nore. It would have
been nice to find it, but in this game you
can't always win.

Much to my surprise, officials of the
Crown Prosecution Service had made the
momentous decision – momentous for
them, anyway – to indict Aniç. One can only
imagine the budget-based arguments that
raged back and forth between them and the
Home Office about the expense of keeping
him in the comparative luxury of a British
prison for many years or sending him back
to Bosnia.

Perhaps the fondant-centred Home Office

had eventually been persuaded by Mr Djork's trenchant avowal that Aniç would certainly be hanged if he ever set foot in his native country again.

Whatever the reasons, we were once more at the Central Criminal Court at Old Bailey.

Aniç had managed to parade an impressive team of counsel led by a well-known QC.

Rising to outline his case, the leader spent a moment or two hitching up his silk gown, polishing his glasses and fiddling with his brief before putting forward a breathtaking range of reasons why his client should not be convicted of the murder of Wilfred Crow. It was a masterpiece of theatre, but no more credible than most theatrical productions I've seen.

'You have before you, My Lord,' he began, 'a poor, innocent refugee, who came to this country to escape a repressive regime. All right, the defence admits that he came here illegally, but that in no way lessens the danger in which he would find himself were he to be returned. Indeed it was for that very reason that he came here in the first place. But almost at once this poor fellow found himself arrested for murdering someone he'd never heard of, and accused of smuggling illegal immigrants into the country in coffins.' Counsel glanced at the jury. 'In coffins,' he said again with emphasis, and afforded the jury a pathetic smile. 'I ask you.'

The prosecution brought Darren Walters

from Parkhurst prison on the Isle of Wight to testify to Aniç's involvement in immigrant smuggling, but his testimony had little bearing on the murder. Some of his evidence, I thought, over-egged the pudding somewhat, but fortunately the fact that he was doing time himself didn't detract from the jury's belief that it was all true, and that he was a credible witness. We don't often have that sort of luck, I can tell you.

But to my surprise, it was the evidence of the fibre that Linda Mitchell found on the door of Crow's room at Battersea that clinched it. Or maybe it was Walters's testimony that Aniç had issued orders for the killing of Pointer.

Personally I thought it was all a bit thin. Nevertheless it took the jury but forty minutes to convict the Bosnian of the wilful murder of Wilfred Crow. Which just proved that we had amassed sufficient telling evidence after all.

On the other hand the jury might just have had a violent dislike of Bosnians. Funny things, juries.

That evening, Dave and Madeleine joined Gail and me for dinner in the West End. It was not a celebration; there is nothing to celebrate in being instrumental in sending people to prison. Particularly for murder, no matter that the victims were themselves villains.

Gail and Madeleine got on extremely well and were soon discussing the technical differences between the demands of high kicking in a constricting basque and high heels when set against the concerns that arose from hoping that your partner caught you in a fast-moving and complex pas de deux.

Dave and I, well we just talked about the Job.

It was two months after the end of the trial that I heard about the death of Ramo Aniç. And it almost certainly resulted from some fool in the Prisons Department at the Home Office who had contrived to have Aniç and Morrison sent to the same prison.

One morning just after slopping-out – it was one of the older prisons – Aniç was found at the bottom of an iron staircase. Dead. It was assumed that the fall had killed him, but a pathologist soon disabused the authorities of that theory. Aniç had been killed as the result of a karate chop to the front of the throat. The inquest heard all manner of pathological mumbo-jumbo about a fractured horn on Aniç's voice box, and how falling down stairs could not possibly have caused such an injury.

I was probably the only person who worked out that Morrison's training in the special forces would have equipped him to launch that sort of attack.

Mind you, it was never proved that Morrison had murdered Aniç, but it wouldn't have mattered anyway. If you're already serving two life sentences, there's not much else they can do to you.